advance praise for *Anarchists in Love*

"Every generation needs to discover Emma Goldman. *Anarchists in Love* breathes new life into the famous anarchist's big ideas, big passions and even bigger hopes for a better future. Robert Hough has written a novel crammed with talk and sex and the heady energy of the times."
— CARY FAGAN, author of *The Student*

"A quick action-filled scan of the highly ambitious plan of two young anarchists whose actions were intended to send a lethal message to abusive greedy industrialists everywhere. Details of the culture mixed with inevitable jail sentences add to the tension and excruciating risks and the critical importance of a close-knit immigrant community to shield each other from overwhelming prejudice and targeted harm."
— CANDACE FALK, author of *Love, Anarchy, & Emma Goldman: A Biography*

"Hough's latest novel is an expertly written, riveting ride through the stark yet full-blooded lives of two revolutionists bound by love, and the powerful desire to thrash against a corrupted social order ... The path of their lives is an almost elemental saga, fraught with drama and violence, but underpinned by a passion that is as important and relevant now as it was at the incendiary close of the nineteenth century."
— KEVIN HARDCASTLE, author of *In the Cage*

ANARCHISTS IN LOVE

Anarchists in Love

A NOVEL

Robert Hough

Douglas & McIntyre

DOUGLAS AND MCINTYRE (2013) LTD.
P.O. Box 219, Madeira Park, BC, VON 2HO
www.douglas-mcintyre.com

FRONT COVER: Portrait of Emma Goldman - BG A5/476/Kent, J.H., International Institute of Social History
EDITED by Pam Robertson
COVER DESIGN by Anna Comfort O'Keeffe
TEXT DESIGN by Libris Simas Ferraz / Onça Publishing
PRINTED on 100% recycled paper
PRINTED AND BOUND in Canada

Canada   Canada Council Conseil des arts   BRITISH COLUMBIA   BRITISH
          for the Arts   du Canada   ARTS COUNCIL   COLUMBIA

DOUGLAS AND MCINTYRE acknowledges the support of the Canada Council for the Arts, the Government of Canada, and the Province of British Columbia through the BC Arts Council.

LIBRARY AND ARCHIVES CANADA CATALOGUING IN PUBLICATION
Title: Anarchists in love : a novel / Robert Hough.
Names: Hough, Robert (Robert William), author.
Identifiers: Canadiana (print) 20250196220 | Canadiana (ebook) 20250199777 | ISBN 9781771624473 (softcover) | ISBN 9781771624480 (EPUB)
Subjects: LCGFT: Historical fiction. | LCGFT: Novels.
Classification: LCC PS8565.07683 A82 2025 | DDC C813/.54—dc23

As always, for Soozie, Sally, Ella

one

IT WAS THE MIDDLE of a broiling August night, and she had yet to fall asleep. Outside, crickets and cicadas hummed; this sound not only maddened her, but contributed to the rashness of her actions. The heat primed her as well; it was suffocating in the room, well over ninety degrees, and a film of perspiration had risen upon her forehead, her upper lip, the skin backing her kneecaps, and the portion of her chest not covered by her nightgown. Her husband, who was sleeping soundly beside her, rolled over, such that he now faced the ceiling, his jaw craned apart, the view all tonsils and soft palate, his snores a series of strangulated gurgles. While he had never been the most attractive of men—he had a long, angular nose, and small eyes just a little too close together—he now looked, in deep slumber, like an eel preparing to feed.

Instead of turning away, Emma kept her eyes trained upon him, for she could feel an impulse, elbowing its way through the turbulence of her thoughts, and she knew it was being aided by Jacob's homeliness. A moment later, she found herself filling a suitcase with clothes, books, and a *tchotchke* or two from back home, most notably an icon that had once hung on her grandmother's kitchen wall, in which a seraphim frolicked around a fountain, a piccolo at its lips. Though she worked quietly—pulling open drawers as slowly as she could, tiptoeing along the bowed floor of their apartment, holding her breath as much as possible in the hot, swampy air—she nonetheless assumed that there would come a moment in which Jacob's prenatal eyes would open and catch her in the act of flight. They didn't; he remained in deep slumber, and this strengthened her resolve to flee as well.

She was twenty years old. Moonlight washed through the window, casting the room in a sullen glow. She peeled off her nightgown and dressed in a grey skirt, hobnail boots and a dark-blue blouse with white edging. Still Jacob did not waken, so she picked up her sewing machine and clumsily lugged it down the narrow steps leading from their second-storey apartment, her breath coming in short, shallow gasps. She stopped to rest at the side of the house, her arms and shoulders aching already. Fortunately, one of the neighbour's children had left a wood-slat wagon in the front yard; Emma placed her sewing machine and suitcase upon it, the wheels grinding as she pulled, her burden sufficiently heavy that she was forced to walk at a forty-five degree angle to the sidewalk. After a laborious half hour, she arrived at a station servicing the New York Central Railroad. Here, she stopped, and felt battered by sadness: in a better world, women with poor marriages wouldn't have to flee at three o'clock in the morning, their worldly possessions teetering atop a liberated wagon.

The station was deserted—the doors locked, the windows covered with pull-down shades, a single, off-yellow light shining within a belvedere that topped the small wooden building. Emma sat on one of the outside benches and lit a cigarette, the smoke hanging thick and motionless in the heavy air. Slowly, the sky changed from pitch black to indigo to a sallow, luminous grey. Three feet away from her were railway tracks. Beyond them, there was a small field, a copse of trees, and a field of corn that reached upward, as if the ground itself had been tilted to benefit her view. She rubbed her eyes; fatigue was making her feel wistful and sore. After a bit, she heard steps, turned her head, and saw a distant figure nearing the station. As the man grew closer, she could make out a station master's hat, a dark-blue uniform, and a lunch box in his freckled right hand. When he was a dozen feet away, he smiled and nodded and continued approaching.

"My goodness," he said. "You're here early."

"I was too excited to sleep."

"Where is it you're heading today?"

"New York City."

"Well, no wonder. Have you been before?"

"Oh yes," she said. "I *have*."

* * *

Slowly, the platform filled with passengers. A train pulled into the station, wisps of coal smoke trailing behind it; Emma boarded with the assistance of a strapping young man who placed her sewing machine in the luggage racks servicing her compartment. He then tipped his hat at her and wished her a good day.

It was just after 6 a.m., and the skies had come up a dull, pewter colour. The train, it seemed, wouldn't leave the station, no matter how badly she willed it, and she worried that Jacob would appear on the platform, his shirt untucked, his hair uncombed, his eyes crusty with sleep, bellowing to anyone who might listen that his wife was on this very train, and that she was hysterical, perhaps out of her mind, and that if he didn't find her, there was no telling what harm she might come to—it happened all of the time, men getting their way by convincing authorities that their wives had been driven mad by the corrosive energy of their reproductive organs. When the train finally did pull out of the station, she leaned back in her seat, closed her eyes, and felt a relief so profound it bordered on the narcotic. Thanks to an almost seductive rumble, which travelled up from the wheels, passed through the floorboards, and massaged her body, she began to feel as though her flight to New York was a tangible entity, and that her marriage to Jacob was already a chimera from her past.

Within minutes, she was asleep. She stayed that way for much of the trip, missing lakes and towns, mountains and farmland, wheat fields and grazing cattle, large wood-slat barns and red-brick farmhouses and old cedar fence lines. She awoke about an hour from her destination; the window next to her was streaked with rain, beyond which lay a wall of forest. In the town of Weehawken, Emma boarded a ferry that slowly chugged down the Hudson River, her view of the great city lost to the rain blowing against her face. After a time, the ferry passed the massive Castle Garden immigration complex, where the city had welcomed her when she came to America four years earlier, in 1885. The ferry continued, rounding the southernmost tip of Manhattan, till it reached a pier servicing local passengers; here, she discovered that, for a moderate fee, she could have her sewing machine sent to a depot on Forty-Second Street, where she would retrieve it once she had a place to live.

She stepped outside of the building. The weather had started to clear, the clouds looking like streaks of pulled-apart cotton batten that pillars of sun shone through. Emma put down her suitcase and smiled, for there it was, the clanging megalopolis, that cacophonous burgh, with all of its clamour and promise and noise and dirt and people, like a mammoth entity in combat with itself. As she absorbed it all, the smell of the city invaded her nose, a scent that was equal parts salt and oil and fish and sweat and concrete dust, all mixed together like a brine, causing thoughts of possibility to race through her head.

She purchased a bagel and a bottle of seltzer from a dockside vendor and ate as she walked north, uncertain of her direction, though she felt reasonably sure that, as long as she stayed to the east side of the island, she'd reach her intended destination sooner or later. The heat was evaporating the rain that had fallen earlier in the day, causing mist to rise from the teeming thoroughfares. She kept walking, block after cobblestone block, until she reached Houston Street, a broad avenue lined with shops and noisy, open-air markets. Everything, it seemed, was sold from overflowing wood-slat bins: she saw mounds of rubber boots, turnips, brassieres, fabric bolts, copper tubing, carrots, onions, washtub parts, fish heads, rolling pins and, in front of a butcher shop with sawdust spread upon the floors, beef hearts, which looked so fresh and bloody as to still be beating. The shoppers, most of whom were women, helped them-selves, tossing whatever they wanted into bundle buggies or large canvas sacks, the store owner collecting a few coins in return, which he'd then toss into the trough of an apron. Amidst this frenzy, chil-dren played and grandmothers gathered to chat and police officers blew their whistles and old Italian men with brightly painted carts pushed through the throngs while calling *Chestnuts! Chestnuts! Get your fresh hot chestnuts!*

Emma found a bench where she sat while attempting to collect her thoughts; her feet hurt, her face was a ruddy flush, and her mus-cles ached. Just then, a man came by; he had a damp nose and was singing to himself in a low, tenor mumble. His beard was grey and untrimmed, and his eyes were watering. He stopped singing, and looked toward Emma.

"Could you give me some money?" he asked in Russian.

"I would if I could. I just spent my last on a bagel at the docks."

"So, the old story, then." He grinned, his teeth the colour of tea. "And here I figured you were the lucky one."

"I guess not."

"Still. You've got nice clothes."

"Thanks."

"The same couldn't be said of me."

"One day, that'll change."

"Ahhh, it's not your fault. I'm not to be pitied. I have a nice dry room to sleep in, you know. The only problem is that I have to share it with a madwoman. We've been married for thirty years. She talks to herself all day."

"What does she talk about?"

"God and whatnot. She thinks that Jesus speaks to her through the radiator. Sometimes she hollers in the middle of the night. Our landlord—a real son-of-a-bitch from Minsk—tells me if I can't get her under control he'll throw us out on the street. I tell him that sadness broke her but you think he cares?"

"I'm sorry."

"Things could be worse. She makes delicious fish soup. Imagine that! Mad as a hatter and yet she can still make fish soup. It's amazing we aren't all crazy, in this city. Do *you* have a place to live?"

"Not yet. But I have the address of a distant aunt and uncle of mine. I'll be heading there now. In fact, perhaps you could help me. Do you know where Essex Street is?"

"Sure I do. Why wouldn't I?"

He pointed and lowered his head while scratching his scalp, his expression now one of exhausted concern. Emma rose and thanked him; five minutes later, she found herself in the shadow of a five-storey tenement with a butcher shop on the ground floor. After taking a deep, anxious breath, she entered the soppy heat of the building. It was dark inside, and everything smelled of coal and turnips. As she climbed the first flight of stairs, she couldn't help but notice the building's contradictions—yes, the pressed-tin ceiling was beginning to undulate, the linoleum flooring was peeling away, and the walls bore small, leaf-shaped scorch marks every five feet or so, right above the little niches where lit candles were placed. Still, at some point, someone had taken the time to sculpt the wooden hallway arches, and someone else had hand-painted pastoral scenes onto the faded yellow walls: shepherds with their flocks, flower girls at a wedding, a dog sitting by a fire. She reached the third floor and knocked on the door of room 302. Though she could hear noises from inside, there was no answer. She knocked a little more forcefully, and this time the noises ceased. A woman came to the door, affording Emma a view inside of the apartment; there were three tiny rooms, the middle one containing a large, coal stove. Next to the stove was a small, lumpy bed and a stand with a wash-up basin. Beyond this, in the living room, next to the apartment's sole window, was a desk supporting a sewing machine, as well as a dummy garbed in a pinned-together dress. There was also a boy of about six years of age, and a girl who might have been a little younger. The boy was sewing buttons onto the front of another garment, while the girl, who was a little farther away from Emma than the boy, looked to be attaching laced cuffs to a sleeve. They both stopped and peered at Emma, a needle and thread in their thin little hands.

"Can I help you?" the woman asked in Russian. She was about thirty years of age, and dressed in a threadbare blouse. Her cheeks, Emma noticed, were hollow.

"I'm looking for Abraham and Lily Goldman. They would've arrived, mmmmm, two years ago. I believe they might have had a photography studio here."

"I don't know them."

"Were they living here when you moved in?"

"We came a year ago. I don't know who was here before us. I'm sorry."

She closed the door. Emma stood in the hallway, feeling unnerved—on the chit of paper she'd brought from Rochester, she had one other address. She knocked on the door again, the woman opening immediately. "Look," she said, blowing a fallen strand of hair out of her face. "I've told you, there's no one named..."

"No! That's not it! I was just wondering... could you tell me where Montgomery Street is?"

"Oh."

"I've someone else who might be able to help me. He's at 37 Montgomery. A friend of mine."

The woman softened, and turned to her children. "I'll be back in a moment," she told them, and then motioned for Emma to follow her to the street. There, she pointed south. "It's simple. Walk a few blocks, turn right, walk a few blocks more, that'll get you there."

"Thank you," Emma said, the woman turning back toward the tenement, lifting her skirt as she stepped over a stream of raw sewage. Emma moved on, her way impeded by children, young mothers, shopkeepers, strollers, bins, stray dogs, and low-hanging awnings. For a minute or so, she tried walking on the actual roadway; this was no better, for it was crowded with horse-drawn carts, their drivers yelling if she happened to get in their way. To make matters worse, she had to be on continual lookout for horse droppings, her eyes down as she walked, all of which made her less alert for fast-moving carriages—really, Emma thought, this was a dance she'd have to learn, for everyone around her seemed to perform it effortlessly.

Upon reaching Montgomery Street, she climbed the steps of a tenement that hardly differed from the one she had just left, except that her destination was a room on the fourth floor and not the third. She lifted her hand to knock, and stopped when she noticed she was trembling. *Damn you*, she thought, *this is just like you, leaving Jacob on the spur of the moment, without any sort of strategy or plan, no money to speak of, you'd think you would've learned from the first time you left him, but no, oh no, you'll never learn, with you it's either a rash blunder or nothing at all*, and still she stood there, fearing that her political friend Hillel Solotaroff might have moved on, and what would she do then?

As if commanded by her worried mind, the door opened and there he was, dressed in a decent jacket and trousers, her tall lanky comrade from New Haven, *Hillel Hillel Hillel*, she was too relieved to speak, she clutched her hands to her chest and squealed.

"My God!" he blurted. "Emma Goldman! Is that really you?"

She nodded, tearful with relief. He picked her up and twirled her in the hallway, her feet brushing the walls. When he put her down, she felt dizzy, thankful, resplendent and, most of all, alive.

"What are you *doing* here?" he asked.

She couldn't speak, she really couldn't, all she could do was laugh at the intensity of her own emotions, her heart pounding and her face turning as red as a beet. Solotaroff laughed as well. "Let me guess—you left your husband again."

"I did!"

"You're really starting to make that a habit."

"I couldn't take it another second."

"You'll stay here?"

"Oh, Hillel, only if it's not an inconvenience."

"Of course not, you'll take my room, and I'll put a cot in the kitchen. My parents sleep in the other room."

"But I couldn't! I couldn't put you out of your own room!"

He leaned toward her, grinning. "When the revolution comes, my diminutive comrade, there'll never be a shortage of space. We can all spread out then."

Emma clasped her hands to her chest, unable to stop smiling, her heels lifting off the ground, her body weightless. "You don't *know*," she said, "how relieved I am to be here."

"Well then. I'd say that calls for a drink."

two

HE TRUDGED ALONG Suffolk Street, his lungs filling with air so hot and moist that it felt like simmering liquid. Feeling faint, Sasha stopped, put a handkerchief to his forehead, and looked up at a low dirty sky, thinking, *this heat... this infernal heat... how does anybody stand it?* All he could do was steady himself by leaning against a gas-light standard; still, the sidewalk continued to eddy beneath his cloddish feet. It was a sickening feeling, as if some unseen presence had sucked the muscle from his frame, leaving behind a body supported solely by bone and gristle and thin, pallid skin. He lit a cigarette, and while this didn't help with the assaultive humidity, it did combat the ennui that was clawing its way into his mood. Then it occurred to him: he hadn't eaten a proper meal in days, his hunger presenting itself not as pangs or a watering mouth, but as a feeling of overall illness. Thankfully, he'd just been paid, and while the amount of money in his pocket wasn't enough to live on—not really, not in any sort of dignified way—it was enough to buy a meal at that moment, the rest of the week be damned.

He stepped into Café Sachs, one of a thousand plank-floor supper houses on the Lower East Side, where you paid a quarter for whatever they were cooking that night, be it chicken cutlets or pig knuckles or beef brisket, most often served up with boiled potatoes, sauerkraut and, if you were fortunate, a sprinkling of parsley. As always, it was brightly lit, and full of cigarette smoke; he found that he could barely hear himself think over the sound of clinking dishware and hollering waiters and the unrestrained chatter coming from all around him. He chose a small table near the restaurant's rear wall. There, he lit another cigarette, and watched a taciturn waiter approach. The waiter lifted an eyebrow.

"Supper?" he asked.

"What is it tonight?"

"Steak."

"Good. Bring two. And coffee. Lots of coffee."

Sasha's food came on a chipped plate, the meat, potatoes and cabbage all swimming in a gravy tasting of salt, celery and blood. He tucked in; within minutes, he felt sufficiently strong to get into an argument with a pair of Moscow-born communists who were seated at the adjacent table. Soon, they were really going at it, voices risen, spittle flying, incisors showing, Sasha's combatants insisting that a highly governed, collectivized economy was the only way forward, whereas Sasha maintained that any type of formalized economic system would, with time, exploit the very people it purported to serve, and that communism would only work when playing second fiddle to a new system of thinking known as anarchism. "If there's no government at all," he challenged, "how will it find a way to enslave you? Well?" At this, they threw up their hands and turned away. Sasha was relieved. Suddenly, he no longer had the stomach for this constant nit-picking of ideals—they could have their communism, their socialism, their Bolshevism and Menshevism and Leninism and syndicalism, some nights a man just wanted to think about his food and his cigarettes (or, better yet, nothing at all).

Soon after, he was joined by a pair of young Russian sisters whom he knew from political circles. Anna Minkin was nineteen (or was it twenty?) while Helene was just eighteen (or was that nineteen?). Both were petite and Jewish, with dark bangs, pale skin, pitch-black eyes and plump, flaking lips. Their personalities, however, were at complete variance: Anna's manner was playful, even joyous, and this gaiety converted her natural prettiness into something approaching beauty, while her sister, Helene, was a burdened soul, reluctant to show her teeth, with gnawed fingernails, creased forehead, a taste for vodka, and a pale despondency in her eyes. Both were active comrades, known for their adherence to Mikhail Bakunin, their willingness to serve on committees, and their recipe for ground-meat pelmeni.

The sisters sat, and ordered glasses of a wine so purple that it darkened their teeth. Anna, meanwhile, was describing a mishap she'd just witnessed, in which a baton-swinging copper, who'd clearly had more than a few at one of the local taverns, tripped on a loosened cobblestone and toppled headlong into a fruit vendor's display, apples and pears rolling everywhere, only to be scavenged by street urchins who then fled in every direction. "It was all so *funny*. You really had to be there, Sasha, I swear I almost peed myself, it was the look on the fruit vendor's face, like he couldn't believe what had just happened!"

She had just finished her story when the door to the café creaked open. Sasha looked up and watched as Hillel Solotaroff entered. He was not alone; his companion was blonde, had striking blue eyes, and was radiant with youth. She wore hobnail boots, a grey skirt, and a blouse that struck Sasha as looking like the tunic worn by a sailor.

Hillel spotted the group, and came over. "Sasha! Anna! Helene! I'm so glad you're here. Allow me to introduce my good friend Emma Goldman. She just moved here from Rochester."

"Hello," she said, her eyes casting over the group.

"So," said Anna. "Given your accent, I'm guessing you're not originally from upstate New York."

"No no," Emma said. "I'm from a place called Kovno, it's in—"

"It's in western Russia," Sasha declared, his eyebrows arcing. "Deep in the pale, where the people grow silver beets and speak Lithuanian. You're not going to believe this, Miss Goldman, but I spent my teenage years there myself."

"Really?! What street did you live on?"

"Ilyvinsky Prospekt. It's on the outskirts."

"The outskirts to the west, or the outskirts to the east?"

"The outskirts to the north."

"Ahhhhhh," she said with a grin. "So you were a rich boy."

"On the contrary. My father died and we were penniless. We had to flee St. Petersburg and take refuge with my uncle. He was well-heeled, though. I'll admit that."

"I can't believe it! A Kovno boy, alive and well in New York City! Let's have a look at you..." She leaned forward, her chest pressing against her blouse, and gazed into his dark-brown eyes, as though studying, and even understanding, all that lurked inside them; she then grinned in a way that struck Sasha as devilish.

"Who *cares* what provincial Lithuanian backwater you two come from," Hillel said. "All that matters is that you're both here, now. We need to celebrate! This is Emma's first night in the city... Waiter! Bring us a bottle of whatever swill the sisters are drinking."

The waiter scowled, and returned with a large ceramic jug, which he placed on the table with a thud. When he set out another three glasses, Hillel handed one back and pointed at Sasha: "This one doesn't drink. It makes him morose. Though if *I* know him, you better keep the coffee flowing, isn't that right Sasha?"

Sasha smirked. "I do like a cup from time to time."

"Emma," Helene said while lighting a cigarette, "what brought you to New York?"

"The same thing that brought us all here, I'd imagine—I read about the Lower East Side in *Freiheit* and thought it sounded like the place for me."

"Really? You can get *Freiheit* in Rochester? I didn't think the anarchist press made its way outside of New York City."

Emma's eyes widened, and she placed a hand on her chest. "Oh but it does! You just have to know where to look. There's a bookstore on Genesee Street. You know the type—old, dusty, clandestine, smelling of mould and old cheese. They keep the political stuff behind the counter. You just have to know to ask."

"And how did *you* know?"

"I suppose I just did. I'd been attending some meetings at Germania Hall."

"Meetings?" Anna asked. "What kind of meetings?"

"Socialist meetings."

"So," said Helene. "The old story, then—socialism took you halfway there, and *Freiheit* finished the job."

"That's about it!"

"You know," said Hillel, "our friend Sasha knows the editor of *Freiheit*."

"Really?! Is this true, Sasha?"

Sasha waved away the idea. "No, no, no, I met him once, briefly. We did have a nice chat, though." He lit a cigarette of his own, inhaling so deeply that the smoke seemed to vanish.

"In that case," Emma said, "I'm impressed, I really am, that's the sort of thing *I* want to do in New York."

"Where are you staying, Emma?" asked Anna.

"I'm with Hillel and his family. But I feel terrible! There're only two bedrooms. His parents are in one, and Hillel insisted that I take his room, meaning he has to make do with a cot in the kitchen."

"Bahhh," Hillel said, waving a hand in the air. "When winter comes, I'll be in the only room in the apartment that gets any real heat."

"You're just saying that," said Emma. "The kitchen is tiny. With you in there, your poor mother will barely be able to move."

"I have an idea," said Anna. "Helene and I live with our father. We each have our own bedroom. We could double up and you could have your own room."

"But I couldn't!"

"You can and you will," said Anna. "Then, when you've found work, you can find a place of your own. We'd enjoy the company. Really, we would."

"Yes," Helene said in that deadpan voice of hers. "There's no room for discussion. You will come home with us. Hillel's apartment is far too small. Case closed. End of story."

They said their goodbyes on the street, under a full moon, the night a song, New York a fantasy, all of them smoking, everyone kissing and embracing one another, though when Sasha went to do so with Emma, she backed away and, once again, gave him a look that shimmered with understanding. She extended a hand; it was small and plump and warm. When he took it, she leaned close to his left ear and spoke softly.

"You know where the Minkins live, do you comrade?"

"I do."

"Well, then," she said.

three

THE FOLLOWING MORNING, Sasha Berkman awoke early, drank coffee, ate toast, smoked a half dozen cigarettes, and proceeded to his job at one of the cigar factories across the river in Brooklyn; here, he spent ten hours per day, breathing in fetid, particulate-thickened air, the one exception being Sunday, when he was granted the afternoon off. For this, he earned about three dollars per week, or barely enough to pay for the Broome Street hovel he shared with his cousin, a libertine artist named Modska.

Upon arriving, he took his place at his work station. To his right sat an old Hungarian woman who smelled like a damp sponge, and to his left sat a poor soul named Marku who, it was said, hailed from some sorry mule-trodden village in Albania. He was a small man with sunken eyes, frail arms and a perpetual three-day growth on his face. As the skin beneath his eyes looked like purplish half-moons, everyone assumed that he had a second job somewhere, or that he was unable to sleep in whatever tenement madhouse he lived in. Each morning, when he started his shift, he'd remove a small, framed photograph from his waistcoat pocket and place it so that he could glance at it when his labours allowed; in the photo-graph was a tight-lipped woman and three small children, two boys and a girl, all looking plaintively forward, as though suspicious of the camera's intentions.

The floor manager, meanwhile, was a despicable individual named Spiros. He was about forty, petulant, sour-smelling, bald, hunched, flat-footed, double-chinned, and possessed of the stubbiest fingers that Sasha had ever seen—they reminded him of kielbasa sausage. Spiros used these appendages like a weapon; whenever he felt that an employee wasn't working hard enough, he'd come up behind him (or, yes, her) and jab a forefinger between his victim's shoulder blades. Yet he was hardest on the Albanian, his cruelty aroused by the little man's helplessness: with Marku, he'd often jam his forefinger into the exact spot in which the ribcage no longer affords protection to the kidneys, the poor man howling like a possum caught in a trap, his vindictive boss sauntering away, chuckling to himself. The Albanian would then take a consoling look at his photograph, take a deep breath, and continue rolling cigars with his spindly, nervous fingers.

On that particular morning, Marku looked to be suffering from a cold, for he kept coughing into the back of his hand, the pouches clinging to the underside of his eyes having progressed from a purplish brown to an inky, midnight black. Meanwhile, the pile of tobacco in front of him was disappearing at a rate far slower than the piles deposited upon the workstations of his co-workers. By mid-morning, his head was bobbing toward the surface of his desk; he'd catch himself and sit upright, eyes blinking, but then, a minute or two later, his head would tilt forward once more, Marku coming awake just as his bobbing forehead grazed the table surface.

"Psssst," Sasha said.

Marku blinked, and took a raspy breath.

"*Pssssst*," Sasha said again, a little louder. Marku looked over as Sasha reached into his pants pocket and pulled out a palm full of raisins, thinking that a little sugar might revive the poor fellow. Marku waved them away, either because he was too proud, or because

Sasha's offerings, which were mixed with little bits of pocket lint and tobacco, looked unpalatable.

Marku yawned, coughed, and returned to his labours. A few seconds later, he once again drifted into semi-consciousness, his head a marionette, bobbing at the end of an invisible string. This time, he slumped fully forward.

"*Marku*," Sasha hissed.

It was no use: the little man was sound asleep, his face flat against the top of his workstation, his eyebrows dusted with tobacco shavings, a gentle snore escaping from his dry, flaking lips. Within seconds, Spiros came over and stood next to his sleeping employee, his hands on his hips, his chest rising and falling, his face pursed. Then, he picked up Marku's family portrait and brought it down on the sleeping Albanian's head.

Marku popped up, confused and groggy, not yet realizing that his photograph was in tatters. He rubbed his head. "Sorry sorry sorry," he said, at which point he noticed the shreds of his family portrait, lying next to his toppled mounds of tobacco. A look of unspeakable sorrow, one born of disappointment in all that life had to offer, crossed his already forlorn features. Sasha saw that look, and while he'd seen many instances of abuse at the factory, directed at both himself and others, it was this pathetic expression, transforming the man's face into a representation of all that was mournful and weak, that was a trigger: Sasha rose, his heart pounding, for he couldn't believe he was doing this, that he was actually backing his foreman toward a wall, the two men so close that the air between them warmed. "If you do that again," he said. "You'll have me to contend with."

For one moment only, the boss looked unnerved. But then he filled his chest with air and spat, "Get out, you're fired, Berkman, I've never liked the look of you, I'll have your spot filled by the end of the day, don't you think I won't, get out get out you son-of-a-bitch, *out!*"

Sasha collected his things, which were a precious few, just a packet of tobacco and a brown paper bag containing a liverwurst sandwich he'd made for himself that morning. He left the factory and stood outside, eating; it was barely ten o'clock, he had just lost his job, and it was quite likely he'd soon find himself eating at one of the many soup kitchens in downtown Manhattan, where you had to listen to a ten-minute speech about God's will in return for a cheese sandwich and an apple. It was even possible that he'd find himself homeless—it wouldn't be the first time, Sasha Berkman knowing full well what it was like to be woken in Tompkins Square Park at five o'clock in the morning, his back aching and stiff, his arms numb, a red-faced officer of the law tapping the bottoms of his shoes and saying, *move it along, Mac, move it along.* Yet he didn't feel distraught. At first, he couldn't understand why, given his was a personality prone to worry, catastrophic thinking and dark, brooding spells. Then, it came to him—it was that young woman from Russia, the one with the penetrative gaze and a sailor's tunic, she'd want to hear about *this.*

* * *

Twenty minutes later, he arrived breathless at the Minkins' door.

"My goodness," Emma said. "Sasha Berkman! Look at you. Has something happened?"

"I just got fired."

"What did you do?"

"My boss was harassing a fellow worker. A poor little man from Albania. I told him to stop."

Emma clapped her hands, yelped, and threw her arms around her new friend, giving Sasha a brief hug before jumping back and beaming. "Bravo, comrade. You *had* to do something. It was your duty as a human being."

"It felt good. I wish I'd done it earlier."

"You know what I think? I think little acts such as yours are happening all over the country. People are fed up. The United States of America, at this moment in time, is a pot of simmering water. A fed-up cigar factory worker confronts a despotic employer? That's escaping steam. A woman refuses to sleep with her drunken husband when he comes home, stinking of rye whisky on a Saturday night? More steam. A group of fish plant workers decide to go out on strike? It's steam, Sasha, steam steam steam. But I tell you, one day the water will boil furiously, and the lid will fly off, and we'll all have our day."

"I don't know what came over me. I could've throttled him."

"You should have. It's not healthy, you know, locking in all that emotion. Better to give rise to it and let the chips fall where they may. But still, *mazel tov*, the point is that you acted. The real immorality, as far as I'm concerned, is doing nothing at all. I take it you're now between jobs."

"I am."

"You'll find another, *boychik*. Come inside, please, come, have a look at my New York abode."

It was yet another dim railroad apartment, with each room doubling as a hallway, a single window embedded in the wall of the final bedroom. The light coming through it barely illuminated the window frame, leaving the rest of the apartment in a gloom. Sasha nodded, and asked, "Is everyone else out?"

"Anna and Helene are at work. As for their father, I couldn't tell you and I can't say I really care. He really is a pig, you know."

"So I've heard."

She stood looking up at him, arms crossed, her eyes sparkling with thoughts. "You know what, you could really help me with something. My sewing machine is in a storage room on Forty-Second Street, and I need a strong man to help me carry it. Would you mind terribly? You can't tell me you're busy."

They walked down a groaning staircase and started walking, the day hot and bright. "Emma," Sasha said. "How do you know Hillel Solotaroff?"

"It's a bit of a story, actually. I came from Russia four years ago, when I was just sixteen, and lived with my sisters in Rochester. They really didn't have room for me, so after a while I got married to a man named Jacob. I was barely eighteen."

"You're kidding."

"What can I say? He spoke Russian. I think I just wanted someone to talk to in my own language. Plus he'd read Tolstoy. Or, at least, that's what he claimed. It was a disaster from the very beginning. So I left him, and got a job in a corset factory in New Haven. There I met Solotaroff, who was giving a talk on anarchism in one of the union halls. He's a terrible speaker, you know. So gregarious and voluble in his everyday life, but as soon as you put him in front of a crowd? He starts mumbling. And his speeches! They sound like lists. I suppose I felt sorry for him. That's enough, for some women."

"That's true. I've heard him speak."

"Say what you want about him, but he does have his charms. Have I mentioned that my husband was completely impotent? If it wasn't for Solotaroff, I'd still be a virgin. He wanted to express himself sexually with me last night as well, but I told him, no, those days are over, ours was a time and a place only. He grinned and said he figured as much."

Sasha nodded, a little surprised by Emma's immediate willingness to divulge. The street, meanwhile, churned with people, such that Sasha and Emma kept brushing against one another, little moments of contact that occurred again, and again, and again.

"At any rate," she said, "Jacob found me and told me he'd commit suicide if I didn't go back to him. I was foolish enough to believe him. But that all ended a few nights ago. Really, I just couldn't stand the sight of him any longer."

"Is he looking for you?" he asked.

"Who, Jacob? My guess is no—he always was a bit of a coward. No doubt he'll find some other lonely teenager, impress her with a passage or two from *Anna Karenina*, and enter into another humiliating union. Still, I'm glad I knew him. He was kind enough to show me the true nature of marriage."

"Which is?"

"Exploitative to the core," she said while jabbing a forefinger toward the sky. "You see, Sasha, *I* believe that people are designed to love fiercely, and then wish to do so again—under any other circumstances, we shrivel as humans. We become meek, physically ill and easily manipulated. We grow ulcers, suffer acne and begin to smell like vinegar. This isn't just *my* opinion, by the way: studies from Europe have shown this. There were times back in Rochester when I didn't get out of bed for a week. I'd sleep all day and simper all night. We're all driven by demons, you know. It's the human condition. I'm just honest enough to admit which ones are mine. For a while, my doctor even thought I needed to go to a sanatorium. Meanwhile, I knew very well what I needed, and it wasn't rest or relaxation, if you get my meaning. Ah, here's the station."

Emma and Sasha joined a queue beneath the elevated tracks. Soon, they were riding in a shaking wooden car toward the middle of the city, Emma gazing out of the opened window, the breeze ruffling her hair. "I can't believe this place," she said. "The sheer madness of it."

"I had the hardest time getting used to New York."

"Every square inch is just *teeming* with life. I've never heard so many languages spoken in one place."

"Sometimes I think that the whole of the world has either come here, or is about to come here, or wishes they could come here."

"Tell me, Sasha, do you think that cities have souls?"

"What do you mean?"

"I'll give you an example. The soul of Kovno is characterized by shame. The city is embarrassed that it's such a little backwater, that the language spoken there is used nowhere else on earth, that it has no famous poets or revolutionaries and is governed by Moscow, some fifteen hundred kilometres away. It's embarrassed, Sasha, that its only contribution to world cuisine is a beet soup variation in which parsley is substituted for dill. It's not even particularly good."

"Ha!" Sasha exclaimed while slapping the tops of his legs. "You're right! It's *not* that good. What about St. Petersburg?"

"That's easy. St. Petersburg is a city operated by fear. It's a city of bats, golems and secret police, lurking around every corner. It's a place where people awake in the middle of the night certain that the branch tapping against the window is some sort of vengeful ghoul. Is it any wonder that so much great art has emerged from there? Every groundbreaking novel is a cry for rescue, every plié is an expression of sadness, every note of every symphony is a lament. There's a reason you can't swing a dead cat in St. Petersburg without hitting a poet in the face. Don't misunderstand me, St. Petersburg is a beautiful place—too beautiful, in fact, for the cretins who run it. But its soul? Bah, it quivers with terror."

Sasha thought about her words, his expression souring, for there was no doubt that she was right again. "What," he asked, "about New York City?"

"I've only been here for two days. I haven't decided yet."

"For some reason I don't believe you."

They were riding over Fifth Avenue. As they bustled along, Sasha gazed into those apartments that were at the same level as the elevated train. It was like watching a procession of photographs, come to life in vivid colour: a young couple embracing, a woman wagging her finger at a red-faced child, a pale fellow attempting to slice brisket with a bread knife, an old man with a large belly in a soiled undershirt, his face shaking as he bellowed into the street.

"Now that I think of it," Emma finally said, "New York City is a child. Yes, that's it, it's a terrifically excited infant, it's a caterwauling brat with no self-control. Every desire, every need, every ambition, every passion—here, it's immediately expressed, without any of the self-monitoring or self-containment practised by an adult. In fact, it would be dangerous to *not* do so here—you'd be left behind. Oh yes, the more I think of it, the more I believe I'm right. New York is a city without propriety, without half measures, without fear of consequence or reprisal. New York is a toddler running into traffic in order to retrieve a ball, without a moment's thought to the carriages that might run her over. What do you think?"

"I doubt you're the first person who's felt that way."

Emma's face brightened. "I've always wanted to live in such a place! It suits me! It fits me to a T. Oh look, this is our stop."

They deboarded and found a storefront crowded with newcomers, all waiting to claim steamer trunks filled with their possessions. After a long wait, Emma regained her sewing machine, which Sasha lugged back to the train—"I know it's heavy," she said, "but be careful, it's my meal ticket, without it I don't know what I'd do." After they rode back downtown, he carried it through busy streets, his forearms howling for relief by the time he set it down on the cutting board spanning the Minkins' bathtub. He was breathing hard, and was forced to wipe his brow with a handkerchief.

"Thank you," Emma said. "I don't know what I would've done if you hadn't dropped by. You really are as strong as an ox, you know. I'll find a better spot for it later. But listen, I've got an idea."

"Yes?"

"I'm free, you're free, all of New York is out there. Why don't you ask me to do something?"

* * *

The Pioneers of Liberty clubhouse was on Orchard Street; it had peeling light-green walls, wood-beam floors, teetering tables, rattling old windows, and air thickened by steam rising from a brand new coffee percolator, which sat bubbling all day on a battered electric stove, creating an acrid brew that stained the teeth and made one's fingertips tremble. Emma stepped into the noisy room, a grin of expectation on her face, and gestured toward the six-inch-high stage, where an unburdening soul was droning on about the emancipation of the proletariat, his voice low and uninflected, his hands clamped tightly to a text he'd no doubt prepared the night before, staying up so late that when he finally went to bed the rest of the city was beginning to awaken.

Sasha gave Emma a cigarette, their smoke adding to the thin blue-grey cloud that, at all times, clung to the rafters. The room was quiet that day, just a handful of members sitting at long, wooden benches, drinking coffee and half listening to the speaker, who was now punching his free hand into the air while shouting, in German, *Long live freedom! Long live liberty! Long live anarchism!* As the lecturer walked off the stage, Sasha touched the small of Emma's back and directed her toward the corner of the room where, as he'd expected, his cousin was sitting, a sketchbook and charcoal stick in hand, his once-fine clothes rumpled by his time in the city.

Modska looked up, his face lightening. "Sasha!" he said. "Who's this?"

"Emma Goldman, this is my cousin, Modska Aronstam. We share a room on Broome Street. Modska, this is Emma Goldman."

Modska stood, and cradled Emma's outstretched hand in both of his. "Ahhhhh," he said, "so this is the comrade from Rochester."

"Rochester, St. Petersburg, Lithuania, I'm from all over, actually."

"Who isn't these days? Maybe New York will agree with you. It's a pleasure to meet you. Please, please, join me, you too cousin."

Sasha was about to tell him that they couldn't, that they had all of New York City to see, when Emma interjected: "You know, I wouldn't mind sitting down for a drink."

"Wonderful!" said Modska, clapping his hands. Sasha fetched coffee; by the time he came back, Emma was telling Modska about her husband, her hands gesturing as she spoke.

"Really," she said, "his impotence wasn't his fault. He couldn't find a job, the poor wretch. I don't know what it's like here, but in *Rochester*? Bah, a factory closes every day. The bread lines keep getting longer and longer. It was the system that robbed him of his manliness. To tell you the truth, I'm not sure visiting a doctor would've done him any good anyway, not with the beating his libido took while out of work."

"It happens," said Modska with a grin. "Or at least that's what I've been told."

"Then again, he *was* a compulsive gambler and a pathetic mother's boy, so maybe he was to blame after all."

They all chuckled, lit cigarettes and sat smoking, Modska and Emma trading memories of the Kovno they knew as young children: the rides in the regional park, the store with the best candy, the narrow streets of the old city, where a five-year-old could reach out and touch both walls at once, and where water ran in singing rivulets after every rainfall. "I remember!" Emma kept saying. "I remember, I do, my heart is aching with recollections, it really is!"

Someone started playing German music on a wheezy phonograph; to this accompaniment, Solotaroff happened to wander in and joined the table. It was late afternoon when the Minkins arrived, looking for an escape from their living situation. They were also joined by a poet named David Edelstadt, who had spent the morning spouting revolutionary verse at the corner of Essex and Delancey, where his booming voice had startled children, caused stray dogs to start barking and attracted the attention of the police. (He was in a sour mood; mostly, he sat quietly, a cigarette clamped in his orange-stained fingertips.) The others talked, the conversation flitting from the Haymarket bombings to the price of apples, from the recent fire at a Canal Street sweatshop to the pigeon problem in Tompkins Square Park, from police brutality to the speech that Johann Most, *Freiheit*'s renowned editor, was slated to give the following Sunday at Cooper Union.

Hearing this, Emma turned to face Sasha, her eyes staring into his, one of her chubby little hands alighting on the top of his leg. "You and I, we'll go see Johann Most together, I'd really like to hear him speak, you'll take me, yes?"

"Of course," he answered. "Of course."

A short while later, Emma left to walk home with the Minkins, leaving Sasha and Modska behind. Soon, others came, all of them labourers by day and anarchists by night, with names like Drostofsky, like Bernstein, like Strashunsky and Yudelvich and Wein. There was vodka and loud chatter and sandwiches.

As Sasha sat, smoking and drinking coffee, a strange feeling came over him; it felt like a vapour, inflating his lungs, lightening his thoughts, invigorating his legs, his reverie ending when Solotaroff punched his arm and said, "What's gotten into you, Berkman? You seem almost... hmmmm... what's the word I'm looking for? Oh, I know, *happy.*"

four

AS SOON AS EMMA GOLDMAN met Anna and Helene Minkin's father, an obnoxious lout named Vasily, she knew she'd have to leave. It wasn't his drinking, or the hair that grew in wiry clumps upon his shoulders, or that he barked orders at his eldest daughter—*fer chrissakes Anna, wouldja get me a drink?*—or that he lay around, all day, in a stained undershirt, his mouth and fingertips turned orange, moaning about the fact that nobody would give him a job, god damn it. What truly revolted Emma was the way in which his eldest daughter responded to his brutishness; he picked on Anna more than he picked on Helene, who, in all honesty, seemed to scare him a little. Yet it was *Anna* who was the cheerful one, the perky one, the one who never had a bad thing to say about anybody, and that included her rancid, abusive, dipsomaniacal, mustard-stained paterfamilias. It was clearly a case of compensation run amok, and it saddened Emma more than she could have imagined, in that it replicated the neurotic relationship that she'd once suffered with her very own father—*if he strikes me*, she'd often told herself, *it must be because I'm a bad girl.*

She started searching for rooms for let, a chore that involved walking up and down the streets of the Lower East Side, searching for notes, handwritten in Russian or Yiddish or German, taped to smeary windows. She saw three or four each afternoon; all were filthy, lonely little abodes, with grimy hallways and a single shared bathroom down the hall. At the final place she visited, a fetid little room on East Broadway, she realized she was too tired to look anymore, so she turned to her future landlady, a wrinkled crone with a lazy eye, and muttered, "It'll do."

When she told the Minkin sisters that she was leaving, their reactions could not have been more different. "Why wouldn't you?" snorted Helene while tilting her head in the direction of their father, who was slumped in his chair, snoring. Anna, on the other hand, started to sniffle, and nodded her acceptance of this sudden new truth.

"I'm sorry," Emma said, writing her new address on a scrap of paper. She handed it to Helene. "Could you tell everyone that I've moved?"

"Of course."

"I'll be busy the next few days, so it's important."

"Don't worry."

"I'm going to the Johann Most lecture with Sasha Berkman, and I don't know where he lives. So it's important you give him that address when you see him."

"For Christ's sake, Emma, I said I'd do it."

Emma was about to roll her eyes at Helene's reliably caustic disposition when she felt a different emotion rise within her, an emotion that caused her cheeks to redden and her eyes to glisten. "You know," she said in a thin, croaking voice, "I love you both. I didn't realize it until this moment, but I do, I really do, you took me in, you're like my real sisters, how could I not adore you, could you please please tell me *that*?"

* * *

Now that she had her own place to live, Emma started visiting the garment factories in the neighbourhood; mostly, she was told to beat it. At those few shops in which she did manage to speak with a floor manager, she was told that there were no positions available. Yet there *were* a few who told her that, even though they had no full-time jobs, they often sent out excess piecework, and if she was willing to attach buttons, seams, piping, collars, eyelets and sleeves, and could also perform a little decorative stitching should the situation arise, they might have something for her to do. By Saturday morning, the middle of her apartment was piled high with semi-completed dresses. *Look at me*, she thought, *a bored housewife turned Lower East Side seamstress. Will I ever be anything beyond a cliché?* She placed her sewing machine on a teetering card table she'd found abandoned on an empty Grand Street lot. Then, she got to work, pins between her teeth, her sewing machine trundling away, stitch after stitch after stitch, the room otherwise dead quiet, her hands soon working independently of her mind, thus allowing her thoughts to roam and quickly land upon a topic far more pressing than home, work, or life in New York—on that hot August afternoon on the Lower East Side, Emma Goldman could think of little else than the young, brooding anarchist who had helped carry her sewing machine.

Normally, she did not like to examine the cause of sudden and intense attraction—to her, such moments were nothing less than instances of magic, and attempting to unlock the mysteries of the heart was not only disrespectful but futile, like trying to scale a mountain with shackled feet. Yet on this occasion, with a river of dresses, corsets, skirts and petticoats flowing through her sewing machine, she couldn't stop her thoughts from landing upon, and wishing for, this man named Alexander "Sasha" Berkman. On the one hand, he was built like a small rhinoceros, with his barrel chest, sturdy legs and tree-trunk forearms. From the neck up, however, his appearance could best be described as interesting—those small eyes, those jug-handled ears, those thick, rubbery lips; at the tender age of nineteen he could have passed for thirty, a widow's peak already forming at the crown of his head, worry lines having etched onto the broad expanse of his forehead. This was all beside the point, as Emma was a woman who favoured men with an aura of tragedy about them, along with an appearance suggesting complexity, or duality, with both sides of the psyche duking it out for supremacy; in fact, she couldn't help replaying the night when she'd first walked into Café Sachs and spotted him tearing into a raw steak, a spot of gravy on his chin, his fork hand the size of a cantaloupe. But then, he'd looked up and gazed at her with such a sad, languid dolefulness in his eyes that her heart, for a single, enraptured moment, stopped beating, only to restart with a cadence so irregular that it hurt. This was another thing that she knew for certain: it wasn't his soulfulness or his vulgarity that had snared her, it was the fact that the two coexisted, seemingly with ease, within this single, overwrought person. This, for Emma Goldman, was entrancement itself.

Emma stayed up all night, working. She did this often, as it was the only way to get everything done she wanted to do in life, while still generating enough income to, however modestly, feed and clothe herself. Outside her building, the sky eventually turned yellow, the shouts of cart vendors floating through her wide-open window. Only then did she lie upon the lumpy single bed that had come with the room and fall into a colour-soaked dream. Five hours later, she awoke with the knowledge that she was running late. She ran to one of the shared bathrooms in the hallway and quickly bathed, the water all but cold, and then she ran back to her room and dressed in the only nice clothes she happened to own, a grey skirt and that white blouse with white piping (if *only* she'd brought more clothes from Rochester, if *only* she'd given some forethought to her extrication from the marital home, *if only if only if only*). She then pinned her hair, patted down her skirt, and attempted to appraise her appearance in the reflection thrown by a large silver spoon that she'd found in one of the drawers.

There was a rustling in the hallway, followed by a knock. Emma opened the door and gave Sasha a light kiss on the side of his face. Then she stood back, a hand on one hip, surprised by how well-appointed he was: he wore narrow, striped pants, a pressed white shirt, polished leather shoes and wire-rimmed glasses.

"You look handsome," she said.

"I don't, but thank you."

"Don't do that," she said.

"Do what?"

"Denigrate yourself. It's a bad habit to get into. There's a whole world out there, just waiting to make you feel bad about yourself. If you start doing it too... well, all is lost, really. Come in, please."

As he stepped into the apartment, he gazed over Emma's head, taking in the two large piles of clothing in the living room, one a mound that had been completed, the other a heap that still needed Emma's attention.

"It looks like you've been keeping busy."

"I'm taking in piecework. I tell you, Sasha, I've sewn on so many buttons this week I see them in my dreams. I'm glad you came. Honestly, I'm about to lose my mind. I do that sometimes, you know; then I have to go to bed for a week. It really is good to see you. I can't tell you how much I've been looking forward to this. Do you want some coffee? There's some made. I just need to warm it up."

"Mmmmm... I'd prefer to get going. I'm a little worried about getting a good seat. We're talking about the king of the New York anarchist movement. Sometimes I think that every garment worker and cigar roller in this city depends on Most for a little bit of hope in their lives."

"Yes! Yes! You're right!"

Emma paused to scan the room, a portion of lip between her teeth, as if gauging the amount of work that would be waiting for her when she returned. She took a deep breath, and looked back at her comrade. "Well then," she said. "Shall we?"

* * *

They wound their way through the city, passing tenements and townhomes and Gothic stone fire stations and city squares colonized by the homeless, until they reached the Cooper Union building, a beautiful Italianate mansion with vaulted windows and tall stone arches. After finding seats near the front of the stage, just off to the right, they spent the next half hour watching the hall fill with people whose manner of dress contrasted sharply with the elegance of the venue. The man seated beside Emma had a torn lapel, and was sipping from a bottle of schnapps; when he offered her the bottle, she gamely took a sip before passing it back. As the start time came and went, the audience quickly grew restless, its discontent beginning with coughs and quickly turning to loudly expressed sentiments. Someone called out "Where the hell's Most?" in a raspy voice, and someone else lobbed a half-eaten apple at the curtain. This toss seemed to provide a spark: people began to chant *We want Most! We want Most!* and soon they were whooping, the stage a target for lobbed bottles, half-smoked cigars and even an old boot, its tongue flapping as it soared through the air. Emma and Sasha glanced at each other, eyebrows arched, for they both knew that this venom, this absolute disregard for propriety, when channelled in a single direction, would change everything. It was exciting, this rage: the crowd began to stomp the floor, at first in a random cacophony, but then, after ten or twenty seconds, in a coherent, almost military tattoo.

"Sasha," said Emma. "Isn't this wonderful? Isn't this terrific? Isn't this... isn't this... *glorious*?"

The curtains parted. There was a roar of applause. The stage was bare save for a lectern and a glass of water. A man walked out—not Most, but some toady with the Knights of Labor who was met by boos as he attempted to announce that this meeting was being held in furtherance of solidarity, and that if he could please just say a few words about...

He could not; the crowd wanted Most and only Most; the derelict beside Emma stood, cupped his roughened hands, and yelled, "Shut yer fookin' yob ya tosser you." This prompted a roar of applause, the poor Knight having no option but to shake his head, raise his hands and, in his loudest voice, announce, "Ladies and gentlemen, I give you Johann Most!"

It was deafening, the eruption of cheers and whistles as Most walked upon the stage. A moment later, there was a slight hush, for there were many in the audience, Emma included, who had never before seen Johann Most, and did not realize that flesh-eating diseases had laid waste to the left side of his face when he was young. While he did his best to camouflage his deformity by growing his beard thicker on the left side of the face, thereby filling the crater left behind by the disease, the trick worked in only the most rudimentary of ways.

Most gestured at the crowd to quieten. He then began to speak in a heavily accented English.

"Louis Lingg," he said, his eyes shifting from right to left. A murmur issued through the audience.

"George Engel," Most said in a slightly louder voice.

More whisperings.

"Adolph Fischer! ALBERT PARSONS! AUGUST SPIES! Oh yes! I can see that most of you know who these brave men were. But for those who do *not*, allow me to tell you. A few short years ago, during a demonstration in support of an eight-hour workday at Haymarket Square in Chicago, police arrived to disperse a crowd. A riot ensued, with someone throwing a bomb that killed eight police officers. In return, eight anarchists were arrested, five of whom were later given the death sentence. Four of them, namely Spies, Parsons, Fischer and Engel, were hung. As for Louis Lingg, he died by his own hand in a Chicago jail cell, having swallowed an explosive device that robbed the state of the satisfaction of killing him. They were heroes, martyrs to the cause, every one of them. And do you know what their crime was?"

"Tell us!" yelled an audience member.

"Yes! Tell us!" yelled another.

"Oh don't you worry," continued Most. "I shall enlighten you, my good people! I shall enlighten *all* of you. But first, I will tell you what they did *not* do... these men did *not* throw the bomb that killed advancing police officers at the Haymarket labour strike, thereby causing a riot that injured hundreds. I repeat, they did *not* hurl a homemade, brittle-casing incendiary device! This is not just *my* opinion, by the way. Oh no, it was never even *contended* that these five comrades were even *at* Haymarket that day. The judge knew it, the prosecution knew it, indeed *everyone* knew that the five men who were about to be sent to the gallows did not hurl that fated bomb. So what happened? Why did they have to die?"

Most paused, his face roiling with disgust.

"I shall tell you!" he continued. "The police, following the fracas, simply arrested every well-known revolutionist in Chicago, and then settled on these five as patsies. Oh yes, these men died for a crime all right! But the crime was not a bombing. Oh no, their crime was being anarchists! Their crime was being in favour of humane working conditions! Their *crime*, I tell you, was being *German*!"

Sasha and Emma, like the rest of the audience, cheered, for they all knew that Most was right, that to be German in New York City was to be feared by the authorities.

"Please, please, let me continue. We all *know* that these five men were unjustly condemned. If you ask me, the fateful bomb was detonated by provocateurs, hired by factory owners to discredit the great labour uprising that has seized our country. But I ask you, good men and women. Would it really have been a crime if these five men *had* thrown that bomb at advancing police?"

He looked over the hushed assembly. "No!" he yelled, his fist striking the lectern. "Of course not! Pinkerton agents, hired by the establishment class, had opened fire on the demonstrators the day before. *This has been well established.* Viewed this way, the bombing—if in fact the device *had* been thrown by one of the accused—would have merely been a case of self-defence. In *fact*, if it was a crime at all, I'd say it was a crime of aiming too low, of picking the wrong target, of injuring a handful of lowly police officers, who were merely doing the bidding of their autocratic overlords. Oh no, if an anarchist wants to commit a completely justifiable attack on another individual, better that individual be some titan of industry, a beast of property, a viper of capitalism!"

Emma stood, as if pulled skyward by the power of Most's delivery. Sasha rose to his feet as well, if only to see over the people now standing in the row in front.

"Please, please," Most continued. "Settle down, let me speak. We are talking about serious things, my good men and women. So calm yourselves, and listen. Open your ears, and digest. Let me pose another hypothetical question. Say you have a notoriously oppressive factory owner. For the purposes of this game, he need not have a name. But he IS real, he pays starvation wages, his factory floor is dangerous and unsanitary, he demands a seventy-hour work week, he gropes his female employees, and, whenever the mood hits him, he fires a few good employees just to demonstrate that the welfare of his workers is something he can fritter away like day-old confetti."

"Boooooooo! Booooooo!"

"And so, a good anarchist, dedicated to the betterment of humanity, working tirelessly to undermine the yoke that is capitalism, decides that he is *more* than justified in creeping into that factory owner's office and ending the oppressor's life with a pistol."

"Yes!" howled the crowd, as this was the reason they had all come—to hear Most's thoughts on the moment in which violence became the favoured option.

"Please!" Most continued. "I ask you. What is the point of this? Is it to eliminate one more beast of property from the face of this good earth?"

"Yes!" yelled someone in the audience.

"God damn right!" called someone else.

"NO!" retorted Most, again banging his fist upon the lectern. "And I'll tell you *why*. Where there is one Rockefeller, there are a dozen like him, all keening to take his place. Where there's a loathsome Vanderbilt, there are a dozen underlings, only too happy to step into his shoes! Where there's a single Carnegie, there's a conference room of Carnegies, all champing at the bit to get started!"

He paused. Confusion hushed the crowd. Someone coughed.

"And yet, there IS a real benefit to the assassination, for it raises the temperature of the proletariat, and inspires it to similar actions. Soon, there is full-fledged revolution. We call this *propaganda of the deed*, and it is a very important concept: if an attack is carried out, it should be carried out for its inspirational value. Here I'll quote the Italian revolutionist Carlo Pisacane, who famously said, "Ideas spread from deeds and not the other way around." I'll also quote Mikhail Bakunin, one of the fathers of modern anarchism, who said, "We must spread our principles, not with words, but with deeds, for this is the most potent, and most irresistible, form of propaganda."

"Do you hear?!" Sasha yelled into Emma's ear. "*Bakunin!*"

"I'll give you another example: the murder of Alexander the Second in Russia. Has the tsar's death ended oppression in Russia? Of course not. In fact, under the new tsar, it has triggered a wave of retribution too sickening for me to describe. What it *has* done, however, is embolden those forces in Russia who are toiling to see the end of tsarism. And trust me, good men and women, I have many contacts in Russia, good anarchists all—though over there they refer to themselves as nihilists—and they assure me that the revolution will OCCUR AT ANY MOMENT!"

"Yes!" Emma yelled, her hands cupped around her mouth, "yes yes yes!"

Most now raised his voice, so that he was all but yelling: "THIS IS WHAT I AM TELLING YOU! THE TIME FOR THEOR- IZING, FOR STRIKING, FOR FORMING UNIONS, FOR TYPING UP LEAFLETS, FOR PROSELYTIZING FROM SOAPBOXES ON BOWERY STREET CORNERS... ALL OF IT IS OVER, MY GOOD PEOPLE, ALL OF IT BELONGS TO A DIFFERENT TIME, TO THE PRE-REVOLUTIONARY PHASE... BUT NOW WE ARE MOVING INTO A NEW EPOCH... OH YES... IF I CAN DO ONE THING TODAY, IT IS TO WELCOME YOU ALL, WHOLEHEARTEDLY AND WITH ALL THE FERVOUR CONTAINED WITHIN MY HEART... TO THE TIME OF THE *DEED*!!!!!"

* * *

It was this declaration, this call to angry order, that lifted the speech into the realm of the incantatory, creating a spell that in no way dimmed as he continued speaking. Midway through his speech, with Most railing about the value of the *attentat*, a word he used to describe any violent action taken against the state, the hall's elec- tric lights began to flicker, plunging it into darkness for a second or two, before reawakening the crowd with a light that seemed slightly brighter than it had been just moments earlier. This kept happening; it seemed to Emma that these brief flickerings of darkness tended to follow the completion of a distinct idea within Most's speech, such that a striking rhythm began to emerge, a pattern marked by asser- tion, darkness, rebirth... assertion, darkness, rebirth.

Most spoke for forty-five minutes. His speech culminated with an anthem he'd penned called "Hymn of the Proletariat." The audi- ence members all sang, arm in arm, eyes damp, swaying like trees on a breezy night, alive in their hearts and minds and souls. Then, they calmly walked toward the exits, eyes glazed, looking beatific and spent. Emma and Sasha now understood Most's appeal: his speeches provided a release from the stressors of life in immigrant New York, a release so intense as to be almost carnal.

Sasha and Emma lit cigarettes as soon as they stepped onto Third Avenue. They did not speak, though Emma slipped a hand into the crook of Sasha's elbow as they walked. The Cooper Union was located at Third Avenue and Seventh Street, right at a boundary between rich and poor, the owners and workers, the haves and have-nothings, the socialites and the social outcasts. As they strolled along, Sasha and Emma tried to imagine the neighbourhood when the revolution finally came. That fat man over there, with his tailored suit and two-dollar stogie? He'd become a fossil. That face-smudged urchin, searching in the gutter for dropped apple cores? He'd be lifted, as if by a magician's spell, into relative comfort. That velvet-gloved matron, stepping into a horse-drawn carriage? She'd be obliterated by the dialectical forces of history, along with her personal maid, her livery staff, her summers spent on the continent, and the stuffed egret mounted on her hat. Or, that emaciated wastrel, poking her head out of an alley, peeping, "Have a go, mister, I'm the best, I really is, have a look at these knockers, too good to pass up now, isn't they?" Oh yes, Emma and Sasha knew too well, meaningful work would be found for her, her life of degradation no more.

They reached the doorway to Emma's building; "You'll come up," she stated. They climbed in half darkness, Emma's hobnail boots tapping against the stairway. She reached her doorway and crossed her lips with a forefinger. "The walls are as thin as paper. If I make the slightest noise, the old woman who lives next door yells at me to be quiet. She's as mad as they come, that one."

They stepped inside her room. Emma lit a candle, filling the room with soft light. The air was thick and hot. Wordlessly, she began to unbutton her blouse; Sasha stood watching, attempting to disguise his amazement, as she casually removed her boots, her sailor's blouse, her skirt, her undergarments. Then, she stood before him, hiding nothing, her expression one of serene intensity. She walked toward Sasha and kissed him, softly. "There are two types of men," she whispered. "Some are idealists. Some are vulgarians. You're both. I know this as surely as I have ever known anything. Now please, Sasha, my darling revolutionist, get out of those clothes."

He did, undressing in a far more rushed and nervous manner than Emma. He stood before her, breathing heavily, becoming emotional when she said, "You're beautiful."

"I'm not."

"Yes," she said, moving around him. "You are." Even in the room's low light, she discovered the tiny, pinprick scars. "Ahhhhh," she said. "So, you had a father like mine."

"No..."

Emma squinted. "Your mother, then?"

"Not really. Hardly at all. Only when I was little."

"A metal hair brush?"

"Yes."

"Why?"

"She said I deserved it."

"Did you?"

"Most likely."

"Of course you didn't," Emma said. "You were a child. You'll need to rid yourself of this belief. This is important. You'll be trapped until you do."

She slid her arms around him, and rested the side of her face on his shoulder. "My father tried so hard to make a lady out of me. It was futile, of course. I am who I am and will not make apologies. He'd make me walk around the room with a book on my head, and if it dropped off he would strike me. It only hurt because I loved him so."

Sasha felt her small breasts pushing against his back. He turned to face her. He was taller than her, but not by much. He kissed her hotly.

"Sasha," she murmured. "You have the chest of a bull."

"I don't."

"You do. You could carry me as though I were a child."

"That's true," he said, gently lifting her. Emma's muscles, he noted, felt soft and dense and sublime. Her bed was a few steps away. He lowered her to the mattress, his arm muscles flexing. There were beads of sweat on her upper chest. A delightful throb spread through his pelvis, the top of his legs, his lungs. He kissed her neck, her mouth an inch from his ear.

"Sasha," she whispered, "the woman next door... please... she's insane, she'll murder us both in our sleep, muffle your cries against the side of my neck. Express yourself any way you like, but keep your mouth sealed to my skin."

And so, he did.

five

THEIR DAYTIME LIVES felt imagined, now, as if they had both stepped into a tactile fever, the city a chaotic, grey-mash dream. Sasha found another job, this one at a cloak factory in Manhattan, while Emma continued to take in as much sewing as a single person could possibly manage. Yet their real existence, apart from political activities, now occurred in the evening, in Emma's stuffy and thin-walled abode, where Sasha stifled his cries of exultation not only upon the side of her neck, but upon her stomach, her right thigh, her left calf, the recession between her shoulder blades, her gently sloped forehead, the small of her waist, her girlish breasts, her plump-ish mouth, and, on a night in which their sexual congress approached the acrobatic, the instep of her right foot. One evening, the inevitable happened, for Sasha must have selected a part of Emma's body too angular to make a seal—a clavicle, perhaps—thus awaking the woman who lived next door. In a flash, she was pounding on Emma's door, yelling, "You harlot, you Jezebel, how am I supposed to sleep with sin in my dwelling place, with the long arm of Mephistopheles reaching for me, plucking at me, dragging me toward the fires of retribution, sentencing me to the inner circle of Hades, I CONDEMN THEE! I CONDEMN THEE TO HELL!"

Looking for new quarters was a dispiriting task, for the city was a crowded place, with new arrivals coming every day, wide-eyed hopefuls fleeing Europe, their worldly belongings packed into a single tin-cornered steamer trunk. At least Sasha and Emma were in love—this helped maintain their spirits. They had pet names for each other—Emma was sailor girl, Sasha her fishlips. They kissed hotly upon waking; they made toast and eggs while smoking; they trudged through streets in soft light, holding hands and talking about nothing and everything, all at once, and in so doing discovered the remarkable number of things that they had in common. Both were from that portion of western Russia where the people survived on root vegetables, lived in crumbling houses, and spoke a strange language called Lithuanian. Both had spent time with their families in St. Petersburg, during a brief period in which the rules governing the Pale of Settlement had been relaxed. Both had fractious relationships with their opposite-sex parent, and had the scars to prove it. Both loved smoking cigarettes and drinking coffee, though if there was beer or vodka around, Emma didn't have to be persuaded. Most remarkably, both had uncles who were revolutionists: Emma's was a well-known nihilist, while Sasha's had been a founding member of Land and Liberty, perhaps the largest revolutionary society in St. Petersburg.

"Sasha," she said, lying naked beside him one evening. "How many poor and oppressed Jews live in Russia?"

"Too many to count."

"And how many workers are slowly murdered in the factories of America?"

"Even more."

"And how many devote themselves to creating a new and equitable world?"

"Hardly any."

"Have you ever thought why that might be? Well, have you? It needs to be in your blood, Sasha. You can't overthrow unless someone in your family has already overthrown. Look at my uncle: by day he worked as a milliner, by night he threw bricks through factory windows. Or *your* uncle, the poor bastard, banished to Siberia by the state apparatus. If he's still alive, he's probably building a railway that starts in the middle of nowhere, and ends in the middle of nowhere, and covers plenty of nowhere in between."

"He was innocent."

"Who isn't? Here's my point, my lovely little fishlips. You and I—we can't help ourselves. We were programmed to right wrongs. Someday, scientists will figure out exactly how this happens."

"You might be right."

"I am right."

"Well..."

"What is it? You suddenly look upset."

She was right—Sasha was suffering a recollection that, while entirely germane to the topic at hand, had always caused him a great deal of distress. He lit a cigarette, the smoke pluming thick and blue toward the ceiling. Finally, he asked, "Can I tell you a story?"

"Yes," said Emma, "of course."

"You already know that my father died of a heart attack when I was twelve?"

"Yes... when you were still living in St. Petersburg, I believe."

"We were. When he died, my mother discovered how broke our family was. It seems he'd borrowed money from people all over Russia to fund his business. Now they were all at our door, hands out, wanting to collect, like buzzards. We packed up in the middle of the night and moved to your hometown to live with my uncle. Modska was his son. That's how we met—my family moved into his house."

"I think I knew that too."

"Well here's what you don't know. When I was about fifteen, my uncle hired a servant girl named Rosa. She was seventeen years old.

A quiet, serious girl with plain features. I saw myself in her. How I loved her! I used to follow her around like a sick puppy. She was all I could think about."

"Did you kiss her?"

"She considered me a child. There was one time, we ran head-long into each other in the hallway. I was about to tell her how I felt when she told me to make sure I ate my oat cakes, as I'd awaken hungry if I didn't. I decided, right then and there, that I'd bide my time, grow a little bit, and then tell her."

"That's too bad, but I understand."

"Early one Saturday, Rosa emerged from her room, chamber pot in hand. She was coming down the stairs leading from the third to the second floor when something startled her. It was me, of course, lurking in the doorway of my room, hoping to catch a glimpse of her. She tripped, and caught herself, though not before slopping a bit of the pot's contents on the stairway runner. Unfortunately, my mother had just come out of her room."

"Uh-oh..."

"She glared at Rosa. 'You ignorant peasant,' she seethed. Rosa said nothing. What *could* she say? That's when my mother slapped the side of her face. Rosa yelped, her knees buckling. Naturally, I rushed to assist her. She looked up, a fury in her eyes. That's when I realized how she saw me—in a world divided by class, *I* was one of *them*. I reached out to help her up, and she swatted my hand away. After that, everything changed."

"I bet it did," Emma said, raising an eyebrow.

"I went from being a quiet, studious boy to a hellion. I started smoking, I cheated on exams, I talked back to my professors. I formed a reading group; there were six of us, misfits all, and we only discussed revolutionary texts. I even got suspended for submitting an essay on the death of religion. When they finally let me back in, I was behind by a year. I lasted for a week or two, and then quit."

Sasha paused. He looked weary.

"So," Emma said, "you're saying that love made you an anarchist?"

"I suppose it did."

She grinned, and patted his chest. "Good. That's just the way it should be."

* * *

Again, it was a matter of spotting signs, scribbled on cardboard panels, though the neighbourhood was starting to change, the couple now seeing "To Let" signs in Italian, in Portuguese, in Hungarian. They viewed room after room. One particular abode was still inhabited by a sallow-faced woman and her three children; as the landlord showed Sasha and Emma the apartment, the poor family hunched by a window, looking pitiable and worn, their expressions pleading, as if Sasha and Emma might have had the power to prevent their eviction.

"Oh don't worry about them," said the landlord, "they're out tomorrow, haven't paid their rent, they're no good, no good no *how*."

"You should be ashamed," Emma told him.

"And *you* can leave now."

"Don't worry."

"Then go."

"We will."

"Then why in the hell aren'tcha?"

Sasha was rooted, motionless, bristling with rancour, when he realized, with some degree of surprise, that his fists had tightened at his sides, so much so that they'd turned white at the knuckles.

Emma noticed, and grinned. "You wait," she said to the landlord. "All of this, every brick and floorboard, yours no more, you got that?"

They saw a few more rooms that day, each one worse than the one before, the last smelling so badly of sewage that Sasha had to cover his face with a handkerchief. Afterward, the couple retired to Café Sachs. Modska was there, drawing, as always, in the corner, his grin falling away when the couple approached.

"Why the long faces?" he asked.

"Bah," Sasha said. "There isn't a decent apartment in all of New York City."

"What? You're moving? Cousin? Is this true?"

"We're going to live in sin," Emma joked.

"Take me with you! We could all live together, and save on rent! Say yes. *Please* say yes. You know I can't afford our room by myself! Besides, you know how bad the place is. Just the other morning, Emma, that widower who lives above us opened his window and tossed out a bucket of fish heads and they landed with a splat on the windowsill. I tell you what. I'll forgive you both for not telling me sooner if I can live with you. So can I? Join in on the fun?"

Sasha was about to say no, not this time, for if the truth be known, he was growing tired of the way their room was always covered with art supplies, such that he couldn't walk across the floor without stepping in paint, an annoyance nearly matched by Modska's habit of washing his socks in the kitchen sink, only to become distracted by some artistic notion and leave them there, forgotten, the water murky and brown. Yet before Sasha had time to open his mouth, Emma clapped her hands and said, "Of course, Modska."

Modska jumped to his feet, and kissed both sides of Emma's face. "You won't regret it!" he shouted. "Let's have a toast! We need some beer!"

Just as Modska was pulling steins of lager from the tray of a passing waiter, the Minkin sisters came through the door. "Why so happy?" asked Anna. Modska hugged her, too, and said, "Sasha and Emma and I are going to live together."

"Could Helene and I come too?" she asked. "Papa's getting worse. The other day he got so drunk he wet himself." She leaned forward, and lowered her voice slightly. "I've been doing some reading. Do you know about repressed memory? The Viennese have just discovered it... I believe our father may have touched me when I was younger."

"I'm not surprised," Emma said. "It happens all the time. With mothers and their sons, too. Taboo only increases temptation, you know, not the other way around. That's why it shouldn't exist. This memory has just come to you?"

"No, this is what I'm saying, it's a *repressed* memory. I'm not yet ready to face it."

"Then how do you know it happened?"

"I have no other memories to replace it. It's all a blank. Everyone else I know has all kinds of memories of their childhood. But me? I remember nothing."

Helene spoke up: "That's because you have the brain of a gnat. *Look.* The man's a lazy drunk with a foul mouth and body odour. Anna can't accept that we hate his guts, pure and simple. She has to look for an excuse. She can't let herself feel that intensity of emotion. She's repressed all right, just not in the way that she thinks. Then again, he is a lying sack of shit, so who knows? But we're getting off topic. Will you take us or won't you?"

"Of course," said Emma while turning to Sasha. "What do you think, fishie? It sounds like we have ourselves a collective. Is there any other way we could possibly live?"

* * *

The search continued, the inventory of apartments even smaller now that they needed a place that could sleep five adults. They split up, the theory being that five people could scour the city more effectively if they worked alone, reporting back with any promising leads. This caused Sasha to grow even more disconsolate—without Emma at his side, the chore of finding an apartment was just that, a lifeless, spirit-mulching obligation. He grew weary of the uniform adopted by every landlord in the city: the three-day beard, the untucked shirt, the scant hair swept over their scalps and adhered with a perspiratory dew. Their behaviour, meanwhile, spanned the gamut, from the officious to the plainly barbaric—he saw one railroad apartment on Suffolk Street that, according to the landlord, had housed a family from Riga, all of whom vanished one night, leaving rent unpaid, a kitchen coated with grease stains, and a litter of motherless kittens, who were found mewling in one of the cupboards. As Sasha went from room to room, he began to grow optimistic, not because the rooms were particularly nice, but because there was nothing terribly wrong with them. This changed when he came to the last room. "*What*," he asked, "is that smell?"

"Smell? You smell something?"

"Don't play stupid. Something died in there."

"No, no, such is not the case. I believe you are imagining it!"

One evening, the group met up at Justus Schwab's, an anarchist watering hole that operated out of a street front on First Street; here, Anna informed the others that she'd changed her mind about living with them. "I'm the eldest daughter," she said with a sniffle. "It's my duty to take care of my father." The tabletop was covered in beer bottles and coffee cups.

Emma looked furious. "Familial obligations! Those are the ties that bind, and then cut off circulation to the brain." She stormed off; Sasha found her near the window overlooking the street, shaking with anger.

"It might be a good thing," he told her. "It might be easier to find a place now that there's just four of us."

"But you don't understand?" she countered. "It was *supposed* to be all of us. That's the way it was *supposed* to be. The more people, the stronger the collective. This isn't just about us! I shouldn't have to tell you this..."

* * *

Late one afternoon, having spent the day hawking caricatures near Central Park, Modska was walking home along the East River when he saw a "To Rent" sign in the window of a handsome apartment building on Twenty-Third Street. He hid his brushes and paints in a shrub, straightened his lapel, checked his hair in a store window, and entered the building, at which point he discovered that the landlord was, in fact, a landlady; this caused him to grin, for he knew the battle was already half won.

"I'm in sales," he claimed, and, before she could ask for authenticating details, he complimented her on the brooch she was wearing. She blushed, and Modska told her that he was surprised—no, he was astonished—that a woman of her tender years could have acquired the responsibilities of a property owner. "My wife and I," he told her with a straight face, "are thinking of starting a family, she'd really like three children, she herself had a brother and a sister, in her mind a family isn't a family unless there are three little tykes running around, so God willing the extra rooms will fill up quickly, madam, and if I can be perfectly honest—and I believe that I *can*—this abode, at least to me, seems warm and good and ideal for the raising of a brood."

Modska, Emma and Helene, upon moving in, were delighted—the new apartment had a real stove, level floors, four bedrooms, functioning heat, adequate plumbing, a garbage chute in the hallway, and a view of the river, which sparkled with barge lights in the evening. There was even a hallway, running through the centre of the apartment, so that you didn't have to walk through someone else's bedroom to get to your own—it was this feature, more than anything else, that made the group feel as though they'd escaped the squalor of the Lower East Side. The only person who was slightly disappointed was Sasha—he'd thought he'd share a room with Emma, meaning they could keep a spare room available

50

for visiting comrades. Emma wouldn't have it. "Oh no, it'd be too much like marriage if we occupied the same room, can't you see that fishlips?"

She was excited, in other words—she now had an actual anarcho-commune, a collectivized lifestyle informed by a splash of Kropotkin, a spritz of Bakunin, and a dollop or two of Marx, the four living according to their needs and contributing according to their abilities. Sasha worked in the cloak factory. Helene toiled in a corset factory—"you wouldn't believe how many of those fat bourgeois matrons actually wear the god damn things," she'd say whenever she drank schnapps. Emma took in sewing, while Modska peddled sketches in various locations around Central Park.

Despite his initial ambivalence, Sasha grew to love the new arrangement, for it felt as though they were finally *doing* something to further a new concept of society, instead of endlessly talking about it, their breath steamy with cigarette smoke and kielbasa. They had no private possessions, they shared every dime they earned, and they pinned a chore wheel to the inside of the bathroom door. After a long day, they'd unite for supper, and chat about their day over some simple dish that Emma or Modska had prepared; while neither would ever be mistaken for a professional chef, Emma made a highly savoury beet-and-potato borscht, while Modska was particularly adept at chicken Kiev, a dish that some Ukraine-born aunt of his made during family get-togethers.

Helene sewed a pair of curtains with a bolt of fabric she liberated from the corset factory—"the sons of bitches won't even miss it"—while Emma grew dill in a kitchen window box. One Sunday, Sasha and Modska painted the walls, ridding the apartment of an ecclesiastical green that, Emma claimed, soured her mood; the walls were now a pale, restful blue. Using their collectivized funds, they paid a half dollar for a pair of pawn shop lamps, and found a Turkish rug in a used-goods shop on Houston Street: the two cousins took turns thrashing it with a broom before Emma and

Helene allowed it in the apartment. Modska's paintings decorated the walls—he was partial to watercolour renderings of birds, plants and small animals.

At night, they played euchre, drank coffee, smoked cigarettes, and talked of upcoming anarchist events in the city. There was no shortage; they went to anarchist lectures at the Cooper Union, socialist worker rallies in Union Square, boisterous get-togethers at Justus Schwab's, smoke-ins at Frank's Hall on West Houston, all-you-can-eat-schnitzel nights at Café Sachs, plotting sessions at the New York Social-Revolutionary Club, anti-fascist dust-ups at a den filled with reprobates called Zum Groben Michel, and concerts at Battery Park, where klezmer bands would play for tossed nickels and rounds of applause.

Other times, they'd have visitors, the apartment filling with smoke and the scent of unwashed wool. Naturally, debate would occur. Was violence an inevitable component in the coming revolution? (Some thought yes, others weren't quite so certain.) Were political structures necessary following the collapse of the free market? (Followers of Kropotkin envisioned a collectivized power structure, while adherents of Bakunin believed in a completely unfettered anarchism.) Were homosexuals deviant? (No; without instituted norms, there *was* no such thing as deviance.) Should women be allowed to vote, to sock an aggressor on the jaw, to demand an orgasm? (Yes, yes and most certainly yes.) Would the need for prisons evaporate once the revolution came? (Of course it would; criminality was a consequence of worker oppression.) Should religions be outlawed, its leaders shunned? (A tricky point, this—with the coming of anarchism there would *be* no laws, and no way to illegalize anything. Mostly, it was agreed that, following the revolution, religion would be an opiate no longer needed, and the masses would stop smoking it of their own volition.) They weren't alone. Scattered throughout the city were French, Italian, Hungarian and Czech collectives, with whom they intermingled at group events. There were anarcho picnics, anarcho dances, anarcho rifle clubs, anarcho bridge nights, anarcho singing groups, anarcho poetry workshops and anarcho astronomy clubs; there were even anarcho mushroom-hunting expeditions, conducted in the unsettled wilds of the northern Bronx.

One evening, the four took a long trolley ride to a house in Harlem, where they attended a seance governed by a Caribbean woman who was highly recommended within spiritualist circles. She was an enormous woman, well over three hundred pounds, and she wore a green-and-yellow caftan, her hair flowing from her head in long, stiff, braided locks that curled in various directions.

After introducing herself as Madame Hortense, she closed the curtains and lowered the gas-lights. "Please," she said while gesturing at the round table in the middle of her living room, "sit, my *chers*, might as well be comfortable." They all held hands. Madame Hortense closed her eyes and started singing, quietly, to herself, her voice low and rumbling, though after a minute or so she stopped, her eyes opening wide. "Well *mon dieu*," she said with a laugh. "There are spirits here who are having a powerful interest in *you*! Tell me, my *chers*, why do you think that might be? You must be doing something worthy, all right. They don't care about just any old souls, you know, but they *are* watching you! It's like they are sitting back, a cold drink in hand, just waiting for the show to start!"

Then the grin fell from her face, and Madame Hortense leaned toward the centre of the table, as if trying to hear the whisper of a child. "*Hmmmmmmm*," she said, "there's one in particular, jumping up and down, trying to get his two cents in, his name is, mmmmmmm, Otis, or Opus, or Opie... what is it now?"

Modska, Emma and Helene all gasped and looked at Sasha, whose face had drained of colour.

"Osip," he stammered. "It's my father."

"Oh, well!" said the medium. "That makes sense. That makes sense indeed. He's worried about you."

Sasha gulped. "Why?" he managed.

Madame leaned forward once again, her breasts flattening against the table's surface. "*Hmmmmmm*," she repeated. "It's crowded in there. Too many people talking at once." She sat straight up and closed her eyes, as if it might help. A second passed. One of the candles flickered, as if bothered by a breeze. Her eyes then popped open, and Madame Hortense seemed to return to her earthly confines. "Sorry," she said. "I lost track of him. Y'all might want to come back, and give it another go—he's definitely out there, waiting for a visit. I get the feeling he was a little lonely when he was in this world."

"I know," said Sasha, surprising the others. "I know."

* * *

May became June, and June turned into a humid July, and a humid July gave way to the blast furnace that was August. There were days in which Emma and Sasha did little at all, apart from taking a lunch up to Central Park, where they lay on the grass and watched clouds drift by, their pinky fingers entwined.

One Sunday, they all voyaged out to Rockaway, a beach so removed from the Lower East Side it was difficult to believe that, somehow, it was still within the vicinity of New York City. In addition to Emma, Sasha, Modska and Helene, there was Katz, Hillerman, Edelstadt, Michelman, Faltzblatt, Solotaroff, Bernstein, Strashunsky, Anna Minkin... the list went on and on, everyone eager for a reprieve from the city. By the time they arrived, they were all dusty and hot from the endless trolley ride. The food was packed in wicker baskets, the beer and liquor gone tepid in burlap totes. They all changed into swimming uniforms and set up on blankets.

Sasha and Emma looked out over the ocean, which was as calm as they'd ever seen it, the waves too deadened by the marshy heat to bother crashing upon the shore. The others drank and chatted and laughed and passed around fish-paste sandwiches, which, owing to someone having dropped the picnic basket, were crunchy with particles of sand.

"What a magnificent day!" someone crowed.

"Who brought the badminton set?" said another.

"I thought you did!" said yet another.

"My Lord," someone else said, "who's in *charge* here? What's a picnic without badminton?"

Without saying a word, Sasha stood and marched to the edge of the water. He kept going, the water reaching his ankles, his shins, his knees. "Oh look," someone cried, "Berkman's taking a dip!"

When the water reached his thighs, Sasha pointed his hands over his head and dove, windmilling his arms and kicking his tree-trunk legs, the voices of the bathing party receding behind him. At first, he felt divine, sea air channelling through his lungs, oxygen rushing to his heart, his mind, his muscles. He kept going. When he turned his head to breathe, he stared up at infinite blue. He swam and swam, losing himself in the first exercise he'd had in a year, stopping only when he heard the foghorn of a passing steamship. The sun glinted off calm water, the ocean alive with minute dancers, all performing pirouettes. He swam back toward shore and, after a bit, stopped once more, tired and sputtering, thinking that maybe he'd bitten off more than he could chew. He wasn't worried, though; even without his glasses, he was close enough to observe his cohorts, all of whom were drunk and laughing and patting together sandcastles. Katz was smoking a cigar the size of a rolled-up billfold. Solotaroff threw his head back and laughed, holding his stomach like he was an amused burgher. Edelstadt's latest fling—what was her name again? Tanya, was it?—had a parasol, which she was swirling like some grande dame afraid of bronzing. There was no denying it—from this distance, his fellow revolutionists looked like bourgeois vacationers, out for a day of mindless frivolity. Sasha's mood faltered and turned dark, his mind now infected with a worrying preoccupation.

Though keeping himself afloat necessitated the smallest amount of effort—a circling of his hands, a slow revolution of his feet, a slight uplifting of his chin—he stopped moving altogether and started to sink, descending through blue, indigo and black, the weight of his muscles tugging him through watery depths. In those long moments before he kicked toward the surface, the weight of the ocean pressed against his eardrums, and he swore he could hear a concerto, playing somewhere far away, a transmission from a world not glimpsed by the entirely sane.

six

SASHA WAS AT THE KITCHEN TABLE with Emma and Helene, eating a bowl of leftover stew, when they heard heavy footfalls in the hallway. The door flung open—propelled, as it turned out, by Modska's left foot. He walked in, breathing hard, his hands supporting one end of an old sofa. On the other end was a hefty, bearded galoot, damp beneath the arms, who grunted hello in Belarussian. "Over here," Modska directed, and they dropped the couch against the interior wall of the kitchen. The Belarussian nodded and walked out, his oversized boot prints marring the floor.

"Where," Helene asked, "did you get that?"

"I was down at Zum Groben Michel, and I started talking to that very same gentleman who was just here. It seems his brother had just been arrested for something or other, and he needed money for a defence, and did he know anyone who was interested in a used sofa?"

"Modska," Emma said, "we don't have any money."

"True! But I had a couple of my watercolours with me, and I asked him if he might be willing to make a trade. You should have seen his eyes light up. It turns out he'd been a student of art history back in Minsk. Yes, I'm talking about that overfed lug who was just here! Can you believe it? I'd have taken him for a gravedigger, or maybe a debt collector. Suddenly, he forgot all about his imprisoned brother. 'They're beautiful,' he told me, a tear gathering at the corner of one eye. 'These birds in flight, they remind of the starlings I used to see in Neskuchny Garden.' And so, my friends, voila."

They now had a place where they could sit, side by side, in both a literal and metaphorical sense, listening to street noise while discussing the ideas of Hegel, of Rousseau, of Peukert and Susan B. Anthony and Leo Tolstoy. At night, if Emma sought company, she went to Sasha, her own room off-limits to anybody but herself. Helene, meanwhile, began seeing a Calabrian socialist who would come over and make noodles in a bubbling tomato sauce while singing Spanish operas. Modska also had a number of women with whom he socialized; many evenings, he didn't return home, though when he did he was often in the company of a Nadya, an Irina, a Katya, a Gertrude.

One night, after a long day at the cloak factory (his fingers sore, his eyes burning, his lower back aching, his skin clotted with fibres) Sasha came home, shook the snow off his hat, and noticed that Emma was sitting quietly on the sofa. He was about to ask if something was the matter—she was a woman who only sat still while reading, and even then had a habit of pacing while turning the pages—when he noticed that it wasn't Emma at all. And yet, this stranger looked so much like her—the same blond hair, the same stocky build, the same interrogative blue eyes—that he immediately assumed it must be one of Emma's sisters, visiting from Rochester. He was about to say, *Oh, hello, you must be Lena? Or is it Helena?* when Modska came into the room, wearing one of his pairs of paint-splattered overalls.

"Cousin! I see you've met Tatiana."

The woman looked up, smiling. Immediately, the spell was broken, for her smile had none of Emma's delighted, intelligent mischief. Still, it couldn't be denied: this Tatiana, this fish-plant worker from Fulton Street, this round-shouldered darling from the Russian timberland, was a dead ringer for his sailor girl. He stowed this fact away, and allowed it to fester.

Soon after, he began to notice the brief, sidelong glances that Modska directed toward Emma when she wasn't looking. Had he always done that, or was that something new? Or, when Modska reached the end of one of his amusing stories, all of which chronicled his interactions with suspender-wearing tourists (who, without any sense of irony, uttered such provincial nonsense as "golly gee" or "well I'll be a monkey's uncle"), would Modska really turn toward Emma, as though he'd dished up the anecdote for her benefit and her benefit only? Perhaps, perhaps not. When considered individually, even a man as brooding as Sasha could dismiss all of these events as meaningless. Yet when he added them all together, piling them one atop of another like some tower of hormonal rot, he couldn't help but come to a singular, paranoid suspicion: given how lazy Modska was, it was inevitable that, with time, he'd stop bothering to leave the apartment in order to satisfy his libertine desires.

Even Emma, who tended to view everything through the rosy lens of their communal experiment, had to admit that Modska was not particularly productive. On a typical day, she knew only too well, he awoke late, usually around 10 a.m. or so. He then made himself coffee, smoked a cigarillo, prepared himself a breakfast of eggs and leftover kippers, read *Freiheit*, and applied grooming wax to his moustache. Finally, he dressed himself in a waistcoat and brogues, both of which he'd bought on Madison Avenue, justifying his profligacy by saying, "Comrades, please, listen to me, no one's going buy art from a *hobo*."

Whistling, he'd pack up his easel, his drawing paper, his brushes, and a handful of paintings he'd already completed. Then he'd head north, electing to walk up to his favourite spot, which just happened to be near the Metropolitan Museum of Art. Again, he cited the fiduciary needs of the collective to justify his actions: "Think how much money I save on transportation. Riding the El doesn't come cheap, you know."

Hearing this, Emma almost had to laugh, for she knew that Modska's decision to stroll all the way to the steps of the museum, during which time he often stopped to drink coffee at one of the many streetside diners along the way, was prompted by another motivation: it reduced the amount of time in which he had to actually work. Often, he stayed home altogether, pleading that his feet were sore, or the weather was inclement, or he needed to produce some more watercolours to sell alongside his caricatures, despite the fact that he hadn't sold one of his own creations in months. This delighted Emma, however; Modska, despite all of his faults, was good company. They'd work together, Emma sewing away in one corner, Modska manning a palette and easel in the other.

On one such day, Emma happened to look at Modska, who was happily painting a portrait of a marsh wren, and felt a sudden sadness. Modska heard the resulting sigh, turned to her, and asked, "Something wrong?"

She took the pins out of her mouth, and slumped. "It's just that, well, here I am, living in one of the most creative cities on earth, a city graced with the finest artists and writers and dancers of the New World, and I never get to see any of them, since I'm always stuck at home working. It's frustrating and dull."

Modska grinned, and put down his paintbrush. "Well then," he said. "We can't have that."

*   *   *

That afternoon, Emma rode with Modska to the steps of the Metropolitan Museum of Art; here, they stood in misty weather, looking up. "Just *look* at that building, Emma. Just look at those parapets, those cornices, those balustrades! Why, those friezes alone—they could be *inside* a museum, and yet, here they are, out on the street, for anyone to see."

A minute later, Emma was shuffling through the museum, struggling to keep up with Modska, who sped past one salon after another. He pulled up short; Emma, breathing hard, found herself before a depiction of a horse fair in Paris. "This," Modska said, "is one of the most popular paintings here. Look at those animals! The way the light plays off their muscles! When it was first shown in Paris, critics said they felt as though they were about to be trampled, and it's not hard to see why. Do you like it?"

"It's beautiful."

"Of course it is! Come, come, I've got one you're really going to like."

Emma hustled after her roommate, Modska taking her to a painting that depicted a pair of young lovers, fleeing beneath a burst of rain. "*The Storm*," said Modska, "by Pierre-Auguste Cot. It scandalized all of Paris when it was first painted, and you can see why. Just look at where his hand is on her body! Also, their expressions—have you ever seen two people more in love? It's not hard to imagine what they're going to do once they find shelter from the weather! The question is: is it romantic or is it salacious? Is it transcendent or bawdy? Who cares, I say, if it captures a real moment, don't you think? Come on, I've another I need to show you, a recent addition that has really captured my fancy."

Again, he set off, Emma following at a trot, the two stopping before a painting of a woman in a forest. "*Joan of Arc* by Jules Bastien-Lepage. The museum just bought it. What do you think?"

"Her face," Emma said. "It's wonderful. She looks so..."

"I know! It's her spiritual awakening! Look at how Lepage renders the moment: joy, beguilement, wonder, even a little fear—my God, to be able to capture such a moment using just paint and a canvas! How I'd love to be able to do that. Let's just stand here and really take it in."

After a minute or so, Emma looked up at Modska, who didn't seem to be able to take his eyes from the painting. In so doing, she bore witness to a Modska she'd never before seen, his happy-go-lucky artifice replaced by something that was worshipful, entranced and undeniably wise. She wished she saw this side of him more often; quite likely, its animation was the key to his succeeding as an artist. She also couldn't deny how attractive this new Modska seemed to her—he was practically aglow with inspiration. Yes, she had always thought of Modska as handsome, with his aquiline nose, his high cheekbones, his aristocratic jawline, his soft hazel eyes. But Modska's beauty had never meant anything to Emma, beyond something you might mention casually in conversation, like the way in which you would remark on the impressive colouring of a neighbourhood cat, or the deep blue of the sky on a cloudless day. For Emma, physical appearances ordinarily did not influence her heart; in fact, she sometimes regarded them as fascistic, in that they seemed to grant the handsome man or the comely woman an influence over the world that they had not, in any way, earned.

But at that moment, Emma's theories regarding superficiality were trumped by something far more important—looking at Modska in a cavernous salon within the Metropolitan Museum of Art, she was struck by the notion that she had a job to do, and there were few things that Emma Goldman enjoyed more than honest, enthusiastic effort.

"Let's go home," she said.

Modska required a second or two to respond to her suggestion. "What," he said, "now? We've only just got here."

"We'll come back another time. But right now—I feel like I've seen enough."

"Ah yes, I know the feeling. You're *full*. I get that way too. It's too bad, I've other paintings I'd love to show you, this really is a wonderful place. But as you say we can always come back, it's the glory of living in New York City, isn't it?"

The two rode in near silence, Emma so enthralled by unreined horses and young love and divine inspiration—by the mad, untethered sensuality of those artworks—that words seemed ineffective, even cheap. At the El station, they started walking home, Modska humming away, Emma taking the crook of his arm. Once inside the apartment, she turned to him and said, "Wait here."

Emma went into her bedroom. She removed her shoes, her blouse, her skirt, her stockings, her underwear. She put on a robe and walked back into the living room. Appropriately enough, she found him standing by his easel, as though anticipating what she was planning. She stood before him, the robe bunched at her throat.

"Modska," she said. "You've spent enough time painting fat-cheeked tourists and Central Park wildlife. Now, it's time for you to draw something more substantial."

She pulled off her robe, letting it drop to the floor. Though she did not consider herself beautiful, not with her dimpled thighs and her ovoid face, she did consider herself as something genuine, and that's what she wanted Modska to draw—something that was real and present and shuddering with life.

Modska asked her to lie upon the Belarussian sofa; as she did, he found some charcoal and a sketch pad.

"Do I smile?" Emma asked. "Do I pout? Grin? Sneer? Look otherworldly?"

"Just be yourself."

"In that case I'll smile. I'm feeling happy today."

"Good."

"I want you to sketch all of me. Not just what I look like. Do you understand?"

His brow furrowed; when concentrating, he pressed his tongue into his cheek. He drew quickly, without thought or consideration or expectation, an hour passing before he stopped, saying that he couldn't draw anymore, that his wrist hurt and his eyes smarted and, above all else, he could use a thimble or two of vodka. Emma put her robe back on. Even though she had done nothing for the past sixty minutes other than lie on her side, her cheek on a folded arm, she felt exhausted as well. Modska handed her the sketches he'd done—there must have been twenty or more. She looked at them, one by one, and with each sketch she suffered a pedestrian, earthbound response. The charcoal was smudged. Her left leg looked weird. Her eyes were too big, her ears too petite, her breasts more supple than they actually were. Then she reached the four-teenth—or was it the fifteenth?—drawing. She stopped. Her eyes filled. She put a hand over her mouth. This one spoke of the infinite, the sublime, the essence not just of her being but of *all* being. Time swooped, becoming meaningless—then and there, she promised herself that she would keep the sketch for the rest of her days, as she considered it a testament to both the vigour, and the unabashed valour, of this thing known as youth. She held the drawing up to Modska. He grinned, not unlike a proud child.

"This one," she said, before pinning it to the apartment wall.

A few hours later, Sasha returned from his job at the cloak fac-tory. He brushed snow from his hat, sat on the Belarussian sofa, let his eyes travel across the room, and saw the nude sketch of Emma, brazenly thumbtacked to the wall. He reacted by closing his eyes, hoping that, given his fatigue, and the number of cigarettes he'd smoked that day (fifty? sixty? more?), he was imagining things. But no—he stood and stepped closer, and, in that moment, understood that his concern regarding Emma and Modska wasn't some imagin-ative conjuring of his dark, brooding mind. It wasn't that Emma was without clothes, her dimpled thighs on view, her breasts like mounds of vanilla custard. What Sasha hated was the radiance that Modska had captured, not just in her eyes but in the tilt of her head, the fall of her hair, the placement of her arms. With nothing more than a charcoal stick and an eight-by-twelve-inch sheet of foolscap, he'd conjured a gaiety that Sasha did not, and could not, inspire in Emma.

When he looked at the drawing—and he did look, for minute after wretched minute—he saw not only the lustre of her spirit, but a reflection of his own cheerlessness, which was no small accomplishment, given that he wasn't in the drawing. Though he hated to admit it, the drawing was good—this disturbed him more than anything, as he'd always considered Modska to be a journeyman at best, a producer of insipid nature scenes and hastily scrawled caricatures of freckle-faced Midwesterners. But this drawing resonated, somehow. It had a shimmer, a glisten. He could almost hear a hum, coming from an unseen depth. Sasha wasn't sure what he hated more—that Modska had managed to capture Emma's essence on paper, or that she'd managed to extract a level of artistry from Modska that had not been there previously. During the modelling session that had produced this artwork, it was obvious there'd been a communion between artist and subject, a level of communication as intimate as anything that Sasha had ever attained with his sailor girl.

A few days later, he came home to find another sketch upon the wall. This time, Emma was lying with her back to the artist while gazing over an artfully poised haunch. Sasha hated this one even more than the first, Modska having captured a thoughtful quality in her expression that was at variance with the stridency she shared with Sasha.

Over the ensuing week or two, the apartment filled with drawings of Sasha's lover: Emma reclining on her back, her nipples directed toward the ceiling; Emma gazing nude out the window, a shaft of sunlight falling upon her belly; Emma on her knees, hands clasped below her belly, head slightly lowered, face restful, eyes at half-mast, like some Buddhist adherent. Then came the *coup de grâce*: Emma seated upon the Belarussian sofa, peering intently at the artist, legs widened, her expression far-off, her eyes a soft dream. And what could Sasha do? Complain? Place his prudish, bourgeois propriety on display?

Thankfully, it was Helene who came home one wintry night and tore down every sketch tacked to the apartment's four walls. Then she pounded on Emma's door. Emma answered, clearly startled, Helene pushing the drawings into Emma's hands and saying, "I will *not* live in a museum of your body parts, you got that, comrade?"

* * *

Sasha now walked in the shape of a coat hanger, a cigarette lit from the moment he awoke to the moment he went to bed, only to wake in the middle of the night, feeling the irritability known only to those who have suffered from nicotine withdrawal, at which point he'd lie awake, smoke curling out of his nostrils, ruminating. During his time on the Lower East Side, he had attended so many political rallies that his shoes were worn thin; he'd sung the Internationale so loudly and so often that his voice had gone hoarse; he'd read so many issues of *Freiheit* that his fingertips were stained a dark, algae green; he'd discussed revolutionary strategy at so many Pioneers of Liberty meetings that he barely knew what he believed anymore. All of these efforts, he began to suspect, were next to meaningless: if he was making a real contribution, it was by demonstrating to the world how the principles of collectivity worked. Yet if the group fell apart due to his own insipid jealousies, it would not only make a mockery of the revolution, it would confirm his deeply held fear that, as both an anarchist and a person, he was without any real contribution to make.

With this thought, he tried to imagine ways in which he could regain Emma's affections, as he was now convinced that Emma and Modska were engaging in trysts that they hid from the rest of the household. He knew this wouldn't be easy, as he felt inferior to Modska, so much so that he often wondered why Emma had chosen to be with a man as tormented as he was in the first place.

Fortunately, this endeavour was aided by Modska himself, who came home one day, grinning like a pampered child, one hand bent behind his back. With the other he twiddled the ends of his moustache, a tic indicating that he was pleased with himself. His roommates all looked up at him, wondering what had enlivened him so.

"You know that watercolour I did in the park?" he announced. "The one of ducks swimming after tossed bread crusts? The one with the subtle interplay of light upon water?"

"Of course."

"Guess which starving artist just sold it for a pretty penny?"

"Really?"

"I did! To some Pennsylvanian banker! Actually, it was his wife who fell in love with it. I doubled the price on the spot. He didn't hesitate."

"That's marvellous."

"To celebrate, I purchased *these...*"

He then withdrew the hand he'd been hiding behind his back, revealing a bouquet composed of rhododendrons, azaleas, calla lilies, tulips and gerbera daisies, all ballasted by a perimeter of freesia. Emma yelped, leapt to her feet, clapped her hands together, and plunged her nose into petals. "Oh Modska," she said. "They smell wonderful." Helene, meanwhile, raised her eyebrows and said, "Make sure they're not carrying any bees."

This left Sasha, who thought carefully before speaking. "Modska," he said. "What did you spend on those?"

"I won't tell you, cousin."

"By which you mean you spent every penny you got from that Pennsylvania fat cat."

"Not quite. There was enough left over for a cigarillo or two."

"You should've spent it on the movement."

"He's right," Emma sighed. "There are too many starving and unemployed comrades out there for this kind of indulgence. Then again, Sasha, you must admit that they *are* beautiful, and this apartment can be so dreary when it rains. It'll lift our morale, and make us better revolutionists. So look at it that way. But please, Modska, the next time you have a windfall, give a thought to the people."

Modska capitulated, promising that the next time he sold a painting, he'd donate every penny to the Pioneers of Liberty Fund for the World-Wide Furtherance of Anarchism and Its Principles.

A week later, he sold another painting, this one a sentimental rendering of a mother wren feeding worms to its chicks. He returned to the apartment, looking sheepish and drunk, his words slurring. On his way to his bedroom, he slammed his shin on the edge of Emma's work table, causing him to leap about while holding his leg and groaning. This caused a crinkled ball of paper to fall from his jacket pocket. Helene stood and picked it up. After unfolding it against her palm, she gasped, and showed it to Sasha and Emma, who both imagined what must have happened: Modska, overjoyed and peckish, elected to stop in for a quick bite at one of the Gaullist establishments lining Park Avenue, no doubt promising himself that he'd have a quick bowl of consommé and nothing more. According to the receipt, he'd also ordered mussels, trout in a watercress sauce, a joint of lamb, and a not-insignificant bottle of claret.

"Modska," Sasha declared. "You could have fed a family for a week with that! This was not a mere extravagance... this was a crime."

"Really, Modska," Emma added. "You should be ashamed of yourself."

Modska stammered some excuse, the usual doggerel about the artist's ingrained appreciation of elegance in all its iterations. Yet owing to his inebriation, his protestations were unintelligible, and he retreated to his room.

Sasha, Emma and Helene stood looking at one another.

"He really can't help himself," Emma said.

"No," said Helene. "He really can't."

Emma was about to titter, as it was funny, in a way, Modska's shameless flaunting of the rules of his own home, when she noticed the scowl on Helene's face. Emma sobered instantly. Helene was holding a folded newspaper, which she slapped onto the kitchen table before marching out of the room, loudly shutting the door to her bedroom. Emma then turned to Sasha, who bore a look of almost fatherly concern.

"This is a problem," she said. "Isn't it?"

"Yes," he responded, "it is."

* * *

The upper hand was now Sasha's, a steadfast adherence to anarchist principle being the lone area in which he could outdo his dashing, talented cousin. Unfortunately, he pressed his luck—the four of them, about two weeks later, attended a dance at the New York Workers' Hall. Every Russia-born anarchist, syndicalist, communist, socialist and malcontent within a two-hundred-mile radius came as well, the place stinking of cigarette smoke, pine oil and gin. A klezmer band was playing the hits of the day, and Emma, a woman who loved a party above all else, was dancing madly with every comrade who had the gumption to ask her.

Sasha, meanwhile, sat with his arms crossed, slowly convincing himself that, with the criticism he was about to offer, he would further underscore his conviction to the revolution, thus impressing Emma—even though she was the one he was about to criticize. When she next took a rest—breathing heavily, neck dewy with perspiration, blond ringlets affixed to her forehead, a look of resplendent detachment in her eyes—Sasha leaned over and, in a voice lowered by sanctimony, said: "Sailor girl, please, it does not behoove a comrade to dance with such reckless abandon. It undermines the seriousness of our goals."

She glared at him. "You really are a fanatic, did you know that?"

He muttered an apology. It didn't help.

"Oh, and by the way, *fishlips*, if I can't dance I don't want to be in your revolution." She then stood, approached a burly stranger, took one of his hands, and led him to the dance floor.

Two weeks after this incident—an incident that should have been educative for Sasha—he came home from a long day at the factory and found all three of his commune-mates sitting glumly in the living room. The room was dim, and they were all clutching juice glasses that looked to be filled with measures of vodka. No one spoke, their silence indicating that something truly grave had occurred.

"Sasha," Emma finally said, her eyes damp. "David Edelstadt has fallen ill. He's contracted a severe case of tuberculosis."

"Damn it," Sasha said. "The curse of the tenements. He was coughing the last time I saw him. I'm amazed we all don't have it."

"He's extremely ill," said Helene.

"But don't worry," said Modska. "There's a sanatorium in Denver, and the Pioneers of Liberty are going to release some of the fund to send him there."

Sasha considered this, a stiff moment or two passing, before he surprised even himself by saying, "They can't."

"What do you mean," Helene spat, "*they can't*?"

"That fund is to aid revolutionary activity only. We were all there when the motion passed, remember? We can't start releasing funds for private matters. In no time, there'd be nothing left in the fund and then where would the movement be?"

"How about up your rigid ass?" said Helene.

"Really, cousin, how can you be so callous? He's a good friend of yours."

"Yes, but do you consider him a true, active revolutionist? His poetry is beautiful, indeed, and might indirectly prove of some propagandistic value. But that's all. We can aid our friend with our own money, to be sure, but I believe money from the fund should only aid direct revolutionary activity."

Emma brought her hand down hard on the arm of the Belarussian sofa, a puff of dust rising into the air. "Sasha," she said with a withering tone. "I'm getting so sick of you throwing the movement in our faces." She then went to her room, slamming the door behind her.

Two weeks later, Sasha sat on his hands when, at a general meeting, the Pioneers of Liberty voted to fund Edelstadt's treatment in Colorado. Either it was too late, or the mountain air insufficiently recuperative: Edelstadt died a month later. He was twenty-six years of age. In their Twenty-Third Street apartment, Emma and her comrades wept, covered the apartment's lone mirror, found a necktie to scissor, made a pot of kasha varnishkes, and sat quietly. In this mournful hush, Sasha moved next to Emma. "I'm sorry," he whispered. "I never thought this would happen."

"I know, Sasha."

"I was stupid. I'm a monster. My commitment is all I have to give."

"No, Sasha, it isn't. One day, you'll learn that."

There was a long pause. "How?" he finally asked.

"That, I can't tell you. But it'll happen. In the meantime, could you do just one thing for me?"

"It depends..."

"Try to live a little, okay? The time will go faster. Would you at least promise me *that*?"

seven

IT WAS AMAZING, it really was, the way in which two cousins could be so different. When Emma expressed herself sexually with Sasha, it was tantamount to worship, Emma gaining the sensation that she could peer into his very being, a process so transformative that sometimes she felt herself dissociate from her own body, at which point she would float upwards, toward the ceiling of Sasha's musty room, and watch the two of them beneath her, Sasha a mad rutting bronco, his hair streaked with sweat and smoke, she the foot-arching maiden, howling at him to set her free. But then: a shout, a groan, a flailing of arms, and she'd collapse back into her usual form, damp-eyed and weary and, at times, a little fearful of her connection with this ancient, ruptured soul named Alexander Berkman.

But with Modska? It was like a ride on a carousel. It was enjoyment without the shackle of meaning or significance. He liked to tickle her, lightly, even though she was barely ticklish. He was bullish on kissing, not just her mouth but her forehead and her shoulder and her stomach, where he'd form a tight O with his lips and blow, creating a sound like a dropped tuba. Or: he'd collect a length of her hair, tug it till it straightened, and hold it over his upper lip, such that it looked like the moustache of a sultan. It was his eyes that made it funny; she swore he could roll them in opposite directions, even though she knew it was impossible. But still, there it was, an erotic playfulness, arousing her to no end, and then, only then, with his face caught by the sunlight streaming through the window (for they made love in the afternoon, when Sasha and Helene were at work), she'd wish that all of life was like this, a giddy nothingness. But then, it would be over, Modska neatening his hair in his bedroom mirror, and she would look at this man—at this handsome, handsome man—and think, *I've already forgotten what happened between us.*

"Modska," she said one afternoon.

"Yes?"

"We have to tell him."

"I know, my pet, I know."

"His development as an anarchist *depends* on it. You know it, I know it, I think that even he knows it, deep down. I mean, really... who ever heard of a real anarchist man with only one lover? It doesn't make a whit of sense."

That evening, the four of them went to a speech at Webster Hall, a red-brick concert hall that had opened a couple of years earlier on Eleventh Street between Third and Fourth Avenues. They each gave a contribution to the sponsor—in this case the Lower East Side Political Action Committee—and stepped into a large room turned cloudy with tobacco smoke. They stood in the middle of the hall and lit cigarettes of their own. The audience was small and reverential, the speaker a refugee from Ukraine who had recently arrived at Castle Garden, weighing all of eighty-eight pounds. He looked skeletal, his hip bones protruding like spigots over his drooping trousers, his chest so sunken it looked like the contours of a spoon. He spoke of the usual tsarist horrors, of wheat theft and burned-out buildings, of summary executions, of the torture centres that had come to Riga, to Minsk, to Vilna. "They came for me in my parents' house in Odessa," he told his audience, stabbing the air with a spindly finger. "I was eating breakfast. I was literally hauled away with egg on my face. They took me to one of the many detention centres downtown. I was never charged, never interrogated, never asked for any information. They barely fed me; they subjected me to bright lights and loud noise; they made me stand on a box with a bag over my head, for hour after hour, striking me if I dared to step off. And my crime? Can you guess? I wrote about horse racing for the local newspaper. Harness, trap, steeplechase, derby, that's all I cared about. But still, in the mind of the new tsar, I was a journalist, and there was no worse crime. Now, I'm a comrade. *Now*, I've discovered Proudhon, I've discovered Bakunin, I've discovered Kropotkin and Chernyshevsky and Rousseau. Oh, yes, my people, I've discovered anarchism, in all its glory, and I can tell you something—each day, the tsar produces another hundred just like me."

Emma, Sasha, Modska and Helene stepped into the chilly fall air. They all walked up the avenue, strangely silent, Sasha assuming that the others were gloomy from the gruesome details they had just heard. Partway home, Helene announced that she and Modska were going for a drink, and they veered off toward the boisterousness of Union Square; Sasha was about to follow them when he felt Emma's arm slip through his own, such that she could lead him in an opposite direction. Her hobnail boots clacked against the cobblestone path.

"Sasha. I have to tell you something." They took a few more steps. Sasha felt sickened, for he suddenly knew what she was about to relay.

"A person," Emma continued, "can love two people at the same time, as long as it's a different type of love. You ignite my soul, Sasha, and my revolutionary consciousness. You are as much a part of my being as I am, and I know, as much as I know anything, that you and I will always be a part of each other's lives. It's different with Modska. He livens my heart, my sense of beauty, my inner child.

My love for him will be a more transitory experience, for I know that once the wonder expires there will not be a foundation upon which it will continue."

Sasha looked stricken. "But Emma, his belief in the movement, it isn't sincere."

"Oh, but it is! You just can't see it because his sincerity takes a different form. He's an idealist, through and through. He believes the best revenge is living well, that revolution can come through the pursuit of happiness. You, however..."

"Yes, yes, I know. You don't have to say it."

"You don't seem happy for us."

"That's because I'm not. I'm sorry. I can't help it. I was raised under the yoke of monogamy. My father never had another lover. My mother would have beaten him to death with her bare hands. What can I say? My childhood has its talons in me."

Emma gripped his forearm, and gave it a collegial squeeze. "That's wonderful, then! Our new arrangement will help you work on your bourgeois possessiveness. You and I both know that a true anarchist cannot cling to outdated modes."

"I know, I hate myself."

"Well, don't. It's wasted effort. I have no problem with you taking another lover, you know. In fact, I hope that you do. It'd be good for you."

"I'll try."

"Furthermore, I want you and Modska to bury this... this... *testiness* that has developed between the two of you. It's counter-revolutionary, all this one-upmanship. We must direct all of our energies to a singular goal. *You* taught me this, Sasha."

They passed a cart vendor, who called out, "Chestnuts! Chestnuts here!"

"Can I ask you something, Sasha?"

"Yes."

"Do you ever sense it coming? The revolution, I mean?"

He thought for a moment, and said, "Yes."

"It's like the way the wind picks up, just before a storm starts. It really is on its way, isn't it? We just need that trigger, that single deed that Johann Most is always talking about in the pages of *Freiheit*. How I'd admire the person who provides the spark."

Sasha and Emma walked around for hours; Modska was in the apartment when they finally returned, while Helene was out with her Calabrian. Modska looked sheepish. Sasha's head was down; he looked at Modska's shoes. "Emma told me, cousin."

"What can I say? She sees something in me, Sasha. She sees a real artist. I can't pretend that's not true."

Emma made tea. When it was ready, they all sat at the kitchen table and played cards. After a few hands, Emma stretched and said she was tired. There was a brief awkwardness before she took Sasha's hand and led him to his room. They undressed and held each other and that was all. "Sasha," she said, "you are the most committed revolutionist I know. I look at you and see a man longing for upheaval. I see a man who will cause change, by whatever means are required. By the same token, you will find aspects of the revolution difficult. We all will. Modska will have to give up his nice shirts, his nice meals, his expensive cigars. Helene will have to learn to be cordial to others if she's to live communally. And you, Sasha. You'll have to address your clinginess. Everything will be shared in the new society. There'll be no possessions, human or otherwise. It's not your fault. It's merely the adjustment that you'll have to make."

"What about you?"

She thought about this for a moment. "I'll have to learn to stay on an even keel. I make too many decisions based on my furies."

* * *

Following Emma's announcement, very little seemed to change in the Twenty-Third Street commune. At night, Emma would either visit Sasha, or she would stay in her own room, often nursing one of her frequent maladies; she suffered from headaches, stomach pains, tingling fingertips, vertigo, blue moods and crying jags. This was Emma's conundrum; one moment, she would evince more vitality than any woman alive, her very being a blast furnace. But then, at a flip of some invisible switch, she would find herself bed-bound and groaning. "Ah Sasha," she'd say. "I have women's problems, you wouldn't understand, how I hate them. You know what I hope? I hope that one day gender won't matter, that we'll all be the same, and that whatever we have or don't have between our legs won't matter one whit. I tell you, fishie, I'm looking forward to the day in which the words 'man' and 'woman' don't even exist."

If she did visit with Modska—and she did, often, for she cherished the merriment of their time together—it always happened during the afternoon, in Modska's brightly lit room, Emma pushing tubes of paint off of the bed in order to make room. This discretion was Modska's request—he wanted to let Sasha get used to their polyamorous relationship before they started sticking his nose in it. It was a tactic that only served to frustrate Emma. "*Modska*," she told him, "our ménage is a perfect opportunity for Sasha to come to terms with his possessiveness."

"But I know my cousin," he responded. "Sasha is an old man in a young man's body. We need to give him some time to get used to the idea. The one thing we don't want to do is rub his face in it. You don't want him to get petulant. He might throw himself off the Brooklyn Bridge. He thinks about it, you know. The poor bastard— his side of the family is littered with suicides. I've heard whisperings that his father didn't actually have a heart attack."

"All *right*. But I'm warning you. We're going to put an end to this charade sooner or later."

A week or two passed. One evening, Emma and Sasha found themselves alone in the apartment. Both were reading. Emma looked up from her book. "Sasha," she said, "have you taken another lover yet?"

"No. I'm sorry."

"There's nothing to be sorry for. I was just curious. But see that you do, all right?"

Whether Sasha realized it or not, this was Emma's way of informing him that his period of adaptation was over. A few nights later, after a long day of sewing, she told Sasha that she wouldn't be visiting him in his room that night. Yet instead of returning to her room, she knocked at Modska's door. He answered, looking surprised.

"May I come in?" she said.

"Emma, you know I..."

"Don't worry. I talked to Sasha."

"You did?"

"Oh yes," she said. "I did."

Sasha, Emma and Modska were now an unabashed threesome, with all of the complexities that such an arrangement might cause. On nights when Emma needed to exit the confines of her own body, when she wished to commiserate with someone about the hard nature of life, when she needed her sensual pleasures flavoured with the slightest tinge of ferocity, she would go to Sasha. On nights when her heart needed joy, and her eyes a modicum of delight, and her skin a lightness of touch, she would tiptoe down the hallway and tap on Modska's door.

Helene, meanwhile, was spending less and less time in the apartment; early one evening, she appeared before the others, a suitcase in each hand, frowning. "I'm moving out," she said. "I'm sure you can find another fourth wheel."

Sasha, Modska and Emma spoke in unison: "No, please, you can't, you mustn't, let's talk about this."

"I can, I must, and I'm not much for talking. Besides, the three of you are driving me crazy. I can only stand so much *skulking*."

With Helene gone, the three others could no longer afford the apartment. They went looking—after a long month of trudging through surrounding neighbourhoods, where they saw little, if anything, they could afford, they gave up and returned to the Lower East Side, where they resorted to a drafty, three-bedroom railway apartment on Forsyth Street. With Helene gone, the tension existing between Emma, Sasha and Modska only magnified, all three pining for the days in which their little collective had been a safe harbour against the harsh winds blowing outside. Now, they were overly polite with one another. They stepped around each other in the kitchen. They occasionally took their meals alone, in their respective rooms. They didn't laugh as much as they used to, if, in fact, they laughed at all.

One night, Sasha was drinking a cup of coffee at the kitchen table when Emma emerged from her bedroom and sat across from him. A few seconds passed. He could tell from her furrowed expression that she had something unpleasant to say to him.

"Sasha," she said. "You *must* find another lover. It's no longer an option. Even monogamists don't practise monogamy. You think the woman down the hall doesn't invite the fruit vendor in during the day? You think her husband doesn't visit a special friend on his way home from work? No one is faithful, Sasha. The human psyche wasn't built for it. The only thing that we're doing differently is being honest about it. But *you*. It's not that you're clinging to outmoded ways of thinking. You're not even living. You're grasping at behaviour that never existed in the first place! It casts a pall over everything. It makes everything unequal. It's like someone brought out a big cake, and you announced you were on a diet. Fine, okay, that's your choice, but you can't go around dejected and surly because others got cake and you didn't. It's not fair to everyone else."

He put his face in his hands and rubbed his tired eyes; already, his fingertips were beginning to stain a pale orange from excessive smoking. This small detail, for reasons that Emma couldn't quite understand, suddenly made her feel guilty for the way in which she was pressuring him.

"I love you, Sasha, more than life itself. You have to believe me. I really do. So please. Do it for me. Go fuck someone else."

* * *

Sasha now found himself in a deeply ironic bind—in order to salvage his relationship with Emma Goldman, he had to take another lover, even though the only woman he wanted to be with was his sailor girl. His first thought was of Anna Minkin, who was still trapped in that rancid Avenue A apartment with her brute of a father. She really was a lovely woman, all curls and good humour, and if she was as catastrophically repressed as Emma claimed, then she might actually be a good match for Sasha.

He arrived one night at the apartment. Anna answered. She'd obviously been cleaning, for the sleeves of her blouse were rolled to her elbows, and she wore a kerchief around her head.

"Why... Sasha! What brings you here?"

"It'd been a while, and we were all wondering how you were doing."

Her father appeared behind her. His hair was uncombed, his face a shadow of whiskers. "Anna," he grunted. "Who's this?"

"It's Alexander Berkman, Daddy. You remember him."

The old man grunted. Sasha reached into his satchel, and pulled out a box of cigars. "I brought these for you, sir."

"What?"

"They're cigars, sir."

"I can see they're cigars. Why on earth would you bring them to me?"

"I just thought you'd like them."

The old man pulled one out and lit it; the apartment filled with peaty smoke. The father walked off, humming contentedly. This left Sasha and Anna alone, just inside the doorway to the apartment. "I thought," he said, "we could go for a walk."

"Oh."

"I mean, if you're not busy."

The two went to Tompkins Square Park, which, at that time of the year, was crowded with indigents, sleeping rough on squares of cardboard. "Thank you for dropping by," Anna said. "Really, it was most considerate of you, to think of me on such a lovely day!" And so it started—as they strolled the perimeter, she never stopped talking, one banality after another falling from her heart-shaped mouth, and as she nattered away it was easy to get the impression that, despite the squalor in the park, her whole life revolved around the fall colours, the nice children in the neighbourhood, and a cute puppy she'd laid eyes on earlier. Their walk didn't last long; after twenty minutes, or roughly two laps around the park, Anna announced that she needed get back to her cleaning. Sasha didn't argue. He walked her home, and they bid their goodbyes outside of the tenement.

Sasha trudged back to his apartment, more discouraged than distraught, as his thoughts were now directed toward a shopkeeper's daughter from down the street, a pale Estonian named Natalia who, on more days than not, wore a fishing cap bearing a telltale black flag. Didn't she always seem pleased to see him when he stopped in to buy apples? Didn't he see her at Union Square rallies, her tightened fist in the air? Didn't she, on days in which Sasha stopped in to do a little shopping, throw an extra turnip in his bag, and say, "Here's a little something, comrade, no charge, best to keep your strength up, you can't build a new society on an empty stomach"?

Sasha asked her to go for a walk around Tompkins Square Park as well. As they watched ships come and go, they traded their own stories of coming to America in steerage, ten days spent below deck, eating salt beef and potatoes, feeling seasick and worn, and, to add insult to injury, listening to the gaiety occurring above deck, where mutton-chopped burghers drank gin and tonic while playing crokinole. "The number of times," Natalia said, "I heard some loud son-of-a-bitch call out, 'Now this is the way to travel, by George!' And meanwhile, the old woman in the bunk next to me would be on her knees, puking into a bucket."

Sasha laughed; she really did have an acerbic sense of humour. He reached out and took Natalia's hand. She squeezed it, just a little, Sasha feeling the first registering of arousal, a barely perceptible stirring that, if nothing else, made him want to touch this sharp-witted little comrade, with her skinny arms, her frayed black sweater, her lovely little upper-lip mole. He leaned in to kiss her. She, in turn, parted her lips, only to mutter "shit!" at the exact moment in which their lips were about to touch. "Shit, shit, shit," she said again, and when Sasha opened his eyes he saw blood streaming down her upper lip, directing around her mouth, pooling in the tiny cleft in her chin. Natalia threw her head back and pinched the bridge of her nose.

"God damn it," she groaned.

"What's happening?"

"It's a nosebleed. I get them all the time. My blood's thin."

He passed her a handkerchief, which she pressed to her face. She was breathing hard and wincing. The handkerchief turned pink, and then red, and then an ugly, baked-earth copper.

"Are you all right?"

"Do I *look* all right?" she said, the day ending with Sasha squiring her home in a horse-drawn cart he could scarcely afford. Natalia, after a time, tossed the handkerchief into the street; her neck was red, her face a mess, the front of her blouse speckled. Sasha had never seen anything like it. Natalia, meanwhile, seemed too woozy to be embarrassed. He helped her down and she walked toward the apartment she shared with her family above the grocery. The two rarely spoke thereafter, their communication reduced to brief, awkward nods.

After that, there was a buxom Slovenian who hung out at Zum Groben Michel, a stick-thin trade unionist who peddled candles on Delancey, and a motor-mouthed exile who waitressed in Café Sachs, despite having lost two fingers in some sort of incendiary mishap—either they didn't fancy Sasha, or had a preference for women, or, as was the case with the Slovenian, lived in a shack near an East River pier and smelled strongly of mackerel. Sasha began to doubt himself, even more so than he had before—could it really be that every female anarchist in New York City was neurotic and off-putting? Or was he only selecting partners who, on some repressed level, he *knew* were unsuitable, since there really was only one woman he genuinely wanted?

One night, when his self-condemnation grew particularly fierce, he made the long trek to the Brooklyn Bridge and stood in its centre. There, he imagined himself falling through space, striking water, his body drifting out to sea. This helped. Just knowing that he had this option, should things ever become truly unbearable, soothed his nerves, and allowed him to think. At such times, he could picture his life as though it were a tableau, stretched out over black water. Over there was Vilna, lovely Vilna, where he'd spent his earliest days, innocent of the world's failings. And over there, it was St. Petersburg, that city of beautiful ghosts, from which they'd run in the middle of the night, leaving behind all of their possessions in order to buy themselves a head start. And there, directly below him, the village-city called Kovno, where he'd fallen in love with a scullery maid named Rosa.

He climbed up on the support railing and stood, slowly, wind ruffling his hair, gripping a guy wire, gazing at black water, his eyes watering. As sometimes happened, his father appeared beside him, wearing the same concerned expression that he had worn throughout his life.

"So," Osip said. "This again?"

"Yes," said Sasha.

"Do you mind telling me why?"

"Maybe I don't need a reason? Look at you. Tell me, Papa. Was it really a heart attack? Mother was pretty tight-lipped with the details."

"Of course it was. Not that it matters. That was then. I see things differently, now. Would it matter if I told you that life's a gift? That every day is a revelation? That the world, for all its problems, is beautiful?"

"You know I don't feel that way."

"What if I told you that there's a reason things happen in life?"

"I wouldn't believe you."

"Well, that part's up to you. Still, it happens to be true."

"But how would you..."

It was too late; the phantasm was gone, a cool mist in its place. Sasha stepped down, feeling a rare sort of gratitude. Yet as he reluctantly walked home, this impression faded, the real world exerting its dreary hand.

* * *

The weather, meanwhile, was beautiful, as autumn always was in the city of New York. Dish-sized leaves spiralled down from the trees, their red and yellow outlines left upon the sidewalks. At dusk, the sun acquired an almost poetic tone, reflecting dark orange off the windows of the opposite tenement. As for the city itself, it seemed quieter now that its residents no longer had to escape the heat by taking to rooftops, parks and avenues.

While Emma still expressed herself sexually with both Sasha and Modska, she found that she was initiating such interludes less often, and when she did she was merely proving to herself that polyamory wasn't some abstracted pipe dream, dreamt up by theoreticians who didn't get out much. This concern exhausted her, and caused her discomfort; each month she'd take to her bed, holding herself, cursing a malady that seemed like punishment for being born a woman.

Around the time in which snowflakes began to waft from the chunky New York skies, Emma awoke one morning with steel claws punishing her interior. The pain worsened as the day progressed, until she had no choice but to take to the Belarussian sofa, looking sallow and weak, her hair a mess, her eyes red and damp. Modska came home and found her holding herself, groaning pitiably; he was making her tea when Sasha returned from his factory job.

"Jesus!" he said. "Emma, are you all right?"

"She was like this when I got home," Modska said.

Emma sat up shakily, waving away any offers of assistance. "I'm fine, fine, I just need to lie down. Now fuck off, the two of you."

She hobbled down the hallway, sweeping a forearm against the wall for support, until she reached her room. She closed the door behind her. Sasha sat and listened to the groans emitting from her room. After a few minutes, he could stand it no longer—he knocked, and entered. Emma was red-faced and holding herself, her face tracked with tears. "Oh go to hell," she barked, a request contradicted by her fearful, pleading expression. Modska then came into the room and exchanged concerned glances with Sasha. When Emma next moaned, a guttural whimper that sounded like the groan of someone who was weakening with pain, Modska pulled Sasha into the hallway and said, "I know someone, cousin, who can help."

They took the stairs two at a time, dodging children at play and an old cabbage seller and a young mother with a child in her arms. Once on the street, they wound their way north, and then west, and then north again, where Modska knew of a woman who, with a minimum of payment and a guarantee of discretion, might assist their fallen comrade. Sasha and Modska reached the door of a small, battered row house on East Broadway and knocked. It croaked open, revealing the tallest woman either one of them had ever seen; she even towered over Modska, who stood six feet tall. She peered at them both. "I'm needed," she said, "yeah?" As they sped back to the apartment, Sasha described Emma's symptoms as best as he was able, the woman nodding her head and saying, "Right, right, it happens, right right, I know it, nothing strange about that."

She entered Emma's room, telling Sasha and Modska to stay out, no matter what they might hear. There was a surfeit of moaning. After a time, the woman emerged, cracking her knuckles. "Can we sit?" she asked.

Sasha led her to the kitchen. She took a chair, while Sasha and Modska sat on the sofa, like schoolchildren awaiting a lesson.

"Well, it's just what I reckoned. A clear case of the dimitri-osis. It's like she's got talons inside her, and every month they turn savage. It's common enough in Russian women, something to do with the shape of their insides. This month just happened to be particularly bad. Like I say, it happens."

"What do we do?"

"*Listen*," she said, holding up a twig-like finger. "You hear that?"

Sasha cocked an ear, and noted that Emma had calmed. The woman pulled out a little bottle with a stopper from her pocket. "I put a couple of drops on her tongue. She won't feel a thing, or at least she won't until it wears off. Then you give her a few more, right? There should be enough to last her a couple of episodes, but don't let her take any unless she's in pain. That goes for you, too; if you get a taste for this stuff, before you know it you'll be out on the street. Mark my words, I've seen it happen, horrible, horrible. When she's finished the bottle, I'll sell you another. But don't tell nobody, yeah? I don't exactly have a licence to dispense, if you know what I mean. Oh, and there's one other thing. Her case is severe. I doubt she'll be able to have children. One of you will have to break it to her. I'm sorry. That's the way it is."

She said a few more things and then asked for four dollars. Sasha and Modska looked at one another, embarrassed. In the end, she accepted two dollars, along with one of Modska's wren sketches and some tea bags. Then she was gone.

They could hear Emma rustling inside her room. This was followed by a pitiable plea: "Sasha?"

She was sitting up on the side of the bed, her head hanging, spittle at the corners of her mouth, dazed. She didn't look up. Sasha sat beside her. The bed sagged. "Am I dying?" she asked.

"No."

"Oh."

"Do you feel better?"

"I don't feel anything at all."

"Emma... there's something I have to tell you."

"What's that?" she asked in a whisper.

"The woman said that, in all probability, you won't be able to conceive a child."

"Good."

Sasha didn't respond. Emma sighed. "Tell me something, fishlips."

"Yes?"

"What are we doing here? What are the three of us up to?"

"I'll be damned if I know."

"All this tiptoeing around one another, while the sink piles high with dishes. Sometimes I think I might just as well go back to Rochester. I'm worn down, Sasha, and that's just the way it is."

So there it was; his torment, her torment. They were the same person, deep down, no wonder they had connected so easily, and with such immediate fervour. Sasha touched her hip. She reached behind and took his fingers. It was an awkward and lovely gesture; both suffered from unutterable sadness. In Sasha's case, it afflicted him every day, in a continuous, barely managed dose. In Emma's case, it lay in wait, a latent virus, most days not bothering her at all, but when activated it would cause her soul to collapse, her mind to blacken, and the air to seep from her lungs, rendering her breathless and wan.

I know, Sasha thought, *who might make her feel a little better.*

eight

EMMA CIRCLED THEIR OILY LITTLE KITCHEN, smoking cigarette after cigarette, gulping black coffee, wringing her hands, and obsessively adjusting her clothing—she was dressed in a dark skirt and a white blouse she'd filched from her sewing pile. "Oh fishie, I'm so nervous, I can barely contain myself, I know I should eat something, but my stomach's doing flip-flops. I tell you, we should've done this earlier, I wish we'd done this earlier, why *didn't* we do this earlier?" She peered at herself in a hand mirror, using her free hand to straighten her hair and pinch some colour into her cheeks. "Well that'll have to *do*. You can't make pearls from a pig's ear, can you?"

It was late afternoon, shortly after Sasha's day at the factory had ended. They walked to William Street, Emma chatting the whole way, Sasha feeling faint with nerves, for though he hadn't lied to her, he had allowed certain presumptions to go uncorrected, all of them regarding the duration of his one-time meeting with the renowned editor Johann Most. The truth was that he'd spoken to Most for no more than a couple of minutes a half year ago, at which point some fawning acolyte in a beret came running up and breathlessly took Most away. Would Most remember him? The truth was that he probably wouldn't. My plan, Sasha thought, is a folly... no, worse, it is ludicrous, a derangement of the senses.

The wooden staircase groaned beneath their feet, the sounds from the street mixing with the hubbub coming from above. Once they were inside the *Freiheit* offices, no one stopped to greet them or so much as look their way as they moved through the busy front room. Behind them was another, larger room, where the rumble of a printing press provided a constant, chugging backdrop; everyone in the office had to speak in raised voices, which only added to the cacophony of the place. "What do we do?" Emma asked. Sasha pointed to the corner of the main area, his forefinger trembling ever so slightly. There, the great man was standing at the podium where he worked, moving his fountain pen in angry, darting swoops. "Do we just go up to him?" she asked.

Sasha swallowed thickly and they approached, stopping when they were about two feet away. He then cleared his throat and was about to say *Excuse me? Herr Most?* when Most looked up, impatience in his eyes. He returned to his work. While Sasha and Emma remained in place, Most took a breath, looked up a second time, and asked, "What is it?"

"I'm Alexander Berkman," Sasha said. "If you recall, we met at a workers' march? In the spring?"

"Which one?"

"It ran along the Brooklyn waterfront. Sponsored by the dockworkers' union? It was raining, if I recall."

"Oh, right, yes, yes, of course."

"This is my friend Emma Goldman. She's an admirer of yours."

Most glanced at Emma. "Is there something I can help you two with?"

"I just wanted to introduce her to you," Sasha said.

Most gave Emma's hand a perfunctory shake before returning to his work, his eyes sharp with intent. Sasha and Emma backed away. "I'm sorry," Sasha mumbled as Emma neared a large wall covered in bookshelves.

She was now running her fingertips over the spines. "Look at all these books," she murmured. "Gogol, Tolstoy, Dostoevsky, Heine, Chekhov. And Nietzsche! Look at all of the Nietzsche! I've never seen so much in one place."

She extracted a copy of *The Birth of Tragedy*. Upon opening it, she gasped. "Fishie! Look, this one is signed! *To my dear friend, Johann.*"

Sasha looked back and saw that Most had crept up behind them, no doubt preparing to chide them for touching his precious books. Emma turned, and saw him too. "I'm sorry," she said, "I shouldn't have."

Most waved a hand in the air. "It's fine, these books are here to be read. I take it you know German?"

"Yes."

"Smart girl. It's the most educated language on earth. You can borrow the Nietzsche if you like. He's a genius, you know. His theories on the primacy of the individual have contributed greatly to anarchism. A lot of people don't realize that."

"Yes, I agree. Thank you so much, Mr. Most."

"Just make sure you bring it back. I'm very possessive about my library."

"You mean that all of these books are yours?"

"Whose else would they be? But that's not why I came over." He took a deep breath, and looked as though he were about to do something distasteful. "I was rude, just then. I can be that way when under stress. I'm so swamped here I barely know my own name. These damn editors are squeezing the blood out of me! Copy, copy, copy—that's all they want! But when they try to write a single line by themselves... bah, it's so substandard I have to rewrite it all anyway."

"There's no need to apologize."

"I understand that. I wanted to anyway. Why did you come to New York?"

"This is the centre of the revolutionist world."

"So you are an adherent to the principles of anarchism?"

"I am."

"Come back anytime, Miss Goldman. We can always use some help. You too, Berkman. Anytime."

There was an awkward moment, in which Most should have returned to his work but, instead, remained in front of them, rocking on the balls of his feet, his chin in his hand. He raised a finger. "Now that I think of it, by this afternoon I'll have two thousand copies of *Freiheit* that, I can guarantee you, will not assemble themselves. Would you care to offer some assistance?"

* * *

Emma and Sasha retired to a cheap cafeteria in the shadow of the Brooklyn Bridge, where they ate jellied eels, boiled potatoes, walnut cake and coffee. It was a cacophonous place, loud with crashing cutlery and waiters yelling orders from one end of the room to the other. From outside, they could hear foghorns and gulls. "Sailor girl," Sasha said in a bemused tone, "I've never seen you so ravenous."

"I know!" she said with a full mouth. "Fishie, I know! It's because we're finally *doing* something... it's triggered my appetite, I think. What about you?"

"It's hard to say, since I'm always hungry."

When they were done, they smoked cigarettes and walked the maze of streets leading back to *Freiheit*. This time, they were greeted by a tall, thin man with a goatee. "Hello," he said. "The name's Stein. I'd shake your hands, but..." He held up his fingertips, which were damp with ink. "Johann tells me you're going to help fold papers."

"We are," said Emma.

"Thank goodness. A couple of volunteers were arrested last night. If you two hadn't happened by, I don't know what we would have done."

Emma and Sasha followed him into a large alcove just outside the entrance to the printing room; here, the finished pages were piled up in tall columns. "So," said Stein. "As you can see... well, you probably can't see... but if you get a little closer you can see that the sheets are piled into what we call 'forms.' There are four pages per form. This pile of forms right here? Each contains pages one, two, fifteen and sixteen. You take one..." He lifted a form from the teetering pile and laid it upon a long, rectangular table. "You then go to the next pile of forms, and take the one containing pages three, four, thirteen and fourteen, and you lay it atop the first form, you see where I'm going with this? The next form contains pages five, six, eleven and twelve, and so on. Now, when the forms are all together, you fold the paper over lengthwise, like this, and then once again widthwise. Got it?"

"I think so," Emma said.

"Good. If you have any questions, come and ask me. I'll be in the printing room. There'll be a new stack of forms in about a half hour or so."

Sasha and Emma started assembling issues of *Freiheit*. After a few minutes, the printer started making a chugging noise; it was now impossible to communicate without yelling. About twenty minutes later, a strong-armed volunteer, whom they later learned was named Juris, started bringing in new bundles of forms, which he held in his outstretched arms like a man carrying a bundle of logs. The piles grew until they were taller than the height of the folding table, at which point Juris (who, they noticed, spoke with a Latvian accent) started creating new piles, shouting, "If I make 'em too high they tend to keel over." Sasha looked balefully at Emma, who was nervously chewing the end of a lock of hair that had fallen over her face. Still, the forms kept coming, the press chugging like an enraged locomotive, and as the piles grew up around Sasha and Emma, Juris yelled, to no one in particular, "Where the hell's Leon? Where the hell's Natasha?" at which point he walked to the entrance of the editorial room and shouted, "We're short-staffed in the folding room and we need some god damn help!"

When Sasha and Emma returned home, they were both exhausted, and deafened from the roar of the press. They collapsed on the Belarussian sofa and, for the longest time, just sat, staring forward, not moving, breathing slowly. "I've never felt so tired," she said with a mirthful sigh, and for both Sasha and Emma there was a delicious sense that time had become unshackled from itself, with one moment no longer leading to the next, every instance occurring and repeating, circling back on itself, rising toward infinity, the two mired in its endlessness.

* * *

Emma Goldman now visited the offices of *Freiheit* every Wednesday afternoon, where she helped to fold a thousand issues of the newspaper. While she didn't enjoy the work, not particularly, she enjoyed making a contribution, so it didn't bother her that there were as many as six volunteers, all working in a room with a folding table that could accommodate no more than two people—this meant that the majority were forced to work upon the floor. As it was much easier to crawl between each pile to select the appropriate forms (as opposed to stand, fetch a form, and then lower oneself back to the floor), Emma started to go to the offices with a pair of knee pads, as it was a common complaint amongst the newspaper folders that the wooden floor, over a shift of several hours, caused the knees to ferociously ache.

One afternoon, when Emma had been volunteering at *Freiheit* for five weeks, Most stepped into the folding room. "Miss Goldman? May I talk to you?"

She nodded, and followed him to his office, a space defined by a five-foot circular perimeter existing around his work station.

"Emma," he said in his native tongue. "I've been hearing you talk to the other volunteers in German. You really are perfectly fluent, aren't you?"

"I wouldn't say I'm fluent, but I do speak it well."

"You were taught in German?"

"Yes, it was the language used at my *Gymnasium*. They thought that..." She paused, smirking. "They thought that Russian or French was for philistines."

"They were right. I have a proposition for you. My proofreader was just deported on sedition charges and I need someone to take over his duties. You'd come in on Tuesdays as well as Wednesday. I'm afraid I can't pay you, but you'd be taking on a bigger role in the publication of *Freiheit*. Would you be interested?"

"Oh Mr. Most," she said. "Of course I would."

"Good. Thank you for your time. And one other thing. Call me Johann. As such, I will call you Emma. Now please. I have many things to attend to."

* * *

The next week, she came in on Tuesday afternoon. She was given a sheaf of papers to proof, a chipped coffee mug that she could regard as her own, a stained clay ashtray and, most significantly, a desk just ten feet away from Johann Most's podium. From here, she could watch everything the man did: the way he looked up and away when seized with an idea; the way he would write so furiously that, at times, the paper beneath the nib of his pen would rip, causing him to curse, ball up the sheet, throw it away, and start again; the way he would call out "next!" when he was finished, only to start the ensuing article without so much as a moment's rest. *Or*—the way he would look straight at her, his gaze emotionless, as though she happened to be located between him and the existence of some great idea, which he was attempting to pull out of the ether. Working this closely with Most, a man who dedicated as much as eighteen hours a day to the cause, both inspired her and infected her with a degree of energy that, at times, made her feel like one of Nietzsche's supermen.

Now that she was spending two full days a week at the *Freiheit* offices, her sewing commissions were beginning to pile up. Emma confronted the problem by working late, drunk on coffee and tobacco, sleeping no more than two or three hours per night; Sasha and Modska learned to fall asleep to the sound of her sewing machine trundling away, the rise and fall of the needle providing a soporific background. Her energy now limitless, she was also attending more meetings, signing more petitions, and marching in more rallies. She lost weight, which brought her features into sharper focus. Her hands, shed of baby fat, started to resemble the hands of an elegant young woman, even though her fingertips were stained with the cheap ink used to print a political newspaper. Her legs thinned as well, Emma more graceful when she moved across a floor. She attracted stares on the street, now, her admirers coming from all avenues of life. One afternoon, while walking down Second Avenue with Sasha, she passed a cadre of street workers, men in overalls and dirty faces, all of whom turned, in tandem, to look at her, eyes widened, transfixed.

Emma poked Sasha in the ribs. "You see that? Did you, fish-lips? The admiring male gaze will always exist. It's just the way it is. I believe that genuine equality will occur on the day in which a woman can leer at the object of *her* affection, without fear of name-calling or physical retribution. The death of the double standard, I say. For instance, look at that young man over there... the one doing push-ups in the park. Do you see the way his triceps are flexing? It suggests a degree of strength that some women find arousing. I happen to be one of them. In the very near future, I'll be able to stop and stare, eyes wide, drooling if I want to. I might even call out something like *Hey, doll face, how about a smile?* As long as no one touches anyone without permission, it's the way it has to be. At least that's how I feel about it."

"Emma," he said. "You're incorrigible."

"I know! I know! Isn't that why you adore me?"

* * *

One Tuesday afternoon, Johann Most strode from his podium to Emma's desk. "A word?" he said with a characteristic frown. He stood looking at her, as if planning what to next say. He then held up his hands, and looked around the busy room. "You see what it's like here, something always needs to be done. Would you come in on Mondays as well? To perform some basic copy-editing functions? I'd take you off paper-folding. Say yes. I need help."

"Yes! Of course! Whatever you..."

He rapped the knuckle of his forefinger against Emma's desk. "Good," he said before wandering back to his podium, where an avalanche of submitted articles, all of which needed to be improved, if not completely rewritten, awaited him.

The work continued, several busy weeks passing. There was an issue of *Freiheit* devoted to anti-tsarist uprisings in Russia, an issue devoted to the fight for hygienic working conditions, another devoted to housing issues, and one particularly fiery edition that aimed both barrels at the increasing prevalence of child labour in Lower East Side factories. A new fire seemed to have possessed Johann Most, who wrote most, if not all, of the articles appearing in *Freiheit*, many of which appeared under one of his pen names—Wolfgang Mueller, Helmut Schmidt, Fritz Blume, Erik Saltzer, etc., etc. Late one afternoon, around the time in which the majority of his staff was packing up to go home, Most appeared before Emma and said, "Meet me outside. I have something important to discuss with you. Oh, and bring your coat."

He left, Emma trying to gauge his intention by the manner of his walk: shoulders back, head up, feet kicking slightly to the sides, the same as always. She didn't know whether to be nervous or excited, which bothered her: she constantly monitored the man for signs that he was pleased, disappointed, excited, disgruntled, on and on it went, Emma's mood no longer her own but a reflection of Most's. She found him outside, at the end of the block, smoking a cigar, looking slightly impatient.

"Please," he said. "I thought if it was amenable to you, we could have a bit of sustenance. Come."

He charged off, heading toward the El. Emma was barely able to keep up, Most being a man who, above all else, always moved in a hurry. Once aboard they were forced to stand, pressed close to one another, Most frowning at the inconvenience. "This city," he muttered. "It'll kill us all one day." The train shuttled uptown, moving diagonally across the island, the two chatting about an upcoming issue devoted to the writings of Josef Peukert. They stepped off at a leafy, calm neighbourhood that, Emma thought, seemed out of place in New York. They walked a bit, before arriving at a restaurant called the Terrace Garden. "There's something important I'd like to discuss with you. I thought we could have a bite to eat too."

They went inside. Emma looked around, not so much astonished as startled, for this uptown bistro seemed to operate on a different principle than the restaurants of the Lower East Side, where everybody yelled at everybody and the tabletops were messy with gravy splatters. But here, in this different world, in this fashionable boîte, the neatly dressed diners spoke in a subdued volume, the waiters didn't seem to be in a rush, and there were plants, growing out of large, terracotta urns.

A waiter arrived and conferred with Most before leaving them with sheets of paper upon which the kitchen's offerings were listed. Emma's eyes narrowed. "There's so much here," she said. "It seems almost wrong. I hardly know what to order."

Most leaned over and gently took the menu from her. "Please," he said. "I know what's good here."

"So you've been here before?"

"The work I do... it's very stressful. And yet there's so much of it, I could never even think of taking a vacation. Instead I come here. It's an escape, nothing more, my lone indulgence. Otherwise, I live like a pauper, I really do. Do you like soufflé?"

"I don't know."

"You will."

A few minutes later, the waiter returned with a bottle of wine, the label reading *Liebfrauenmilch*. Emma grinned. "'Milk of a woman's love.' What a lovely name."

"Do you enjoy wine?"

"The only wine I've ever had was the swill my mother made at Easter time. It tasted like turpentine."

"In that case, this might be a pleasant surprise."

He poured her a glass. She took a sip. "That's delicious! I never knew anything could taste so good." She took another sip, and when she looked up she saw that Most had already drained his first glass, and was pouring himself another. He drank this as well, Emma noticing, with some degree of fascination, the way in which his ears turned slightly pink and his muscles seemed to soften, his rigid carriage giving way to something more approachable.

"Emma," he said. "The path of anarchism is steep and painful. So many have attempted to climb it and have fallen back. The price is exacting. Few men are ready to pay it in full, most women not at all."

"Are there really no outstanding female anarchists in America?"

"No," he said, his eyes reflecting something that was almost mournful. "None at all. They come to the meetings to snatch up a man. Then they vanish, like silly fishermen at the lure of the Lorelei."

"And in Russia?"

"It's a different story over there. The stakes are higher, the oppression more pronounced. The female comrades—they've seen their husbands jailed, tortured, disappeared. They're more willing to do what it takes. That's why I've invited you here tonight. In you, Emma, I see promise. I see boldness. I see a commitment that's sadly lacking in the movement here. There is great need in our ranks of young, willing people—ardent ones, as you seem to be—and I am in need of ardent friendship."

"You? I'm shocked. You have thousands of admirers in New York—all over the world, in fact. You are loved by so many people."

"No, I'm sorry to say, that's not the case. I am idolized by many, but loved by none. One can be very lonely among thousands—did you know that?"

Emma, despite herself, felt a pang of attraction toward Johann Most, a feeling she chased away immediately, for it felt motherly in nature, and she believed that the maternal drive was a culturally imposed structure, dreamt up by men as a way of keeping women where they wanted them: at home, in the kitchen, a baby at the breast. This sudden desire to make Most's loneliness go away? She wouldn't have it. She stiffened, even shuddered. Most noticed, and ordered a second bottle of *Liebfrauenmilch* when the waiter brought the soufflés. She tucked in; it was delicious, like clouds. When she next looked up, she felt relieved, for that spark she'd felt had gone—probably, she thought, it was just her appreciation for all that he had done for her.

"Emma," Most said. "Where did you go just then?"

"I'm sorry?"

"You went away, somewhere. What foreign land did you just visit?"

"I... I don't know what you mean."

"Well then," he said. "I have a proposition for you."

nine

SASHA WAS AT THE KITCHEN TABLE, smoking cigarette after cigarette, fretting after Emma's whereabouts, as it was late, and there was agitation in the streets—a feral restlessness making people do crazy things—and women were advised to not be out beyond a certain hour. He drank coffee, the brew taking his fears and magnifying them, such that Sasha started to imagine horrific occurrences: Emma robbed, Emma pawed at by mashers, Emma dragged into an alley and ravaged. He lit another cigarette, and wished that the rational side of his brain, the side that *knew* Emma had probably just gone out with some co-workers, was a match for the irrational side of the brain, the side that, once it latched on to a worrisome idea, refused to let go, until that idea had overcome the entirety of Sasha's thoughts. In addition to worrying about Emma's whereabouts, he was now disgusted by his own tendency toward catastrophic thinking, a tendency that, if he didn't think of some way to defeat it, would likely characterize the rest of his days upon earth.

When Emma finally did come home, she kissed him and plopped herself onto the Belarussian sofa. He offered her a cigarette, which she lit with the end of his. "What a night," she said. "I had dinner with Johann Most."

Sasha's eyes widened. "Sorry... with *Most*? And here I thought you were lying dead in a culvert somewhere."

"Hardly. We went to a restaurant on the Upper West Side. He said he wanted to discuss something with me." She gestured with her cigarette. "I tell you, Sasha, the *problems* this world will think up. He brought it up over dessert. Meanwhile, he sat back, smoking a cigar the size of a rolled-up towel."

"Are you going to tell me what he wanted?"

"As you well know, November 11 is the anniversary of the Haymarket martyrdoms. A bunch of anarchist groups are commemorating the night with an event at Cooper Union. Most is booked to speak."

"I know, I've seen the posters."

"He thinks it'd be a great boon to the movement if he somehow got the trade unionists to attend. He thinks it'd be an opportunity to lure them to a more anarchist position. To do this, he needs someone to visit the labour halls and do a little recruiting. You know, encourage them to come? Dangle a carrot, so to speak?"

Sasha shrugged. "That makes sense."

"He wants me to do it. He says a woman would go over well in the union halls of the world. He says I'd be perfect. He says I'm a real pistol. There's just one problem."

"Which is?"

"Oh fishlips, it's just so stupid. I'm... I'm afraid of public speaking. I blame those biddies who taught us at school. I remember this one old witch, Stigler was her name, made us stand up and speed through the times tables. If we made a mistake—bam! We'd get it with a ruler. If we did it too slowly—whap! We'd get it with a ruler. If we hesitated—smack! We'd get it with a ruler. It was traumatizing. I still don't know what eight times seven is."

He smirked. "That was a long time ago, sailor."

"Yes—but I was little. Things that happen to you when you're a young child—they hang around. Now, whenever I stand before an audience, I feel like that old bitch is standing next to me, waiting for me to make a mistake."

"What did you tell Most?"

"What do you *think* I told him? The first meeting is Thursday night. The New York Longshoremen Association." She inhaled on her cigarette, and hissed a plume of smoke toward the ceiling. "I tell you, I'm scared half to death. My heart's pounding just thinking about it. But I was thinking that you could come with me?"

* * *

Two nights later, they stood in a wood-panelled barrack down by the dockyards, a clandestine location underlying the fact that, in America, trade unionism was against the law, the merest whisper of the word "strike" having the potential to land a man in jail. Emma was wearing a dark jacket and long skirt, her hair pulled back into a tight bun; Sasha wore a ragged overcoat and cap. Wind rushed through cracks in the window casements, the floors were littered with scraps of burlap, and the broad-beam walls smelled of cockles and diesel fuel. There were no chairs, so everyone stood, shifting their weight from foot to foot, drinking cups of a pungent black coffee topped with whisky. Emma gripped Sasha's hand; her entire body was shaking. "I think I'm going to puke," she said at the same moment in which the shop steward, a man named Jack Barnes, took the stage, which was not a stage at all, just an oil-splattered clearing existing between a pair of empty drums. He was tall, and had a moustache that wrapped over the top of his mouth before extending down the sides of his face, not unlike an overturned horseshoe. He waved his hands in the air.

"Good evening, everybody. Everybody, good evening."

He waited for the men to settle.

"Good, good, can you all hear? Can you all hear me? Before we get going, I have just a few things to discuss, a few things to go over. First, let me remind you, let me remind you *all*, that the annual

Longshoremen's family picnic will be held this Sunday, this Sunday afternoon at noon, at the riverside, that's Riverside Park, it'll be a potluck with games, with all sorts of activities, you all remember the good time we had last year, so don't forget to come, and if you're a single man, if you don't have a wife, don't be afraid to come, you'll still have fun, you'll still enjoy yourself."

"Could you repeat that, Barnsie?" someone called.

Everyone laughed, including Barnes. Emma was looking at a sheet of paper in her hands, her lips moving, as she was still attempting to memorize the speech that Most had given her. "*Also*," said Barnes, "it's the end of the month, gentlemen, the last day of the month, and at the end of this meeting, I'm going to pass the hat so as to collect your dues, to collect your fees, which I know you don't like, which I know you *hate*, but god knows we need every nickel we make, every *cent* we make, but one day, I promise you, this union's gonna make all the difference."

"Atta boy, Barnes-y," someone else called, a bit of approbation that made the steward grin.

"But first, before we do a little mingling, I have here a little lady who wants to say a few words about the struggle, seems she has something new to say, something we haven't yet heard, so please welcome Miss Emma, uh, Miss Emma Goldman."

There was polite applause. Sasha whispered "good luck" and, when Emma didn't move, gently pushed against the small of her back. Emma stepped onto the makeshift stage and nervously surveyed her audience, all of them American workers, Bronx-born and sturdy, with thick sweaters, black woollen hats and bulbous forearms, their noses misshapen by winching accidents, their faces permanently reddened by exposure to the East River wind. Someone in the audience coughed. A trapped bird drummed its wings against the rafters. Emma blinked and looked pleadingly at Sasha, who lifted his eyebrows, and made a rolling motion with his forefingers. When she still didn't begin speaking, he mouthed the word *go*.

"Good evening," she finally started. "My name is Emma Goldman, and I'm here to talk to you today about possibilities. Yes, that's right, I'm here to talk to you about different courses you can plot in order to achieve your goals of independence."

She was speaking too quickly, her voice uninflected and feeble. She paused, gulped air, and continued, her hands still trembling, her voice a speeding mutter, "Yes, that's right, what if I told you that instead of continually going to your bosses, hat in hand, begging for small concessions, like Oliver Twist wanting more, you could be the bosses, yes that's right you heard me, what if you were the bosses, the owners, the directors and the chairman of the board all rolled into one?"

Again, she paused, not only to fill her lungs, but to gauge the effect this statement had on her audience. There was none, beyond a general confusion; one of the dockworkers turned to the man beside him and asked, "What's she on about?" Seeing this, Emma fought a sudden impulse to walk away, not only from that night's talk but the movement itself, and might have even done so had she not glanced at Sasha, who again made an encouraging gesture. She looked back down at her notes, and continued: "Yes that's right it's called anarchism ladies and gentlemen—I mean, sorry, *gentlemen*... it's called anarchism and in the anarchist political discourse there are no owners, there is just you, and I know this sounds like communism but it's not that at all, for with communism you still have leadership, and as we all know leaders will always become corrupted, and will always exploit the working class, given that they have the time and the means to do so, oh no ladies and... I mean, oh no *gentlemen*, with anarchism we prescribe the complete elimination of leadership so that you, the workers, might govern yourselves."

A second longshoreman, responding to the question posed by his buddy, turned sideways and said, "You got me, Smitty, something about anarchism, you know what that is?"

"Not a clue, Charlie."

"Anarchism, my good friends, will release you from the bondage of workplace oppression, for only in the system of political thought known as anarchism can the worker plot his own course, make his own decisions, forge his own path."

On the other of the barrack, near where Sasha stood, a sandy-haired dockworker turned to the man beside him, a gangly fellow in a zippered corduroy jacket, and asked, "You going to the game tonight?"

"Who's playing?"

"The Bridegrooms and the Colts."

"Jesus, that'll be a game an' a half."

"The two heaviest hitters in the league."

"Burns and Wilnot, you mean? I heard they hate each other, them two."

"And I promise you, gentlemen, if you back the horse called anarchism, you will not be alone, why all over Europe, anarchists are conducting actions to dismantle the free market system, they're called *attentats*, and they are even happening here, I'm sure you've all heard of the protests that occurred following the indignities at Haymarket."

"What?" said Smitty to Charlie. "Did she say dismantle the free market system?"

"Christ almighty why would we want that?"

"I think she might be some kind of commie."

"I've heard of them. Russian, ain't they?"

"Don't know about that but she does talk funny, don't she?"

"Oh for the love of Pete," someone else hissed, just loudly enough to be heard. There were nervous titters; Emma stopped and looked up. Through glistening eyes, she witnessed a sort of ideological standoff—while the dockworkers didn't understood what she was saying, they weren't rude men, at least not all of them, and they didn't wish to make this strange woman uncomfortable, given that she was a guest, and the only woman in attendance, and they didn't often have visitors to their meetings. These contrary desires, to be hospitable to this off-putting little creature while, at the same time, stop her from droning on, deadened the room, the silence fractured when some good-natured soul called out, "Oh don't you mind old Tony, miss, he just forgets his manners now and again." There was a roar of laughter. "Ha!" someone else called out, "you remember that time he drank two bottles of Chianti at the summer picnic and swore he could swim to the far side of the Hudson River?"

"Yeah," said another. "If his wife hadn'ta stopped him he woulda tried it, he really woulda, the mad bastard."

The room filled with competing voices, over which Emma spoke louder, "SO PLEASE JOIN US AT COOPER UNION HALL ON NOVEMBER THE ELEVENTH." She crept away from the ersatz stage, her head lowered, struggling to not weep, and stepped into Sasha's arms, her forehead resting against his chest. The men now moved toward the front of the room, where someone had opened an ice cooler filled with bottles of beer, and someone else was handing out cheese-and-pickle sandwiches wrapped in squares of old newspaper. The men stood around eating, crumbs collecting in their beards, lighting thin cigars that smelled like burning leather. One or two even came up and said, "nice talk miss" or "thanks for coming, miss," which only made her feel worse.

Emma and Sasha walked back through the deserted waterfront, a moist wind lashing their faces. The streets grew busier, and narrower, and warmer, as they neared their home. Beside their stoop, a stray pig rooted through spilled garbage. It lifted its head, displaying cold, gunmetal eyes and coffee grounds in its whiskers. There was a homeless man in their doorway; when he asked for spare change, Emma gave him all that she had. They went up. Modska was in the living room, painting. There was mess everywhere. He took one look at Emma's expression and said nothing. Emma turned to Sasha; her cheeks were damp and white. She took Sasha's hand, and led him to his room. There, they disrobed, Sasha holding her in bed while she sobbed.

* * *

The following night, Sasha came home and found Emma lying on the floor, staring upward, arms outstretched, surrounded by petticoats and waistbands, an overturned mug beside her. Sasha lit a cigarette and sat on the Belarussian sofa.

"I went to see Most today," Emma said in a dispossessed voice. "I told him that my speech had been a disaster. You know what he said? 'Of course it was. Everyone's first speech is a disaster.' Then he told me I was booked Tuesday night to speak before Local 4526, the Union of Asiatic Launderers."

"You refused, I take it."

"He never gave me a chance. You know how he is."

"He's formidable, all right. He trades on his reputation."

"What am I supposed to do? Say 'no' to Johann Most? Then he asked me to sweep the floor. And the worst thing was, I did it! He has no regard for other people, you know. I mean, he has no regard for *individual* people. It's ironic. He's dedicated his life to the advancement of the human condition, and then stomps all over others to get there."

"You're being dramatic."

"I'm a dramatic person. Look at all this, Sasha. Look at all this *work* I have to do. Do I look like someone who has the time to sweep floors? If I'd wanted to sweep floors, I could have stayed in Russia, married a drunkard, and had a half dozen brats. By the way, you will come with me on Tuesday, won't you?"

Over the next three days, Sasha could hear her in the other room, talking away to herself, practising the same speech she'd given to the longshoremen. He found it pitiful to listen to—she kept repeating the same sections, each time stressing different sentences, or different clauses, or different words, all in an effort to punch life into a text that sounded inherently disingenuous, if only because it wasn't her own. At dinner, she picked at her food, too fraught to eat, nervously smoking, bouncing a foot against the floor.

"I could come too," Modska said. "That way, I could applaud at all the right bits. Cue the audience, so to speak."

"No!" Emma said. "It's bad enough I have to humiliate myself in front of Sasha. This is the last time I do this, I can promise you that."

Their destination was Pell Street. Though Most had written the address on a scrap of paper, the two had neglected to consider that there were few addresses or street signs in this part of the city, and the ones that did exist were written in a foreign script, upon squares of pressed tin that had grown blotchy and orange with age. After a surfeit of aimless wandering, they showed the paper to an old woman who was selling fruit from a bin. She took it, studied it for a moment, and then handed it back while shaking her head and muttering, "No, no, no, no." They tried to stop a second person, a middle-aged man in a grey business suit, a cigarette hanging out of his mouth; he waved them away and sped on, clearly too busy to assist the two interlopers. This encounter was witnessed by a tiny, ancient man who was sitting on an overturned crate just a few feet away. He smiled and reached for the chit of paper, his fingers tracing along Most's handwriting. He nodded and stood, his trousers hanging from barely existent hips. Next to him was a trap door in the sidewalk; it was open, revealing a set of stairs leading toward the basement of a noisy, dim restaurant. He bent at the waist, cupped his mouth, and yelled. A child of about ten popped up; she wore a boy's haircut and a pair of overalls. The old man said something to her, and then passed her the note.

"Okay," she said, "come."

She sped away. Sasha and Emma followed, which was not easy, for the girl moved quickly, darting around pedestrians, shops, rickshaws, street lamps and tiny steaming sidewalk restaurants, many just a bicycle with a pair of fold-out surfaces, one supporting a pot of rice and the other a large round pan filled with vegetables and hacked chicken. More than once, they lost track of the girl, only to spot the top of her head, bobbing in the dense crowd. Other times, they lost her altogether, Emma and Sasha glancing in every direction, only to see her pop out of an alcove, a look of amusement on her face. "This way," she'd call while waving them forward.

They reached a tall narrow building. The front door was wedged open, its lower edge ground against a buckle in the sidewalk. The child looked back and motioned with a tiny, cupped hand. By the time Sasha and Emma squeezed around the partially opened door, they had lost her once more, though they could follow the sound of her small feet tapping against the crooked, splintering stairs. By the sixth floor, Emma had to stop to catch her breath.

"You hear that?" she asked.

"I don't hear anything."

"That's my point. She must've turned down this hallway."

They pushed open a thin metal door and found her standing in front of an apartment. When they reached her, she held out her palm, Sasha presenting her with a coin. She nodded and said, "Have a good evening." They entered. A few dozen launderers, all with reddened hands and faces, were in a small room decorated with posters of mist-cloaked mountains. They all stopped talking and stared at the pair; Emma gave a friendly wave and the conversations resumed. A grinning man with slicked-back hair and a pitted complexion approached. "Welcome!" he said. "You enter! You welcome!" A moment later, a tiny woman in a gold dress brought the pair a thin, yellow tea that tasted like grass cuttings. Another woman, this one wearing a red silk blouse with buttons running down the side, gave them buns filled with spicy mashed pork. As Emma clutched her plate, still too nervous to eat, a man in a Western-style suit took to the front of the room and began to speak in one of the dialects existing in Chinatown, his oratory ending with a slight mispronunciation of Emma's name. He then turned toward her and bowed. The launderers applauded, albeit hesitantly. Emma nodded and took the front of the room and, trembling slightly, read through her prepared script, showing no more ease than she had with the longshoremen; if there was a saving grace, it was that the audience understood little of what she had to say. She left, sniffling, her hand in Sasha's.

* * *

There were the Latvian Steelworkers, who met in a warehouse just over the river in Brooklyn. The International Consortium of Porters and Chambermaids assembled in a freezing-cold coach house in the West Village; it was the first time in which women were in attendance, all of them sallow, dark-eyed Europeans who, far from offering a sisterly camaraderie, gazed upon Emma with suspicion, a few hissing when Emma reached the part about the dismantling of the capitalist bonds that restrained them. The members of the Fishmongers Affiliation congregated in a chilly backroom in the Bronx; as Emma spoke, they passed flasks of rum back and forth, taking long slugs that burned their throats and made them feel strengthened. The Ironworkers of Union 361 convened in a basement tavern in Hell's Kitchen; they were rowdy, and whistled when Emma took the stage, one of them yelling, *Well hello there sweetheart.*

She had two or three meetings a month. Though her nervousness still assaulted her, it didn't assault her quite as much, and she now often made it to the stage without shaking excessively. Though she credited Sasha's presence—*fishlips, I love you, I do*—she was also beginning to realize that her speeches were accomplishing nothing, and would continue to accomplish nothing, no matter what she did, thereby removing some of the pressure that had been placed upon her. In other words, she was becoming resigned to the confusion and lack of interest that greeted her when she addressed her audience. Other times, she was met with hostility: "Lady, I heard just about enough," hollered one disgruntled pipefitter in a Greenwich Village garage. "Jesus, why'd you let this red agitator in here?" voiced a disbelieving woodworker in a tacked-together bungalow near Battery Park. "For the love of Mike," called a tanner in a Union Square cafeteria, "we want better wages and shorter days, not a god damn revolution. Who in the hell let this menace in here?" In response, Emma would protest, her anxiety replaced by spleen, her hands waving, her voice rising in pitch, "No! You're not *listening*... I'm not a communist, good people, I'm an anarchist, there's a difference!"

One sultry night, at the boilermen's headquarters, an over-heated hall just over the river in Queens, the members of Local 264 stared at Emma, saying nothing, neither applauding nor hissing, just watching her, possessed by weariness. As soon as Emma stopped talking, they went back to their cigarettes, their frustrated conversations, their bottles of Amstel, ignoring Emma entirely, and while there was probably good reason for their detachment—a boilerman's life was hot, filthy and not particularly lengthy—both Emma and Sasha had to wonder why they'd agreed to let her speak in the first place. They exited the cramped hall, which occupied the rear of a warehouse, such that the door opened onto a darkened alley leading to the street. Emma was disconsolate; halfway along the alley, she stopped and looked defeated. "Sasha," she mumbled. "No one ever said revolution is easy. But no one told me it'd be this difficult."

A pair of boilermen stepped into the alley; both were sturdy galoots, with big shoulders and damp skin. Though Emma was oblivious, her hot face pressed into Sasha's chest, Sasha saw it coming, the men walking toward them, the bigger of the two glancing at Emma while grunting, "Go home, you commie slut." They walked on, chortling, their boot heels clacking against the laneway stones, while Emma looked up at Sasha and grinned, weakly, as if to say *You see? You see how it is, fishlips?* and it was true that Sasha *did* see, he *did* see how it was, his hands tightened at his sides, his body tremoring with indignation, his teeth grinding. "Sasha, no," Emma gulped, for he was marching toward the two men, his shoes smacking the pavement. The mouthy one turned, a smug expression on his face, as if to say, *What're* you *gonna do, eh Russkee?* for he was a big man, clearly used to getting his way, while Sasha Berkman was all of five foot six. Yet Sasha was also a man enraged, a man in love, a man with a whisky-barrel chest and fists the size of bocce balls, so he pushed the boilerman against the alley wall, his forearm pressing hard against the man's throat. The boilerman went silent, his eyes bulging and pink, his breath coming in squeaking rasps.

The other man took Sasha by the shoulders. "Listen Mac," he said. "We didn't mean nothin.'"

Sasha released his victim. This was followed by a long, awkward moment, with one man holding his throat and gasping for air, the other two looking sheepish and unsure. The warehouse door creaked open, and a half dozen union members, all laughing and talking loudly, stepped into the alley. The man Sasha had choked, still incapable of any sound beyond a strangulated gurgle, pointed a forefinger. "Run!" Emma yelled, and then the two were fleeing through a foreign neighbourhood, while the men behind waved their fists and yelled that they could fuck off back to Russia, or Prussia, or Poland, or wherever the fuck it was they came from, and that if they ever came around there again they were dead, god damn it, and through it all Sasha whooped and laughed and felt as close to invincible as it is possible for a grown man to feel. Though their pursuers could have likely caught up to them—neither Emma nor Sasha was particularly fleet of foot—it was also true that the streets were crowded with witnesses, so the boilermen stopped after a block or two, their fists raised, howling invectives.

Emma was never more passionate than she was that night, in Sasha's creaking tenement bed, gasping and moaning and biting her lover's neck and pinching her lover's flesh, leaving welts and bruises, and between gentle slaps to his face she groaned that she loved him, again and again, she couldn't stop saying it, "What you did tonight... what I *saw* tonight... I knew it all along... yes I did yes I did yes I did!" They caught their breath; it wasn't easy; Sasha coughed and chuckled and counted the places where he smarted. There was lamplight shining through the window; it turned the smoke from their cigarettes the colour of copper.

"A commie slut," Emma said. "Can you believe that? It's ironic... if I'd asked any one of them if they felt exploited by their bosses, they'd have told me, 'god damn right, why wouldn't I?, look at what they pay us, look at all the burns on my arms, with what I breathe in I won't see forty.' But *then*, when I suggest they change the system that enslaves them, they feel threatened and resort to slurs."

"People want what they know," Sasha said with a sardonic chuckle. "Not what's good for them."

"This country runs on aspiration. It runs on dog-eat-dog. Even if they feel fucked over, they don't want to ruin any chance they might have to fuck over others once *they* have their turn on top. And they really believe that turn is going to come! They all swallow that nonsense about how, in the United States, anyone can be a boss, how it's equal opportunity for all, how all you have to do is apply yourself and live righteously. At least back home, we all know how rigged the game is, and no one pretends otherwise. It's that American gullibility, fishie. That tendency to look at things through rose-coloured glasses. *That's* the real reason we're anarchists—as Russians, it drives us *crazy*."

"Or maybe, they were just pigs."

"Oh fishie," she said. "It's never as simple as that."

ten

WHEN SHE WAS ALONE, now, the walls talked to her, the air talked to her, the table talked to her, a chorus reminding her of how poorly her recruitment speeches were going. A quick accounting showed that she had embarrassed herself in front of longshoremen and launderers; had failed to impress steelworkers, porters and coal scuttlers; had bored fishmongers and ironworkers and welders. She sighed, stared into space, smoked cigarettes, ate leftover kippers, drank too much coffee, and felt overwhelmed by the amount of sewing she needed to do. Then, she went to *Freiheit*, where she encountered Johann Most on the stairs between the second and third floors, Emma on the way up to the offices, Most on the way to one of the courtyard lavatories that serviced the building. They stopped and regarded each other.

"Emma," he said. "I'm in a hurry."

"I won't do any more of these talks."

"I beg your pardon."

"I won't. I'm sorry. They're useless. I'm useless. If anything, I'm discrediting the movement."

Most peered at her, betraying nothing—not anger, not disappointment, not irritation—and, in this way, seemed all the more intimidating. After brushing a fallen lock of ink-black hair from his forehead, he grunted: "I know, damn it."

"You know?"

"I'm not an idiot. These damn unionists! I thought that they might be receptive to a more progressive message. What I didn't realize is how duped they've become. So no. It was a bad idea. I know better, now."

He continued moving down the steps. Emma—who felt slightly chagrined, as she hadn't imagined how easily she could be discarded—remained still. Most must have sensed it, for after a few steps he turned and looked at her through a narrowed eye. "Wait upstairs for me," he commanded. She went upstairs and sat at her desk, Most returning a few minutes later. Taking her by the arm, he led her to an alcove.

"So," he said. "What do I do with you now?"

"I'm happy with my editorial duties," she said. "I have more of a behind-the-scenes personality."

"You most certainly do not. And I've news for you, you're not much of an editor either."

"Don't say that."

"It's true. And lest we forget, your desk is ten paces from my podium. I can hear you when you discuss politics with your co-workers. You're a spitfire, a firebrand. You might *need* an editor, but you sure as blazes aren't one. I just gave you that job until I figured out how you could better serve our overarching goals. And now I know."

"What do you know?"

"I have a speech scheduled for next Wednesday. In Rochester. It's about three hundred miles north of here, a lovely little..."

"Yes, yes, I know the place, I used to live there. And believe me, it's anything but lovely."

"The subject is the fight for the eight-hour workday. Naturally, my position is that it's a mug's game, that by asking the factory owners for this one consideration we legitimize their existence."

"When, by all rights, they shouldn't exist at all."

"Correct. That's the problem with those damn union leaders. They'll organize several million labourers across America, and for what? So that their enslavement can be dished out in eight-hour portions instead of the usual twelve. Emma—*Freiheit* is hanging by a thread. Each issue, I swear it will be its last. I can't spare a minute away. I really can't. I want you to do it. It'll be a general audience, a crowd of sympathizers—no more hoodwinked unionists, no more drunken stooges, no more beer-swilling apologists. With an audience of anarchists, my speech will work. I can guarantee you."

Emma stiffened, and agreed, only to spend much of the next five days pacing the floor in her room, staying up late, practising the latest speech Most had written for her, massaging each sentence, manipulating each turn of phrase, all in the hope of finding some spark in the text he'd provided: *the fight for the eight-hour workday is pure folly, in that it validates the very system that you, my dear people, should be attempting to overturn.* She'd stop, and fight the urge to give up, only to remember Most's opinion regarding female anarchists. In a deeper, perhaps more authoritative pitch, she'd repeat the sentence, over and over, each time adjusting her tone, or modulating her volume, or punching words that might unleash the energy she sought, *oh YES my good friends, the fight for the eight-hour workday is PURE folly, in that it validates the VERY system that...* at which point she'd falter, and try again, *oh yes my GOOD friends, the fight for the eight-hour workday is pure FOLLY.*

Late one night, the neighbourhood streets having turned vacant and still, she crawled into bed next to Sasha and clung to him as he groggily came awake. "Look at what I've done," she said in a frustrated mumble. "My talks before the unions did nothing, we all know that, and who knows what my talk in Rochester is going to do? If this keeps up, anarchism will amount to a few cranks mouthing off on street corners. And you know what? History will have me to thank."

"Shhhhhhhhhh."

"No really, I'm a buffoon."

He rolled over to face her. "You're anything but that."

"Are you sure you can't come with me?"

"Not without losing my job."

She cupped his face. "So *lose* it. You can always find another."

"I'm the only one of us with full-time employment. Without my wages, we'd all starve."

"So what? So we starve? At least we'd have lived by our ideals! In case you hadn't noticed, I'm a nervous wreck. I walk down the street, no longer sure that, with each step, the sidewalk will catch me. You know what that *feels* like?"

She was eating poorly, smoking too many cigarettes, and taking pulls from a vodka bottle she kept hidden in her room. All day (and, to be sure, all night) she kept coffee grounds simmering on the stove, creating a brew as viscous as gravy. The house filled with improvised ashtrays—a pie carton, a soup bowl, an egg carton, each one full to overflowing. On Wednesday morning, Sasha wished her good luck at the breakfast table. She grew tearful. "*Please*, I'm begging you, quit your job and come with me. You can find another when you get back. I'll make it up to you. I will, I promise, oh what have I done to myself?!"

He walked her to the train station. She'd slept perhaps a dozen hours in the past five nights. Once on board, she rested her forehead against the window, and watched as the city dwindled to farms and fields and neat little white clapboard houses. The man in the seat beside her opened a packet of cheddar cheese sandwiches wrapped in wax paper. When he saw that Emma hadn't a lunch, he offered her one, saying, "Please, miss, my wife, she always makes too much." She thanked him and declined, even though it'd been at least a day since she'd thought to feed herself. The man seemed nice enough—an insurance agent, as it turned out—with three children, their names Edgar, Joyce and Betty, Emma nodding and listening and thankful for any diversion. He got off at Syracuse. The seat beside her remained empty. Then she heard it, *next stop Rochester*, and the nervousness that had abated during the train ride came rushing back. She felt dizzy, and assailed by the eerie sensation that the world was a mirage, and that if she was to stick her arm out quickly enough, she might pierce this veil, her hand plunging into goo. Everyone was standing and retrieving suitcases and Emma did the same, following them off the train and onto the platform and through the train station until she saw a man holding a sign reading, "Johann Most."

She went up to him.

"He's not coming," Emma said.

"I'm sorry?"

Emma swallowed away a rush of nausea. "He's not coming," she repeated. "He's too busy. They sent me, instead. My name is Emma Goldman."

The man shook his head and smiled. "I don't think so," he said, leading to an almost comical standoff, whereby Emma and the driver stood facing one another, not speaking, until it was clear that Johann Most was not among the passengers departing from the train. The driver looked down at this curious little woman and asked, "What did you say your name was, again?"

They clopped along a lane leading into the city, the man whistling away. He stopped before a small stone church and, after helping Emma down, brought to her to a basement full of chattering people. Time leapt forward, landing her before a room of faces, all staring up at her, the only noise a bit of rustling, but mostly it was silence and the feeling that she might plummet through space, the stage too feeble to hold her, and what could she do but extract her speech and somehow get through this? She flattened the sheet of paper against the lectern, her hands shaking. She spotted her sisters, Lena and Helena, in the third row, the look of concern on their faces only making things worse. She looked at the paper. The words on the page coiled like garden snakes and why oh why wasn't Sasha here? If he were here she could look at him and he'd make a fist, as if to say *You can do it, sailor girl, give 'em hell*, but he wasn't, she couldn't read, she had lost the ability, time for plan B—she had rehearsed the speech a hundred times over the past five days, so why not just serve it up by memory? The problem was that here, on this little stage, the church air smelling like muffins, she remembered not a word, not one single blessed word, so what was she to do, *oh fishie my fishie where the hell are you?* She squeezed her eyes shut. She opened them, slowly, and, because she had to say something, began to speak:

"I am a Jew from Russia. I mostly grew up in the city of Kovno, deep in the Pale of Settlement. Opportunities were few, there: some grew potatoes, some shovelled coal, some farmed fields so stubbornly muddy that even rutabagas struggled. And believe me, my comrades, rutabagas will grow pretty much *anywhere*. So I left. I came here, to Rochester, where my two older sisters had already fled. In fact, they are here tonight—hello Lena, hello Helena. Right away, I got a job in a factory that made linen and silk blouses for women. I also got the shock of my life. The factory was run-down, in terrible shape, the air unbreathable, mould everywhere, and the only break we received was a meagre half hour for lunch—we couldn't even go to the toilet without permission. And the pay... it was worse than in Russia. Yes, you heard me, with the cost of things in America, it was worse! Had I not been living with my sister, I would have starved to death! That's when I realized that the ownership class will always find a way to exploit its citizens. In Russia, the tsar employs tyranny. Here, in America, exploitation is economic.

"So one day, I asked to speak with the factory owner, a Mr. Garson. This took some determination, for he was *not* in the habit of talking to his factory workers, but with time I was able to have a brief audience. A secretary ushered me into a luxurious office. There was a beautiful desk and American Beauties in a vase. I had seen these roses in a flower shop downtown—they cost a dollar and a half for a bunch, which was more than half of my weekly wages.

"Mr. Garson was behind his desk, smoking a cigar, like some fat cat in the funny pages: he even had a vest with a gold watch chain hanging out of the pocket. He did not ask me to sit down. Instead, he gruffly asked me what I wanted.

"'I've come for a raise,' I told him. 'The three dollars you pay me each week would not even pay for a room in the lowliest of houses, and now that my sister has had a baby I need to move out.' And do you know what he told me?

"What?!" cried a girl in the audience.

"Yes, what?" cried another.

"He told me, 'Well, you certainly have extravagant tastes.'" Then, he rolled out that old chestnut, the one that has kept the worker down since time immemorial. 'Besides,' he said, 'if I gave you a raise, I'd have to give everyone a raise, and that would ruin me, and then none of you would have a job.' So what did I do? I smiled, pointed toward him, and told him he could shove his job up his fat, ugly, capitalist ass."

Emma was forced to pause—she had been speaking in a fevered rush, thinking that if she kept talking, the audience would be denied an opportunity to boo her off the stage. She took a deep breath and exhaled, quickly, so as to get back to her speech before the inevitable heckling started, at which point she noticed something odd: the people in attendance, staring up at her, each one rapt.

Emma spoke for a full hour that afternoon, her ideas popping up so fast she could barely give them voice—her disastrous marriage to Jacob Kershner, her entree into the anarchist world of the Lower East Side, her thoughts on tenements and protests and factories and love and, above all else, the vast inequalities existing in America. Fortunately, she was there with a prescription, Emma quoting anarchist thinkers, from Kropotkin to Peukert to August Spies, all of whom promised that, once anarchism was allowed to bloom, all men and women would be radiant with freedom, their children transformed by joy and affection. As she spoke it began to feel as though the audience didn't exist: the people had vanished, the hall had vanished, Rochester had vanished, New York had vanished, *America had vanished*, it had all been a horrid dream, and that included tsarism and autocracy and totalitarianism and monarchy, all of them gone gone gone, and in their place was just Emma Goldman and the words flowing from her inexhaustible mind.

The applause was unstoppable, like something that had attained a life of its own, entirely distinct from the smacking hands of the audience, for just when it seemed like it might subside, a new wave would arise, coming from some other part of the church basement, the applause ricocheting from points north, south, east and west, until it all came rushing back to Emma. People crowded her, wanting to shake her hand and thank her for her stirring words and, most importantly, ask her questions about this magical potion called anarchism. There were too many of them, so they formed a queue, almost all of them asking her a variation of the same question: *Are there any of these anarchist meetings here in Rochester?*

This took hours. Her only disappointment was that she didn't get to spend any time with Helena and Lena; one of the organizers tugged on Emma's sleeve and said, "Miss Goldman, the final train is about to depart from Rochester." They raced off. Emma couldn't stop grinning—at last, she could see it, her purpose. Most was right, he'd been right all along, she could move people with her words. She returned in the small hours. Since she was feeling ebullient, and joyful, and desirous only of more frivolity, she crept into Modska's room and, leaning over him, said, "Wakey wakey, artist. Guess what? I'm *home.*"

* * *

Sasha was in his room, having come awake, no doubt roused by the sounds emanating from Modska's bedroom, namely titters, giggles, whispers and sighs. It had been weeks since he'd heard these telltale sound effects; he'd even begun to wonder whether the romance between Emma and Modska had run its course. But there it was, clear as day, the squeaking of bedsprings, Emma's voice travelling through the wall, "Am I? Am I beautiful? Am I really? Tell me again, Moddy." Sasha sighed, and waited for the onset of emotional pain. Her night must have gone well in Rochester—had it not, she would have been in his bed, asking for the sort of love that transcends pain, as opposed to the sort of love that prolongs goodwill and celebration.

A minute went by, and another. Sasha lay still, fearing that if he moved, the ache of jealousy—which he knew was hovering above him, trying to find him in the darkness—would spot his motion and descend, its talons ready to tear out his thumping heart. And yet, for some reason, it didn't, it didn't at all, if the sounds of delectation coming from Modska's room did anything, it was to transport him, back in time, to the ship that brought him to America, where he was assigned to a top bunk, starboard side, about two-thirds of the way toward the stern. In the bunk below was a woman travelling with two small children, a boy and a girl, each with combed hair and scrubbed faces. She was about thirty-five, as blond and blue-eyed as her children, with lovely white teeth and braided hair as thick as rope. She also had a quiet grace that granted her a sort of luminescence; even in steerage, where the light was low at the best of times, her skin seemed to shine. Each night, after her children fell asleep, she'd climb onto his bunk, where the two would sit, chatting, their legs hanging over the top of the bunk. On the last night in which she visited, the dull glow of the gas-lights illuminated the front of her nightgown; it had fallen away, revealing a breast as round as a swelling of dough. She caught him noticing, and grinned. When she kissed him, her breath tasted of sadness and pleasure and need, all of which were things that, prior to that moment, Sasha would have sworn did not have a taste, but they did, they did indeed, the first was a fine meal and the second was almond cake and the third was the coffee that came afterward, thick and rich and hot. *Please*, she whispered, a tongue in his ear, *lie back, don't move, be quiet, there are people all around us, we must do this quietly, we must do this slowly, we mustn't waken the children, this has been such a confusing time, but I'm so lonely, and I believe you are too, so just lie back, my Alexander, lie back lie back lie back.*

eleven

WITH THE WEATHER SO BRIGHT and clear, the tenements didn't seem as gloomy, the children on the street didn't seem so bedraggled, the bats swooping and darting above the tenement rooftops didn't seem so voracious, and even the homeless, who camped out in every small park and square, didn't seem quite so ill and hopeless and wan. Perhaps, Emma thought, they all sensed that change was on its way. Perhaps they could smell it, the promise of upheaval, scenting the air. Emma hummed as she made her way to *Freiheit* and climbed those battered, oh-so-familiar stairs. The moment she stepped into the offices, Most was there, striding toward her, beaming. He hugged her, for perhaps longer than was appropriate, before holding her at arm's length and saying. "I heard everything, my little *Blondkopf*. Didn't I tell you that you were an orator? A communicator of ideas? Didn't I say you were born to give a speech?!"

Others had gathered around them. Someone initiated a small round of applause. "Thank you," she said, looking from face to face to face.

"What was the difference? The new speech? A different audience? Did the train ride invigorate you? What happened?"

"Johann, it was wondrous, it really was... all it took was a little improvisation."

"Improvisation? I don't understand."

"I was so nervous, I couldn't read the speech, the words were floating away off the page. I thought I was going to have to walk off, humiliated. As a last resort, I just started talking."

Most's face went dark, his deformity worsening. The others, having noticed, moved away, leaving Emma to fend for herself. "What," he asked, "did you start talking about?"

"Well... it was my life, mostly. I learned something, Johann. I learned that if you talk honestly, and openly, people will be drawn to you. Believe me, by the time I was done they all wanted to know about anarchism."

"Damn it, woman! I didn't send you all the way to Rochester to talk about whatever happened to cross your mind. The movement needs discipline. It is absolutely critical that the anarchist message be consistently presented. You had no right to depart from my speech. I won't allow it. A revolution depends on strictness, on preparation, on seamless and informed regulation. That audience was there to see me—*me*, Emma, the editor of *Freiheit*. In my absence, the least we could have done was give them my words! Oh no, the next time I send you to a speaking engagement, you will stick to the script, do you understand?"

Emma turned, her face the colour of a roasted beet, and marched home, where she dropped herself on the Belarussian sofa, grabbed a pencil and one of Modska's sketch pads, and began to write a letter. In it, she reminded Johann Most that anarchism was, above all, a progressive ideal, and if he didn't begin to treat her in a more courteous manner, she would make known, to other members of the movement, his outdated opinions regarding women, marriage, children and sexuality in general. She also informed him that, while she'd consider returning to her editorial duties at the newspaper, she would not deliver any more speeches on his behalf.

Finally, she asked him to never refer to her as *Blondkopf* again, as she considered it demeaning.

She never delivered the letter: when she arrived at *Freiheit* the following morning, she found Most in a contrite state, his head slightly lowered, his eyes glassy with fatigue, his suit uncharacteristically wrinkled. He shuffled over to her. "Emma," he said in a soft voice. "I'm glad you're here. We need to speak." He placed a hand on the small of her back, and manoeuvred her into the relative quiet of the hallway. "The last time we spoke, I was impatient with you. I get that way sometimes. You know this. It's all the pressure I'm under. But that's not important. We're all just worker bees, serving the queen bee of anarchism, are we not?"

Emma looked on while Most cleared a thatch of hair off his forehead. He took a breath, and said: "You will accept my apology. You're such a valued member of the *Freiheit* family. I really couldn't do without you. I felt terrible after we last spoke. Please, say you'll forgive me."

"You can be harsh, Johann."

"I know. But please, understand my dilemma. I have to be assured that, at all times, the anarchist position is being represented in a measured and accurate manner. Emma—I'm fully confident that, if you address any crowd with the same fervour you mustered in Rochester, you can reach them with words that I've written. In fact, I'm more than confident—I am *certain*. Would you be willing to try? A hybrid approach? There's an event coming up in Buffalo. If you haven't been, it's a lovely place, full of gardens and trees, I think that you'd like it. And then, of course, there's Cleveland..."

On a warm night in upstate New York, Emma read Most's speech and she did so dutifully, *the fight for the eight-hour day is pure folly, as it validates the very system that you should be attempting to eradicate*, the problem being that Most's text lasted about fourteen minutes, even if she read slowly, giving her no option but to repeat parts of the speech, this time injecting a tone of grave insistence, as well as punching different words within the speech, just as she had practised in her bedroom, *the fight for the eight-hour day is PURE folly, as it validates the very system that YOU should be attempting to eradicate,* so forth and so on, her audience applauding briefly before filing out.

An organizer thanked Emma, and told her that the presentation had been clear and logical. Emma's emotions flared. Clear and logical? This was not mathematics, this was not algebra, this wasn't a primer on cement mixing... this was about happiness; this was about personal evolution; this was about emancipation of the spirit. It was supposed to be messy and dramatic and real. She was presenting them a means to better—no, no, to *reinvent*—their lives upon this planet, and to do this, she knew that she needed arousal, excitement, enthrallment, release. She needed what she'd delivered in Rochester, where she'd spoken candidly, and emotionally, about her own life.

Still, there was Cleveland, where she addressed a room of iron-workers, toughened men with tobacco-stained whiskers and giant hands. Once again, she ran through Most's speech, this time altering it by waving a finger in the air like a hectoring schoolmarm, and, at key moments, smacking a hand against the lectern for emphasis. Yet even as she regurgitated Most's speech, she found herself dissociating, such that she could *hear* herself, droning on, talking about the brutality of capitalism, the alienation of the proletariat, the trickle-up nature of capitalism, while, at the same time, she was thinking about completely prosaic matters, such as the mountain of skirts she needed to hem back in the apartment. She was boring herself, in other words, and in the mind of Emma Goldman there was no bigger sin than allowing oneself to be bored.

Upon completing her speech, she was met with the same reserved, transitory applause she had received in Buffalo, the organizer thanking her politely at the end of her remarks. He then turned to the audience, and asked if there might be any questions.

They were in a basement, somewhere, the room so quiet she could hear the coffee machine brewing. There were coughs and rustling feet. "Very well then," said the organizer, "our next point of order is to…"

Emma heard chair legs, scraping against the cheap tile flooring. She looked up, and saw an old man struggling to his feet; he had long, thin, mottled arms and liver spots on his pate.

"Young lady," he started. "I am an old man. This revolution of yours will take time. An eight-hour workday would benefit me *now*. Look around this room. I see men who've been here for thirty years. Ernie, over there, started the same day I did. This was thirty-eight years ago. Back then we burned coal instead of coke. You can imagine what the inside of my lungs look like. What can this anarchism of yours do for people like Ernie and me?"

Emma turned pale, for she knew that the man was correct, that anarchism likely held no promise for this kindly old-timer, though how to explain that, in every revolution, there are a minority of comrades who must sacrifice their own interests for the betterment of the majority? How to explain that to a man who had worked hard his entire life, and clearly deserved something better in his waning days? Emma froze, for just a few seconds, and then sputtered something about the way in which revolutions can start in an instant, that it just takes someone to perform an inspiring deed—an *attentat*—for the powder keg to go off, and it was quite possible—no, no, it was quite *likely*—that the revolution could start the very next day, and yet, even as the words came out of her mouth, she felt like a parroting fake. The audience, too, sensed her insincerity. There was rustling and a few coughs. In that moment, Emma found she could do nothing other than renege on her promise to Johann Most.

"You know what I think? I think it's time to look at facts. The vast majority of this nation's wealth is held by a tiny sliver of the population. Factories are closing everywhere, the production of goods moving to countries with cheap labour. Fathers exhaust themselves to pay the bills, taking two or even *three* lousy service jobs. Children don't have enough to eat, huge chunks of every American city are lost to homeless encampments, and single mothers have to sell their bodies. Meanwhile, the hospitals are overflowing with tubercular factory workers, and the use of laudanum has reached an all-time high. On top of all *that*, more and more people flood the cities every day, since things are even worse in the countryside, so you have two or three families living in a one-bedroom apartment, sleeping and cooking in shifts, until one day the kitchen curtains catch fire and *whoooosh...* another tenement building, up in smoke, dozens dead, no one cares, the rebuilding starts the very next day."

She paused, breathing heavily, her own anger an intoxicant.

"Meanwhile, corrupt populists are waiting in the wings, willing to say whatever reactionary doggerel it takes to get elected. The police are corrupt. The politicians are corrupt. The church leaders are corrupt. They're all in it for themselves—in the system we have today, the only measure of success is stomping on others. And the worst of it? The Rockefellers and the Vanderbilts and the Carnegies stand around, eating caviar and drinking champagne and laughing, knowing there's no way they can lose." She smacked the lectern. "I can't stand it, it's driving me mad, I fear for my sanity... sometimes I take to my bed, weeping and sore, I feel so discouraged. So I agree with you, sir. It's the waiting that's the worst. It's the standing around. It's the counting-of-days before it happens. Someone has to do something. That's all there is to it. Some brave and half-mad bastard has got to stand up and do what it takes."

* * *

Two days later, Emma Goldman marched up the rickety steps of *Freiheit*, knowing full well that, owing to her performance in Cleveland, her association with Johann Most had likely come to an end. As she stepped into the offices, she swore she noticed a slight drop in the room's cacophony (though she also knew that this could, quite possibly, be the product of her imagination). She strode toward Most, determined to resolve their relationship in a professional, and hopefully respectful, manner. She would not get her wish—he was at his podium, working away, though when he heard her hobnail boots striking the floorboards, he looked up, his face contorted by a sudden fury. He rose and strode toward her, while pointing toward the exit.

"Out," he commanded. "Get out, go!"

Her muscles tightened, and her face reddened. "Don't *worry*," she spat. "I'm leaving. Oh, and one other thing, Herr Most. If I ever see you again, it'll be because I bump into you by mistake at an event. Otherwise, you and I are no longer colleagues, do I make myself clear?"

"Out!" he yelled. "Out!!"

She turning on her heels and abandoned the offices of *Freiheit*. After calming herself with a long walk, she returned home and told Sasha what she'd done.

"So you and Most are through?" he asked.

"Yes."

"The two of you... *kaputski*?"

"Yes."

Sasha thought deeply about this development, his forehead supported by thick, calloused fingertips. "Good," he finally said. "I never liked the man."

Two days after *that*, while walking the streets in the early hours, as he so often did when assailed by insomnia, Sasha came across something interesting—plunked on the corner of Essex and Rivington were four bundles of *Freiheit*, each held together by a length of twine; within an hour or so, a vendor would arrive, cut open the bundle, and start selling. (Mostly, the hawkers were female comrades, dressed in woollen stockings, old sweaters, grey overcoats and Greek fishermen's caps.) It was a cool morning, the sun just beginning to peek over the tenement rooftops; when Sasha exhaled, he could see his breath, condensing in the chilly air. He lit a cigarette while staring at the newspaper bundles. Without thinking, he pressed the tip of his cigarette into one of the sides; it smouldered for ten seconds or so, leaving a small, round, ochre-coloured hole. Sasha admired the burn for a few moments, thinking it evinced a strange, rarefied sort of beauty. Much to his surprise, he found himself untying the fraying string that surrounded the first bundle so that air filled the spaces between the newspapers, the stack seeming to take a breath. This time, Sasha extracted a box of matches, and held a flame to all four corners of the bundle. Smiling, he did the same with the second bundle, careful to avoid the flames licking up the sides of the first. Soon, the two bundles were a single conflagration, the flames of each accelerating the flames of the other, which set fire to the bundle beside *it*, the cache becoming a lustrous, thigh-high pyre.

He watched it, face warming, palms out, flames bobbing in his eyes, feeling pure and honest and irredeemably fierce.

twelve

HAVING SPLIT WITH JOHANN MOST, Emma and Sasha were now the subject of suspicions masquerading as questions—could the pair be trusted? Were they genuinely committed? Were their hearts really in it? Invitations to rallies and speeches were not as forthcoming, and Emma wasn't asked to stuff cabbage rolls at the annual anarchist picnic in Prospect Park, as she had been the year before, and the year before that. When an article condemning individualism within anarchist circles appeared in the pages of *Freiheit*, Emma and Sasha read it as a veiled accusation.

But the worst part? None of this cantankerousness was in the open, for the simple reason that, in anarchism, petty rivalries were not supposed to occur: Emma and Sasha couldn't address the frostiness directed toward them when no one would admit to it being there in the first place. Taking the place of actual confrontation was echoing silence, at least when it came to fellow anarchists. They quickly became despondent—food tasted poorly, their fingertips trembled, their sex drives dissipated, even cigarettes tasted bitter. It was as though the past two years, a period in which they had devoted their every waking moment to the furtherance of anarchism and its principles, had been for nothing.

One week after their excommunication, Modska awoke late on a cool morning and gathered his paints, his easel and an oversized satchel containing a half dozen of his completed paintings. He walked to work, stopping for lunch along the way, and arrived at his usual post around two in the afternoon. He set up his easel, squeezed paints on a palette, and waited for customers. A middle-aged burgher from Cincinnati, in town for some professional convention, contracted Modska to do his caricature. As Modska painted, the man droned on about real estate, banking practice and his inability to find decent employees—"now I don't know how things are up here in New York City, but in Ohio the labour pool has been infected by a laziness that is as pernicious as any physical disease. It's like they don't want to do what it takes to get ahead, wouldn't you say so?"

Modska nodded his head while adding a measure of contempt to the caricature—he made the man's forehead the size of a dartboard, his nose as flat as a pig's, and his mutton chops so voluminous his face looked as though it was in peril of taking flight. The man laughed when he saw it—"it's a masterpiece, kind sir, a masterpiece!"—and then surprised Modska by presenting him with a tip that was almost as much as the agreed-upon commission. "Look at me!" the man howled. "I look like a hog with wings!"

The rest of Modska's afternoon was slow. As always, he had a sketch pad with him; he drew the buildings across the park on Fifth Avenue, the fashions worn by passing women, and a Central Park oak tree (which, it was rumoured, had grown in that spot since before the American Revolution). He was just finishing up with this sketch when a shadow fell upon his notepad. Modska looked up, thinking he had a customer. Instead, two frowning young men stood before him. They wore dungarees, work boots, flannel shirts and suspenders; the bigger of the two had a smear of jam on the corner of his mouth. Modska swallowed, as he knew who they were—the recent swell of immigration to New York had given rise to thuggish gangs with laughable, unironic names like "The Oath Takers" and "The Proud Fellas," and, perhaps most galling, "The Liberty Boys."

"Can I help you gentlemen?" Modska asked.

"You sure can, kike," was his response. "You can fuck off back to wherever you came from."

Modska stood, thinking it was all so ridiculous—as if his presence in the park, selling *art*, was a threat to their way of life. He raised the palms of his hands and said, "Hey, let's start over, I think we got off on a wrong..." when the first punch struck him in the stomach. The second, a vicious uppercut that landed right on the tip of his aquiline nose, landed as Modska bent over to cradle his solar plexus. He fell to the wood-chip path circling the park, and watched as the ruffians destroyed his easel, punched fists through his canvas, squirted out his paint tubes and snapped his brushes in half. Then they ran off, howling.

Modska lay on the ground, struggling to catch his breath. Worse than the attack was the unwillingness of his fellow New Yorkers to offer any kind of assistance; though they walked by in droves, they made sure to turn their heads away from him, his condition an unwelcome glimpse into the city's decaying soul. Luckily, he had the money given him by the Cincinnati businessman to hire a horse-drawn carriage to take him home. The driver was an old Irishman; "Now don't you be bleeding on me seat," he said on more than one occasion.

By the time Modska got home, both of his eyes were blackening and swelling, and his shirt was crimson with blood. Emma gasped, and ran to get an ice pack. Sasha poured him a measure of vodka, which Modska knocked back in a single draft. "They appeared out of nowhere, wearing suspenders and boots, spouting the usual anti-Semitic bullshit. I tell you, they're everywhere these days. I'd have feared for my life if it hadn't all happened so quickly. Honestly, it was over in a minute." His nose had begun to bleed again, so he tilted his head back while Emma ran for an old towel. His voice was now a nasal gurgle: "I wonder how they knew?" he muttered. "I don't look Jewish, do I? And oh, my nose, my beautiful nose... what have they done to it?"

"Don't worry," Emma said. "You'll still be a handsome devil. Only now, your face will have a bit of character. Maybe you should thank those hooligans."

Modska feared returning to the park, so much so that he spent all his time in the apartment, accomplishing little; he'd start a drawing, become frustrated, and then crumple it up. Sasha was suffering from agitated sleep and a cough, and wasn't sure how much longer he'd be able to keep his job at the cloak factory—each day, another worker got fired, only to be replaced by some hollow-eyed, limp-haired, bulbous-elbowed, pale-skinned twelve-year-old. Emma, too, was feeling inconsequential and sad; one morning, Sasha caught her taking a sip from a bottle of cheap Polish vodka that they kept in a cupboard above the icebox. "Why so shocked?" she said. "Don't you know all us anarchists are crazy? Why don't you join me?"

"You know I can't."

"Why, Sasha? Why is that, exactly? Who ever heard of a revolutionist who doesn't drink?"

"It makes me crazy."

"So what? Why shouldn't you be crazy? At least I'd have some company."

Worse, their collective was now a collective in name only: at a time in which they were most in need of camaraderie, they were spending an excessive amount of the day in their respective rooms, eating solitary meals, wishing for something to change. One afternoon, someone knocked at the apartment door. Emma, who had been nursing a headache, emerged from her room, sleep in her eyes, her hair a tousle, and opened it. There stood a comrade named Joseph Barondess; a failed actor, Barondess was now a union leader with a progressive bent, in that he believed unionism to be a necessary first step on the way to anarcho-syndicalism. Emma brightened, for his presence indicated that not every anarchist in New York City, quasi- or otherwise, had rejected her. "Joseph!" she said. "Do you want to come in?"

He did; he sat; Emma gave him a measure of vodka in a teacup, which he tossed back with a single gulp. "Bah," he said. "I'm trying to organize a strike on behalf of the city's corset makers. You know, they suffer some of the worst working conditions in New York."

"I'm not surprised," Emma said, waving a finger. "They're all young women, oppressed not only by horrible working conditions, but by their husbands or fathers or both. This makes them too down-pressed for organization. Women are doubly burdened by the free market system, you know. *That's* why they're the true bedrock of any revolution—not the leaders, not the speech-makers, not the rabble-rousers, not the sign-waving dissidents, but the women who stay home, children at the breast, simmering with rage. Once you light a fire under *them*... well, the powers that be better watch out."

Barondess chuckled. "Well then, you'll be interested in what I have to say. I'm hosting a series of meetings, designed to encourage them to join in a work stoppage. But I need a speaker. I could do it myself, but look at me—I'm a forty-six-year-old man. What common ground do I have with these mistreated teenagers? I need a young woman with a gift of the gab. Of course, I thought of you. I heard about your talks in Rochester and Cleveland. I thought you might be interested."

"You don't care that I've split with Most?"

"Hell no. The man's an egomaniac. Not everyone's in love with every word he says, you know."

"In that case, can I ask one question?"

"Sure."

"Would I have to read a prescribed text, or would I use my own words?"

"Emma, I barely have time to eat these days. Even if I wanted to, I wouldn't have time to write a speech. Oh no, you'd be all on your own, I'm afraid. Is that a problem?"

* * *

Two weeks later, Emma Goldman found herself in front of a stately townhouse on the wealthy end of St. Marks Place, a home with five full storeys, dormer windows, arched porticos, a domed carriage-way, harlequin faces carved into the doorway arch, a wrought-iron fence in which the silhouettes of bluebirds had been forged, and a stately front door topped by an elegant stained-glass window in which the street number—27—was displayed. She gripped Sasha's hand.

"What if I screw up?" she asked.

"Impossible."

"I won't have Johann Most to blame."

"It won't happen."

"It could."

"No, sailor girl, it couldn't."

Inside, they were greeted by a butler who took their coats. They stood for a moment, astounded by the entranceway: the sale of any one of the chandeliers descending from the plastered ceiling could have kept an immigrant family in groceries for a year. They stepped into an enormous, carpeted living room filled with young women, all of whom looked as though they were afraid they might break something; Emma found them both pitiable and beautiful, with their worn-thin dresses, their paper-thin shawls, their sparrow-width ankles, their stick-thin fingers trembling with hesitation as they chose little triangular sandwiches from a circulating platter. There was also champagne; the attendees took tiny, cautionary sips. Soon, they were all chatting loudly. Emma took two flutes from a passing tray and downed both of them.

A woman dressed in high style—gown, necklace, velvet gloves, her hair piled atop her head and held in place with diamond stick pins—spotted the pair and rushed over. Her name was Viola Miranda Merriweather-Cox. Emma knew the type, as every progressive movement had them: indolent socialites with poise, thin waists, private-school educations, horses on Long Island, egregious French and, most importantly, a guilty conscience. Her husband was a banker named Gilfred James Cox; it was rumoured he allowed such goings-on in his home as long as he wasn't obliged to attend.

"Well *hello*," she gushed, extending a hand. "I'm Viola. You must be Miss Goldman."

"I am."

"And this is..."

"Alexander. Alexander Berkman. He's a, uh, friend of mine."

"Lovely! I'm glad you could come. Now make yourselves at home. We'll be getting started in a few minutes."

Emma heard a chime. The hostess located herself at the front of the room, next to a fireplace the size of a truck, and tapped a gherkin fork against her flute. "Welcome," she said over the dwindling chatter. "Welcome, everybody. My name is Viola Cox, and I would like to welcome you to my home."

Emma swayed in tight little circles, her hand in Sasha's. There must have been introductions, for she soon found herself before the corset makers, who all looked at her, blinking, the room turning quiet and still. Emma took a sip from the glass of water on the lectern. "Hello," she started. "My name is Emma Goldman, and I'm so very pleased to be here." She took a deep breath. "I, like so many of you, am from Russia, and I am a Jew. Actually, I'm from western Russia, which, in the eyes of the tsar, isn't quite west *enough*."

The audience tittered.

"I came to America two years ago, living for a time in Rochester before coming to this fair city. And you may ask, 'Why, Emma? Why did you do this? Why would you uproot your life like that? Why would you make such a big change? Why would you leave Russia and come all the way across an ocean, under such uncomfortable circumstances?'"

Again, she paused, allowing for the sort of murmurs that signal camaraderie—everyone in that townhouse, with the exception of the host, had come to America in steerage.

"'I'll tell you. I moved to end my victimization. Yes, I was a victim. I was a victim of tsarist repression, of a brand of anti-Semitism that I can only describe as vicious, and of a patriarchal domination that rendered my home a palace of humiliations. Ah yes, I can tell by your faces that you know what I'm talking about. Let's start with my father. The poor man, beaten down, ignored by my mother, reviled at every turn, sexually frustrated, fond of plum brandy, a man of the Pale through and through. I can't even blame him for his behaviour. It was my mother. She never loved him. He was her second husband, you see. My mother's first husband died, which is why my older sisters have a different father than I. My father loved her, but not the other way around; she just needed someone to take care of her. Imagine the pain he must have been in! So he took it out on his children. While we were all on the receiving end of his bitterness, I was his biggest target, perhaps because I was the most outspoken. 'How I wish you'd been born a boy,' he would tell me, 'since then I'd know what to do with you.' As I was the only one in the family with blond hair and blue eyes, he'd taunt me by saying that he'd purchased me from a market, the seller a desperate vendor whom he called 'the pig woman.'"

There was a hushed gasp; Emma nodded, and continued: "One day I came home with a note from my teacher, reporting that I'd misbehaved in class. I showed it to my mother and she began to cry, saying that I was a wilful and ungrateful child, and that I would be the ruin of us all. But the worst part? The part which made me tremble with apprehension?? She told me that she was going to show the letter to my father. He stood reading it. I waited for his reaction, which, for a moment, I thought might be tempered. Perhaps he had had a good day at his workplace? Perhaps he'd enjoyed a better-than-average lunch? But no. He struck me, hard, with a closed fist, the blow landing on a large, round comb I wore to control my unruly hair, the teeth of the comb driving into my scalp. It felt like I'd been struck with an iron bar. Then he grabbed me by the hair and, over the sound of my screams, yelled, 'You're a disgrace! You will always be so! You can't be my child; you don't look like me or like your mother! In fact you don't act like any of us.'

"Yet it wasn't the blow that bothered me. I was fifteen years of age, and *this* time he came up with something that would really punish. 'Well,' he said, 'if you can't control yourself at school, you won't go. You're old enough to start contributing to this family.' This was terrible for me: I only wanted to learn, to read the works of masters, to see art and listen to great music. In fact, that's what got me into trouble at school in the first place: often, I used to hide a book I was reading behind my notebook, so that I could read Dickens or Tolstoy during one of the boring, infantile lectures. True to his word, he went out and, through a cousin of his, procured me a job in a factory. To be honest, I think the real reason he forced this job upon me was that his business was failing, and he needed my wages. How I begged to continue with my studies. 'Please,' I pleaded, 'my father, don't do this!' His response? He threw my French grammar book into the fire and said, 'Bah. Girls don't have to learn much! All a Jewish daughter needs to know is how to prepare gefilte fish, cut noodles fine, and give a man plenty of children.'

"So my days as an indentured labourer were to begin. The factory was downtown, a long way from where we were allowed to live, and I had to get up at five o'clock in the morning to be at work by seven. The rooms were stuffy, unventilated and dark: the sun never penetrated our workroom. There were six hundred of us, of all ages, working on costly and beautiful garments, day in and day out, for very small pay. And the floor manager! He would stop and say, 'Oh, you are doing well, Emma' or 'No, Emma, the stitching should be like this'—but the *real* reason he paid me any interest was so that he could rest his hand upon me, each time moving a little lower."

"*Yes!*" came a voice from the back of the room, and for the next minute or so the room filled with angry babble. Emma lifted her hands and nodded sympathetically; when the chatter petered out, she resumed speaking.

"But then, my father arranged a marriage for me. My husband-to-be was a gawky Tatar with bad teeth, almost forty years of age, though successful in business. I met him once and hated the sight of him. I'm serious: his ugly face made me want to vomit. By this point, my sister Lena had moved to upstate New York, and I begged my father to let me go as well. He refused, telling me I had to get married and that was that! I told him that if he forced me to marry the man —Igor was his name—then I'd throw myself into the Neva. He laughed and told me to go ahead, it would be a relief. The next night, when the *politsiya* dragged me home, soaking wet, wrapped in a horsehair blanket, my hair hanging in my face, my fingers and toes turned blue, my breath condensing in the cold night air, he looked at me and said, 'All right you little hellion, you win, you can go to America.'"

Emma paused, the absence of words indicating that she was jumping forward in time. For a few moments, the room was completely silent, save for the crackling of burning logs, which emanated from a huge, carved-stone fireplace opposite from where Emma stood.

"Now I was in Rochester, the Flower City—where I resorted to marriage! Having found myself exploited by one man, I simply switched to another. People are like this, you know—they gravitate toward what they know, not what is good for them. His name was Jacob. He, too, was a factory worker. He lived near my sister's house, and we used to walk home from work together. It turned out that he was depressive and a gambler, meaning that he frittered away every penny he earned in card games. So I left him, and he came to me, on bended knee, threatening to commit suicide if I didn't take him back. So I did, for a short period, but then, one day—it was in the middle of the night, actually—I realized that I was tired of it all. I was tired of working at a factory, I was tired of my marriage to Jacob, I was tired of life in general. So I came to New York City, where I swore I'd never succumb to the institutions that are designed to demean us, to belittle us, to impoverish us and, yes, to enslave us. I moved into a tenement and took in sewing. What choice did I have? Nothing changed, not the long hours, not the terrible pay, not the sickening food, not the illnesses floating about. The only difference was that now I had to worry about bedbugs. But there *was* one advantage of coming to the Lower East Side: I met people who felt the same way I did. I met people who were willing to do something about it. Do you see that man over there? The one with the ample lips and the worried expression? His name is Sasha and *he's* willing to do something about it. There are others. There are organizations. There are meetings, parades, planning sessions, all with a singular aim—seeing you get what you *deserve*."

There was sudden applause, Emma again raising her hands to hush it for the moment: "And so I say, that if *any* of you have had any of the same experiences as myself, and you wish to be free of the chains that choke you, I beg you to take an initial step. Organize yourselves. There's strength in numbers. Be ready to strike if your factory owner will not provide you with a living wage. As a first step, you should join a union. I have union cards here. Who will sign?"

They rushed toward Emma; their faces, so timid before, beamed a mixture of anger, hope and determination. They formed a line that wrapped around the walls of the salon, the young women at the rear of the line standing next to the women at the front of the line, each facing a different direction. The first girl, a fawn-like creature with enormous green eyes, wrote her name upon the union card. She then extracted a beaded change purse from an inner pocket of her overcoat (which was a little worse for wear, the hem thread-bare, the collar worn thin, no doubt the clasp would soon break). For a moment, she hesitated, as if this amount was a grand fortune. But then, with a fortifying breath, she placed a coin in Emma's outstretched hand.

"Thank you," Emma said, expecting the girl to move on.

Instead, she said, "I always wanted to join a union."

"Why didn't you?"

"My father always told me that unions were for criminals."

"Even better."

The girl leaned forward, as if worrying about being overheard. "May I ask you a question, Miss Goldman?"

"Of course."

"You said that joining the union was a first step."

"Yes."

"What is the second?"

Emma grinned. "Have you ever heard of anarchism?"

"No ma'am."

Emma reached into a large bag she had brought with her, and pulled out a pamphlet entitled *The Precepts of Anarchism*. "Read this," she said, and then nodded at the second girl in line, their exchange an uncanny duplication of the one that preceded it. The line moved slowly. It was almost one o'clock in the morning by the time Emma left, her arm looped through Sasha's. She was ebullient; she ran along cobblestones; she clasped her hands and giddily spun. "We made progress tonight. Real progress! Oh, Sasha, I'm walking on air! I'm about to explode. I can't stand it, I can't, I'm losing my mind, I'm about to fly into pieces!"

"I better hold on to you, then. Wouldn't want to lose you."

She fixed him with wild eyes, and tugged on the sleeves of his overcoat. "You know I really do love you, you gloomy old fish-face, no matter *what*, I'll always love you, don't ever forget that, I love you I love you I do."

thirteen

EMMA NEXT VISITED a ratty, street-level Bowery apartment, a tattoo parlour on one side and, on the other, a shop belonging to an olive-skinned woman who offered tea-leaf readings, astrological consultations, and cups of a bubbling, red-brown elixir that caused scenes of one's childhood to scroll past the eyes. As Emma spoke, small mice scurried along the baseboards of the apartment, which was owned by an old Prussian dissident named Dieter. The audience was comprised of parlourmaids, young women with pale skin, scalded knuckles and sad expressions. Emma spoke loudly to be heard above the El train, which caused the plates and mugs in Dieter's apartment to rattle every time it passed overhead. This gave her words a higher voltage; in response, the women in the audience howled, gasped, whooped and whistled, for this time Emma thickened her tale with salacious details, most of them regarding her husband's inadequacies. "How I worked away! How I pumped and stroked and dirty-talked! Nothing worked. I tell you, ladies, it was like asking an armchair to pole-vault. Some things can't be done!"

Her host looked on, arms folded across his fat belly, laughing as the attendees shouted, "Tell us more, tell us more!" By the time the last girl had left, two bits poorer and gripping a copy of *The Precepts of Anarchism*, it was well after midnight.

"Well, then," said Dieter. "How's about we toast the evening?"

They sat at Dieter's grimy kitchen table, Emma and Dieter drinking schnapps from chipped breakfast mugs, while Sasha glugged from a cup of black tea. Dieter spoke his native language, his accent northern and brusque. "I was a coal miner back in Germany, in a small town near Düsseldorf. I survived a cave-in, you know. It took them four days before they finally dug us out. I was so dehydrated I pissed mayonnaise for a week. I really thought I was going to die. But I made myself a promise. If I survived, I'd dedicate my life to putting an end to this bullshit. So here I am. More schnapps?"

"It's almost two in the morning," Sasha said. "We should really be getting going."

"Going? You can't go."

"Really," Emma said, "you've been most hospitable. But Sasha's right... tomorrow comes quickly."

"You misunderstand me, comrades. When I say you can't go, I mean you can't go *now*. No one walks around the Bowery at two in the morning. Even the coppers don't come around. Oh no, it won't be safe until it's light out again. I'm afraid you're going to have to bunk here. Don't worry, there's room."

Sasha and Emma ended up in the host's bed, while Dieter took the battered sofa in his kitchen. While the sheets were clean, more or less, his mattress was full of lumps—it felt as though someone had stuffed a pair of blankets with rolled-up socks. Emma and Sasha tossed and turned, trying to find comfort.

"Sasha," Emma said.

"Yes?"

"I can't sleep."

"I know."

"I'm too wound up!"

From outside, they could hear screeching cats and the occasional clack of wheels upon cobblestones. A drunk started yelling, until a woman with a ruined voice screamed at him to shut up. This was followed by relative quiet, though they could still hear wild pigs, snorting as they rooted through garbage. "Remember," Emma whispered to Sasha, "when we first became physically intimate? Do you remember how quiet we had to be, what with that madwoman next door?"

"Of course."

"How's about pressing those ample lips of yours against the side of my neck? For old time's sake? I don't care if you leave a bruise, it's cold out, that's why turtlenecks were invented. Now pucker up, Sasha, I'm wound up tighter than a drum, sleep won't come easily tonight, I can promise you that, it could be I'll never sleep again."

* * *

There was a schoolhouse in Morningside; a barroom in Mott Haven; a gymnasium in East New York; a warehouse in Yonkers; a church basement near Rockaway. She spoke at a small bandshell near the south entrance of Central Park, an event in which she prompted the young women in her audience to punch their fists in the air and howl, their frustrations rising high into a grey-cloud sky. With each appearance, Emma's audiences grew in size and complexity. Older women with drawn faces and babies were now coming, at first looking somewhat sheepish, as though embarrassed by the way in which their lives had developed. But these sad, angry women, burdened by factory labour, childrearing and housework, needed only a few minutes before they began cheering at every indignation suffered by their speaker. In return, Emma lengthened her speech, in order to address what she termed "the rights of women": she believed in birth control, in access to safe abortions, in equitable divorce (or, even better, the abolishment of marriage altogether). She even hinted that, should patriarchy prove too durable to overcome, women should dispense with the opposite sex altogether, and turn to other women for physical satisfaction.

Yet the meat of her speeches never changed: as long as there were people on top, be they capitalists or communists, those on the bottom would suffer. Word spread that a tiny Russian woman with a round face was spreading a new sort of gospel that went by the name "anarchism." Her audiences now included disgruntled union men, some of whom had ignored her during the original speeches she'd given in their chilly halls. She also started to attract radicals who had come to New York from other parts of the country, and had nothing whatsoever to do with the immigrant coffee klatches of the Lower East Side. There were loggers from the Pacific Northwest, with missing fingers and steel-wool beards; ex-convicts who'd grown hard of hearing in prison workhouses (and who, as a consequence, would yell, *wouldja speak up fer chrissakes* during her speeches); labourers from the Deep South, on the run from some huge-bellied sheriff who had it in for them; Oklahoma roughnecks who could neither read nor write, and had permanent oil stains in the creases of their necks; and PhD students from the country's better universities, serious young men in pleated trousers who yearned to get their hands dirty. The list grew with each meeting. Even Joseph Barondess became one of Emma's converts, his desire for membership dues taking a back seat to his newly liberated mindset.

Before long, Emma was invited to speak at Columbia University, the dean of political science having grown curious about the way in which radical political ideas were being brought to the city by its immigrant population. It was her largest venue yet, the air musty and damp, the acoustics tomb-like, with small friezes of robed scholars sculpted into the domed ceiling. Sasha stood near the entrance and watched as the hall filled with the city's discontented.

Emma was backstage, suffering from her usual, though somewhat diminished, nerves.

Out front, Sasha was wondering if he should go and assist her in some way—sometimes a glass of water and a soda cracker helped calm her stomach—when he turned and saw Johann Most enter the hall. Most spotted Sasha and approached.

"Well, well," he said. "Alexander Berkman. How are you?"

Though surrounded by people, Sasha felt as though the two were locked into a tiny room, just the two of them, gauging each other. "I'm fine," he said.

"It's been a while. I understand these little talks of Emma's have grown quite popular."

"There's a lot of interest out there."

"And I *hear*," he said with a smirk, "that you're acquiring a reputation as her faithful companion. What's it like? To be Emma Goldman's sidekick?"

Sasha narrowed his eyes and said: "Would you excuse me, Johann?"

"By all means," he replied. "Clearly, you have important matters to attend to."

Sasha found Emma in the backroom, hunched over a table, the arch of her spine visible through her sweater, mumbling to herself. "Emma," he said. "Johann is here."

"What... *Most*?"

"Yes. And he's as insufferable as ever."

"What's he want?"

From the main room, they could hear Joseph Barondess address the crowd—*never has a speaker so electrified a city, so ignited a citizenry, so aroused a collective passion...*

"I have no idea. I was too busy resisting the urge to punch him in the face."

Ladies and gentlemen, I give to you, Emma Goldman!

"Well," she said, "I guess I'd better show him a thing or two."

* * *

On stage, Emma grinned, her eyes scanning from side to side to side, the audience no doubt thinking that she was acknowledging them. Yet Sasha knew better, as he'd seen it so many times before: she was tracking the thoughts in her head, trying to decide which one she'd snare and put to use. Just then, her eye movements froze, and she began speaking. "My father managed an inn, his clients all peasants; they'd come in from the fields, faces smudged, trousers worn, exhausted from picking beets all day, thirsty for the cloudy schnapps that my father made himself. Even with this built-in clientele, he couldn't make a go of it, largely because he spent most of his time telling tales, offering credit and buying drinks in a misguided bid for popularity. He was also lazy as the day was long, but that's another story. Anyway, to round out his salary, he also kept a few cows and sheep, which were looked after by a local shepherd named Petrushka. Even though I was still a young girl, not yet seven years of age, I took notice: the young man happened to play the flute, and I loved the simple folk tunes that drifted in from the fields."

She paused, and slyly grinned before continuing: "So I'd visit him. With little else to do, Petrushka would play for me while I listened, rapt with appreciation. Then, at the end of the day, he'd carry me home on his back. He was a lean young man, barely sixteen years of age, grown thin on a diet of root vegetables and biscuits. So that I didn't fall off, he hunched over a little, causing his spine to gently arch. This curvature, meanwhile, made contact with me right where I had to widen my legs in order to wrap them around his spindly torso. Though I didn't understand why, this felt wonderful! Then, one dusky evening, following a day in which Petrushka's playing had been particularly tender, and the air was musky with the scent of pollinating flowers, it suddenly felt much more than wonderful. I cried out, half believing I'd hurt myself somehow. When Petrushka stopped and asked what had happened, I pretended I had a pain in my hip. He put me down and we walked home side by side, though I tell you: he must've wondered why the innkeeper's little daughter was as red as a beetroot."

A few of the audience members gasped; others guffawed, and a healthy percentage managed to do both. Emma grinned, more than a little mischievously, and continued.

"When I was fifteen, my family moved to St. Petersburg during a brief relaxation of the rules governing the placement of Jews in Russia. There, I worked as a seamstress in a factory. Each day, upon leaving the shop, the young women who worked there would be waylaid by a group of young Russian officers who were training in a military academy just down the street from the factory. In short time, all of my co-workers had Russian sweethearts, pale and pimply young men who'd give them flowers and escort them to one of the pastry shops along Nevsky Prospekt. In *my* case, I fell for a clerk who worked in the hotel next to the factory. How did I meet him? My eldest sister, Helena, worked there as a chambermaid. One day I popped in for a visit. Ivan introduced himself with a bow."

She paused, letting a bit of tension build.

"He was twenty, give or take, and charming. We met for a couple of weeks, taking walks along the Neva, drinking cups of hot chocolate on park benches, stealing kisses in clammy stone-wall alcoves. One afternoon, when he asked if I'd like to see one of the hotel's luxury suites, I surprised him by saying, 'I was wondering when you were going to ask.' He took me in through a side entrance, and we walked along a thickly carpeted corridor. I remember that my shoes sunk with each step, as though wading through a plush, fragrant mud. He reached a doorway and, after checking left and right, opened it with a key the size of a baby's arm. The room was sumptuous: he told me that the tsar's niece, some tubby princess named Tatiana, had once slept upon the huge four-poster bed. The ceilings were twenty feet high, the leaded windows arched and ecclesiastical. There was a seating area, and an end table supporting a vase filled with a dozen pink lotuses. The carved mahogany sideboard was topped by a carafe of amber liquid and a pair of crystal glasses.

"'Would you like a refreshment?' he asked. 'Yes, please,' I said, though I'd never before taken a drink. I sat and he handed me a tumbler. I giggled, and took a sip. It tasted of cloves, and it raised a heat in my lungs. 'Do you like it?' he asked. 'Yes," I said, licking my lips, and it must have been this sight, the tip of my tongue protruding from my slightly parted mouth, that caused something to snap in him. He pounced, tearing open my blouse, gnawing my breasts, slapping me when I beat my hands against his chest. I screamed, and heard my sister's voice call out from the hallway. So I pushed the bastard off me, ran half-naked from the room, and took shelter in my sister's arms. Of course, Helena told me to never tell a soul, that the clerk's father ran the hotel and pulled a lot of strings in St. Petersburg. I agreed, and then told anyone who'd listen about what had happened—turning a blind eye has never been a game that interests me, and I recommend that none of you play it either. We have all had things done to us; when we pretend we haven't, it only makes us ill. I felt neither guilt not self-recrimination following the incident. Instead, I felt educated, as well as a little corrupted. From then on, I've been drawn to thugs as well as angels, to vulgarians as well as idealists. In this way, I submit, I'm only human."

She spoke like an electrical storm, that night—perhaps it was the larger crowd, perhaps it was her growing confidence, or perhaps it was the presence of Johann Most, who sat watching, a discomfited expression upon his blighted face, as she raged against the privileges of the rich, the tyranny of the family, the suffocating institution that was marriage, the pipe dream that was capitalism, the backroom racket that was socialism, the parlour trick that was the judicial system, the brutal tool of repression that was the police, the three-card monte that was organized religion. She spoke for over an hour, never once referring to her speaking notes, the longer running time accommodating a prescription for the future—her solution was freedom, her solution was a collective consciousness, her solution was a genuine respect for others. "My *solution*," she said at the end of her address, "is love, in all its pure and anarchic forms. Thank you."

There was a moment of silence. Then: applause. Then: cheering. Then: the pounding of boot heels, along with the voices of women calling "Emma! Emma! Emma!" Many of them looked almost possessed, not by religious fervour but by hope, Emma having made them aware of ideas they could never have conjured for themselves.

Meanwhile, Sasha looked on—this, he realized, was Emma's gift. She gave voice to desires that existed within others, without them ever realizing that those desires were there, and had always been there, and always *would* be there. Yet as soon as Sasha was possessed of this notion, a painful corollary poisoned his thoughts: What is *your* gift, eh fish face? All this time in New York, and you still haven't figured out this one little thing? Or maybe, just maybe, you *have* no gift? He stopped clapping, and watched as Emma left the dais, only to be surrounded by fans, handlers and newspaper reporters who had come to report on her talk; she blinked and covered her eyes each time a flashbulb erupted.

Outside, Sasha waded through throngs of people, the majority of them women, still red with excitement and exhibiting little desire to go home, where there was laundry to be done and children to be diapered and dishes to be cleaned and a moping husband who always seemed to need something. He pushed through them and marched south, walking block after block along an avenue filled with trollops, confidence men, pickpockets, stray dogs, whiskered pigs, chestnut vendors and sidewalk braziers, and if someone had asked where he was going, he would've turned to them and, a charge to his voice, said, "I don't know, chum, where are *you* going?"

When he could stand it no longer—the smells, sights, sounds, heat and noise—he happened to come upon the police precinct servicing the bottom half of Manhattan. What a lovely building, he thought, a Romanesque pearl sandwiched between derelict tenements. Yet inside? Petty scoundrels, every one of them, for as everyone knew, the city police ran the numbers rackets, and decided who was mayor, and clubbed the homeless for sport, and trafficked the working girls along St. Marks Place, and if you'd ever enjoyed a tumbler of smuggled Canadian whisky... well, then, you had the boys in blue to thank. And to think that the city built them this palace to house them! To think the city would grant them such splendour! Such recognition! The street beneath Sasha was in patches. He bent over, retrieved a chunk of pale-red stone, and, with all the strength he could muster, threw it at one of the first-floor windows. Glass flew everywhere. From inside the building he heard voices, which replaced Sasha's fury with something more self-preservational; he hustled away.

Reaching Mott Street, Sasha forced himself to move in an unconcerned saunter, like a gentlemen out for a walk. He reached another darkened street and began walking west when he came to a small, triangular parkette he'd never seen before: in its middle was a statue of an angel gazing skyward. A line from Pushkin came to him, *She's all just harmony and wonder, higher than passions and the world*, and there was something about the moment that filled Sasha with wonder and dread and every emotion that lurked between the two.

At the northern tip of the parkette was a store, gas-lit and humble, with a few stools near the rear. He went up to the counter, his fingertips shaking. The storekeeper was low and wide and had a creased, mahogany face. He took a bottle of grappa and held it up, as if to ask *Is this what you're looking for?* Sasha nodded, surprising himself; the barkeep filled a small glass with a resinous liquid that smelled of licorice.

Sasha took it to one of the stools and sat. There was a man beside him, reading a newspaper. Behind him were shelves filled with bags of flour, dried corn and tomatoes. Sasha drank the noxious liquid in a single, incinerating gulp, and immediately regretted doing so, for he knew that, in a very short amount of time, when the intoxicant erupted in his brain, he'd be possessed by the hopelessness that existed in his core. He closed his eyes and waited, practically counting off the seconds before the arrival of despair, when something entirely different happened: he was enveloped by a warm giddiness. With this sensation came a vision of that cobblestoned chunk, sailing through the precinct window—the eruption of glass, the risen voices, the ignition of lights, the mad scurrying, the unalloyed fury of it all.

He stayed for a good long while, his sense of elation wearing off with the drink in his system, until he felt nothing but drained. He left and walked home, confident that the police had called off their pursuit, and were likely taking out their frustration on some poor sap sleeping rough in Union Square. Sasha reached his building and trudged up to the apartment. Modska's door was closed; Sasha could hear snoring. He sat on the Belarussian sofa and smoked, waiting for Emma to return. Around three in the morning, he heard footsteps in the hallway; Emma came in and sat next to him. He gave her a cigarette and she lit it from his.

"Where did you go?" he asked.

"There was a party. Thrown by the organizers, in some huge, wood-panelled hall, I swear I met every chancellor, dean and department head at Columbia. It was one of those nights, the air thick with the scent of fine perfume and canapés. I swear I'll never get used to it. I ate caviar while discussing propaganda of the deed. I tossed back champagne while talking about the assassinations back home—when I told them I was all for it, they topped up my glass. Sometimes, I swear they think I'm kidding. Where were you, by the way? I looked and looked and couldn't find you anywhere."

"I needed a little air."

"Oh. You should've come."

"You were magnificent tonight, sailor. There's no other word for it."

"They say that other universities are going to want to hear me speak."

"As well they should."

Emma smiled. "You know, I spoke to Johann afterward. He came up to me and said, 'Congratulations, Emma.' His voice sounded odd."

"How so?"

"It was completely flat, like he'd taken some laudanum. Then he took my hand and kissed the top of it. I tell you, Sasha, I didn't know how to react. His mouth was so dry, like sandpaper almost. I'm not sure he's well. I think maybe he's been poisoned by his own bullshit."

"What happened next?"

"He turned and left. Can you believe that?"

"I can."

"What do you mean?"

"No one likes being bested. You really put the boots to him. "

They finished smoking. She slipped her little hand into Sasha's. They were both in oddly contemplative moods, in which there was nothing in the world they wanted to do—they didn't want to eat, or smoke, or drink coffee, or kiss, or laugh or cry or so much as move. In this complete absence of want or need, they did nothing but sit, looking forward, both feeling as though they had been cleansed, somehow. Soon, the sun started to rise, a smeary orange sphere that brought warmth to the sidewalks, and caused their living-room window to glow. The two wordlessly retired to Sasha's room, where they held each other while sleeping.

fourteen

WITHIN THE CREAKY OFFICES of *Freiheit*, Johann Most walked away from his podium and held his hands in the air, as he always did when preparing to make an announcement. He then gazed about the room, a soft grin on his ruined face. "Ladies and gentlemen," he started. "Friends and comrades, fellow journalists. I have spent ten long years at the helm of *Freiheit*. During that time, I have watched it grow into the foremost journal of anarchist thought in America." He paused, as he would have during one of his speeches, thinking that applause would follow. Instead, his staff looked back at him, blinking. "It has been a most gratifying time, I cannot stress this enough. I cannot think of any human endeavour that would have caused me more satisfaction than working with all of you here, in these humble offices. But there have also been costs. The demands on my time have been extreme, to say the least. For ten years, I have worked fourteen-hour days, only to take more work up to my attic home, where I would often write and edit until the wee hours, only to fall asleep and, upon awakening, start all over again, seven days a week, fifty-two weeks a year.

"The truth is... I am tired. Everyone needs time to rest, to reanimate, from time to time. My friends, that time has come for this faithful editor. On Monday, I'll be leaving for California, where I will help mobilize agricultural labourers in the Salinas Valley. Why? There also comes a time in a man's life when he wants to stop commenting on the events around him, and start creating those events. I'm sure you all understand. Perhaps it will happen to you one day. If so, I'll be the first to congratulate you. I look forward to my sabbatical. While away, I will file stories, via wire, to Ludwig, our esteemed managing editor, who, as always, will conduct the day-to-day operation of the publication. But I assure you, comrades. I will be back. I consider you all to be my family, and I consider *Freiheit* to be my life's work. Yet I really feel that, to fulfill my dreams for the publication—and I have many, please don't doubt that—I need a change of venue, a change of pace, a change in my routine. Are there any questions?"

His editors, who had gone unpaid for the past month, drifted back to their workstations and resumed their labours. Some, however, snuck out for a cigarette break, thus allowing the news to leave the confines of the William Street offices and travel throughout the rest of the Lower East Side. Soon, it was being discussed in all of the usual places: Café Sachs, Justus Schwab's place, Zum Groben Michel, the Pioneers of Liberty clubhouse, the Workers' Hall on West Houston, the soup kitchens along Canal Street, the immigrant camps of Tompkins Square, as well as the hundred-and-one nooks and corners of the city where revolutionists met and, with little else to do in the city's fragile economy, gossiped. Reaction was mixed. Some were distraught, feeling that Johann Most, whether you liked him or not, was inarguably the glue that bonded the city's anarchist community. There were also some who were pleased, believing that Most was a self-aggrandizing ideologue, and was simply publishing *Freiheit* because he liked the sound of his own voice. Many, too, accepted the news with something approaching equanimity: Ludwig Mueller, the managing editor, was a capable individual, and might just be convinced to let other voices into the publication's mix. Yet whatever their reaction—be it positive, negative or some-where in between—the anarchists of Manhattan's lower quarters took note, as Johann Most, if nothing else, was regarded as a father figure, and now that he was gone most wondered what would hap-pen to his ideological family.

Sasha Berkman heard the news on his way home from work, having stopped at Café Sachs for a cup of coffee and, if he felt like it later, a sandwich. As he waited for his order, he noticed that the res-taurant seemed excessively loud that night, as though the patrons all had something terribly exciting to discuss. That's when he over-heard two men talking next to him.

"I can't believe he's going," said the shorter of the two.

"I know, I know, who's gonna be top dog now?"

"I can't get my *head* around it. Johann Most, leaving. I figured he'd never get tired of hearing his own voice."

Sasha interrupted. "Sorry, I couldn't help overhearing... but you said something about Johann Most?"

"Where you been?" asked the taller one. "He's leaving for California. Says he's had enough. Says he wants to pick raisins or some damn thing. Help with the rights of fruit pickers. Can you get a loada dat?"

Sasha nodded and turned. There was a mirror over the bar, and when he caught himself grinning he thought: *You should show your dimples more often, fishlips, isn't that what Emma is always saying?* His coffee came; after taking a few sips, he waved to the bartender and said, "You know what? I changed my mind. Get me a bottle of ale."

The bartender snapped the cork off a bottle and handed it over. "Quite a night," he said, Sasha nodding in agreement as he took a long, thirst-quenching gulp. After downing the bottle, he asked for another; he sipped this one more slowly, enjoying the taste of the beverage as he cast his eyes over those who, only partly jok-ing, would sometimes refer to Sachs as their second home. They were all loudly talking and drinking beer and tucking into plates of that night's special, a pork meat loaf swimming in thin gravy. Yet there was one woman, sitting near the rear wall, all by herself, scribbling in a notebook, distinguishing herself by looking downcast. He immediately recognized her from the Pioneers meeting place—wasn't she some sort of writer? One of Edelstadt's bunch? A moody poetess with an intensity that could not be denied? She looked up for a second and, for the briefest of moments, produced a pale imitation of a smile. He stood, beer in hand, and walked toward her. Her eyes were pale green, as was her sweater.

"Don't I know you from the clubhouse?" he asked.

"Yes. You're Berkman. You don't know my name. It's Sofia."

Her hand was cool and pale. Sasha could see that she chewed her fingernails. "Please," she said. "Sit."

"I don't want to disturb you. I can see that you're working."

"Bah. Who cares? The truth is, I'm a terrible poet."

"I'm sure that's not true."

"It is. I'm a scribbler of dogma." She leaned toward Sasha; her breath smelled like burning leaves, which was something he liked. "Sometimes I think that I'm in hell. Imagine, wanting nothing more than to be an artist, and having no artistic talent whatsoever."

"We're in the same boat," he said with a shrug. "I'm a revolutionist with no idea how to revolt."

"*Really?* In that case, have a seat, comrade. Keep a sad girl company."

He sat, and said, "Anyway, I'm sure you're plenty good. Where do you read?"

"Oh I never read in public. I wouldn't dare. Actually, I once read one of Edelstadt's, at some memorial after he died: "But we will not be frightened from our path / By darkness, prisons or by tyrann-ee / We must awake humanity from sleep / Yea, we must make our brothers glad and freeee."

"Oh yes, I know that one."

"You know what? I think it's impossible to create true art in the middle of the revolution. Everything's too infected with politics, with it's-got-to-be-this-way-or-nothing. When everyone's mad, all art becomes dogma."

"I found Edelstadt's work quite beautiful."

"No you didn't. You agreed with it. There's a difference. Ah well. Maybe I shouldn't be so hard on him. We were lovers for a time. I miss him. He was a wonderful man, he really was. Considerate and kind. Gentle, too. No wonder his writing was so bad." She looked close to tears. "Ah well. Enough of that. The past is the past. Tell me, Alexander..."

"Please. Call me Sasha."

"Tell me, Sasha. Where are you from, originally?"

"Western Russia, among other places."

"I'm a Tallinn girl. Do you miss home?"

"Not really. I have nothing but bad memories."

"I'm not surprised. I've heard the Pale has that effect on people."

"It does."

"I miss Tallinn every day. What a beautiful place. My parents, too. They weren't bad people, you know, but there are times I find myself, sitting here with Michelman or Solotaroff or Yanovsky, you know, the usual suspects, pretending like my folks were monsters. But they weren't! They weren't at all! When they noticed me writing all day, they bought me a beautiful, leather-bound notebook. Sometimes I wonder what I'm doing here. I tell myself: Sofia, that's what you should be writing about, the longing for home, that's your real story. But I'm too embarrassed. I'm worried that my comrades will find it sentimental. So instead, out comes, 'oh my brethren, come and see / the righteous march toward puri-teee.'"

She was drinking wine. Sasha bought her another glass, as well as another bottle of beer for himself. "Do you know what I did the other night?" he asked her.

"No. How could I?"

"You know the Fifth Precinct on Elizabeth Street?"

"Don't get me started on the police. They beat up a friend of mine."

"I threw a rock through one of the first-floor windows. It felt glorious. I don't know what came over me. I felt changed, somehow."

They kissed in the vacant lot siding Schwab's tavern, the ground littered with fragments of brick. He slid a hand between her legs while she held his shoulders. Then they ran through the street, past street lamps and sausage carts, laughing at life and liberation and art and madness, and how they were all intertwined, as if by physical law, and when they reached her room on Norfolk Street, Sasha kicked at the door and tossed her upon an unmade bed. She pulled off his clothes, he tugged off hers. Together, they were a study in contrasts, her skin as white as alabaster, his as swarthy as a Tunisian relic. She had a mane of reddish hair that, when loosened, fell thickly over her shoulders; at age twenty, Sasha had a widow's peak so pronounced it looked like a trowel. None of this felt important. The bedsprings were ancient and it felt as though this repetitive noise—this enticing *squeak squeak squeak squeak squeak*—was the drumbeat to which the revolution would be conducted.

In the morning, he dressed and kissed her and told her that one day she would become a great poet, just as he would be a great revolutionist, and that, between the two of them, they would remake a cruel and unfathomable world. She threw her head back and laughed.

"Goodbye Sasha Berkman," she said. "You're funny."

"Goodbye Sofia," he said. "I don't even know your last name."

"You will," she said, and closed the door behind him.

*　*　*

Sasha began seeing the lovely Sofia, though there were still many evenings in which he shared his bed with Emma, loving her and caressing her and leaving his body *with* her—he noticed that their love was now expressing itself in a way that was less ferocious and more gradual, and that often, when they finally left each other's embrace, he felt a rich contentment that he had never imagined could be possible. "I wish there was a word for the way in which we feel toward one another," she said one night, the two entwined in both bedsheets and each other's arms. "*Love* doesn't quite do it. I mean, I love a lot of people. Modska, for instance. Solotaroff. The Minkins. Now that Most is gone, I realize that I even love him a little—sure, he was a massive prick, but without him I'd have never found my feet as a speaker. Did I ever tell you that I fucked him once?"

"You didn't."

"What can I say? It was late at night, we'd been working together on a piece, he pulled out some of that white wine he likes so much, *Liebfrauenmilch* my eye. Now that I think of it, it may have happened more than once. I guess I was just so full of gratitude. That can be a powerful aphrodisiac—the feeling that you really owe someone. Plus, you know how I feel about vulgarians. But I tell you—his talents as a revolutionary far exceed his talents as a lover. Imagine, telling a fellow anarchist that there are things you *just won't do*."

Sasha snorted.

"But you and I... ours is some sort of essential bond. Unfortunately, we still have to describe it with the word 'love,' which is cheapened by all the other ways in which it's bandied about. I mean, mothers love their *children*. Oh no, there needs to be a better term for what we've uncovered. I know. How about cherishment? Does that sound good? Or treasuredness? Hmmm, I don't know, they both sound so earthbound."

With Sasha often away, visiting his Sofia, Emma began seeing a goat-like physician named Reitman, who, it was rumoured, had bedded every other female comrade in the lower part of Manhattan. Modska, whose visits with Emma had grown rarer and rarer, until petering out altogether, began seeing a freckled Milanese journalist named Gabriella who always carried a small notepad on her person, upon which she scribbled her personal observations. (She had hopes that, one day, they might be drafted for use in a novel.)

Yet they all had a more pressing, and far more pedestrian, concern than erotic desire: Sasha arrived at his workplace one morning and found that it was no longer there, just a few tired immigrants staring forlornly upon a padlocked door with an accompanying sign that said, in Yiddish, *factory closed*. For the next few minutes, Sasha stood among them, listening to them grumble in the new foreign languages of the neighbourhood, be it Catalan or Slovakian or Polish, and when it occurred to Sasha that some of them couldn't read the sign, and that they were hoping the padlock represented nothing more than a temporary work stoppage, Sasha told them that it was time to get another job. A few walked off. Those that remained spoke no English. This time, he pointed to the padlock, drew a forefinger across his neck, and said, in the unnaturally loud voice of a man trying to make himself understood, "FACTORY, GONE, NO MORE, GO HOME." Soon, he was the only one left. He looked up at the factory wall and felt wistful. The hours he had spent there. He lit a cigarette, thinking *the hell with this place*, and went home, hoping to commiserate with his sailor girl, only to find the apartment quiet and dark. He called out for both Emma and Modska, his voice fading to a reverberating nothingness. Then he went to a certain address on Broome Street.

"Sasha," Sofia exclaimed. "What are you doing here?"

"The factory closed."

"Good. You were a slave there."

They pulled each other to the floor. There were groans and titters and mad, savage laughter. Side by side, facing upward, they held hands; hers were long and lithe, like a piano player's, while his were fat and round. "I tell you Sasha, any day now, I'm gone, I'm out of here, I'm back to Tallinn, this land-of-the-free business is for the birds. You want a bowl of soup? I made some yesterday. It's got ham in it. My God I'd give anything to write just one original word."

* * *

The next morning, Sasha got up, dressed, and went looking for work. He wasn't worried (or, at least, he wasn't worried at first): experience had taught him that, in the upside-down economy of New York City, there was always another factory owner setting up shop somewhere, eager for another group of immigrants to exploit. Within the hour, however, he began to notice something a little troubling: gone were the signs in the windows, advertising for help. Okay, he thought, that's strange, but not unduly alarming, for there were many ways to find work in New York City. He purchased a *Herald*, and uncovered another discomfiting indicator: gone were the help-wanted ads that, in more propitious times, crowded the back pages. Gone, too, were the little scraps of paper tacked to the bulletin board in the kitchenette of the Pioneers of Liberty headquarters, on which members wrote down the addresses of establishments looking for workers. Gone, too, was what was known as the "word on the street," there being a time in which Sasha could have just planted himself in one of the steamy lunchrooms on the Lower East Side, and, by listening to the conversations around him, hear about the latest workhouse that had set itself up in the neighbourhood, a place where any man or woman who wasn't afraid of a little hard work could find him- or herself a job piecing together fabric, or rolling cigars, or hacking cows into single-portion steaks. But now? The talk around Sasha was bleak, the voices desperate—there was no work, the rent was due, winter was coming, the landlord was threatening, the kids needed shoes, even the quality of coffee served in New York City delicatessens was suffering.

Another dire sign: Modska, who had finally returned to a different spot in Central Park, was failing to attract customers, as the business of sketching tourists required just that—*tourists*—and they no longer seemed to be coming to the city. Yet another indicator: Emma was finally getting ahead on her consignment sewing. While this initially pleased her, the small mountain of clothes in her bedroom grew smaller, first becoming a hill, and then a mound, until there was nothing left aside from a few scattered blouses, needing a button or two.

One night, the anarcho-economist Irving Stollowitz found himself drunk in their apartment, explaining the state of the world to Emma, Sasha and Modska. "Well it's official," he said. "The banks are finally admitting what us regular people have known for quite a while: we're in a recession. Maybe even a depression. We're midpoint between the two. We're in an economic repression."

Only Stollowitz laughed, and he did so grimly.

"What caused it?" asked Modska.

"You name it, my artistic friend: failing banks in Argentina, devastated wheat crops in the Ukraine, a collapse of speculation markets in Australia, an outbreak of tuberculosis in Portugal, a run on gold in the United States. The problem is that everything's all interconnected, now. Everything's global, now. Everybody trades with everybody. It doesn't matter what country, or what language you speak, if you've got what I want, and I've got what you want, then presto! Those things are on a boat or train, tariffs be damned. And it works, too, except during periods when it doesn't. Then everything collapses, since no country has any sort of broad-based economy to fall back on. No one grows their own food now. No one makes their own clothes now. No one forges their own steel. Either you do it for the whole world or you don't do it at all. The very concept of an economy is a fiction, it's all just things moving from one place to another, and when the movement stops, everything falls apart, which explains why the American dollar is now worth about the same as the drachma. Now where's that wine? I'm going to get roaring drunk, my comrades."

Sasha, Emma and Modska continued to scour the city, looking for any kind of employment, reasoning that they'd cover more ground if they split up. They went as far south as the Battery, as far north as Harlem, and as far east and west as the perimeter of Manhattan permitted. Meanwhile, the streets were growing thick with beggars, the parks were filling with families sleeping rough, and the sounds of the city, all that clanking and revving and whirring, were fading, as though the island itself was running out of fuel. The three started to grow hungry. Sasha's hair thinned, Modska grew a set of ribs, and Emma's face hollowed. Anarchist activity dwindled, as everyone was too busy trying to stay alive. The speeches, the marches, the protests, the political theatre, the rewritten puppet shows for children (in which Judy hits back and then tells Punch what she thinks of him)—they all vanished, leaving no trace they had been there in the first place. The soup kitchens reappeared, the lines stretching around the block. The three ate their cheese sandwich and an apple on street corners, Sasha and Emma growing despondent while Modska, impressively, remained positive—he claimed that he was talking to people who were talking to other people. "Comrades," he told them, "don't *worry*, all of this is temporary, I have irons in the fire and I can tell you, one in particular is getting hot."

One rainy afternoon, Sasha and Emma were both in the apartment, feeling gut-empty and sad, when Modska came home holding a celebratory bag of groceries. He placed it on the kitchen table. His hair was wet, and water dripped from the tip of his nose.

"Well," he said.

"Well what?" Emma asked.

"Our problems are over."

"And how might that be?"

"I have just been offered a *job*."

"Really?" Emma chirped. "A job? Moddy... if this is one of your money-making schemes, in which a thousand things have to go right before you see a nickel, I swear I'll..."

"No! Emma! It's an actual job. As a photographer's assistant. And look! I bought a salmon!"

Sasha looked at Emma. There were tears of relief in her eyes. "That's wonderful, Modska," she said.

"Yes, cousin, you really saved our bacon."

"There's just one tiny catch."

"Yes?"

"It's hardly worth mentioning, given the pickle we're in, but here it is. The job's in Springfield, Massachusetts."

"Springfield!" Emma cried. "Why Springfield?"

"The boss is the brother of a friend of a client here in New York. If we all live together, my paycheque will keep all three of us alive, provided that we live simply. Please say yes! I'll miss you both too much if you don't come."

Sasha agreed at once. The truth was that he was tiring of New York City. He was sick of the noise, the vermin, the rain, the overflowing sewers and, perhaps most of all, the homeless sleeping on cardboard squares while, a few dozen blocks away, socialites yawned their way through performances of *La Traviata*.

Emma, however, balked. "There're no bagels in Massachusetts."

"Oh for fuck's sake," Sasha said. "We'll bring some with us."

"Front porches make me angry."

"You'll look the other way," he countered.

"New York City is like a virus. Once it invades your blood, it has you forever."

"Consider this your antidote."

"Serenity makes me anxious."

"*You*," Sasha said, while gesturing with a lit cigarette, "are incapable of serenity."

"Where would I get my knishes, my rugelach, my borscht?"

"You'll learn to like chowder, apple pie and hot dogs."

"I'll miss Russian and Yiddish and German."

"At least *you* speak English well."

"What do people do there?"

Sasha threw up his hands. "The same thing they do here. They go to work and grow old and die thinking that there was something else they should've done with their lives."

"I just don't know."

Modska now spoke. "I do. A week from now, hired goons are going to throw our stuff into the street, so that some hope-inflated Baltic family can take our place, and then wait around until the same thing happens to *them*."

"I don't care. I hate my possessions."

"Do you hate eating, too?" Sasha asked. "And sleeping indoors?"

"You're being melodramatic."

"I want you to come. Modska wants you to come. Don't you, cousin?" Modska nodded. "Still, if you really want to stay here, we'll have to go without you."

"You can't mean that!"

"It's the bread lines for us if we stay. We'll be fighting for tidbits."

She stomped her foot on the floorboards. "I can't," she peeped. "I won't, I'm a city girl, fresh air gives me headaches. Please, Sasha, Modska, you have to believe me, they walk so slowly in small towns, plus they laugh at anything, at anything at all, oh fishlips, ask me to do anything but this!"

* * *

Emma finally relented—despite her love of New York, despite her affection for the Lower East Side, despite her fondness for the offerings of Houston Street diners, she visited the satyr Ben Reitman at his clinic on Pike Street in order to say goodbye.

"I have to leave New York for a while."

"I'm crushed."

"Ben, *please*, how many women do you have on the go in this city? A half dozen?"

"That's not the point. The point is that I love each one for a different reason, and that, when my time with each one nears its inevitable end, I feel a sorrow, as I know that I'll never feel that particular type of love again. It's the same with you."

"I believe you. I don't know why, but I do."

"Well you should. It's true."

"Goodbye for now, Ben Reitman."

"Goodbye for now, Emma Goldman." Reitman gave Emma one last hug, and then held her at length by her shoulders. "Say... I have ten minutes before my next patient. One last kick at the can?"

Modska, meanwhile, said farewell to his Italian-American journalist in a café on Suffolk, a brightly lit place run by Hungarians, who served glasses of a gummy white wine that, when held to the light, swam with sandy flecks. When he hesitated at Gabriella's suggestion that she go with him—his brow actually furrowed—she tossed a half glass of said wine in his face and stormed off as he sat there, dripping.

Finally, there was Sasha, who bid adieu to Sofia in a tub full of steaming water. She sat in one end, he in the other, a candle burning on the coal stove. The tub dominated the kitchen. "Can you believe this place?" she asked, more than a little rhetorically. "No electricity, virtually no heat in the winter, no direct sunlight, screaming neighbours, more rats than people, the smell of decomposing cabbage... and yet, I have plumbing and hot water. It comes tumbling out of the spout above the kitchen sink at any time of the day or night. There must be a boiler the size of a locomotive in the basement. I take three baths a day. It's the only luxury I have."

Wet hair fell upon her shoulders. Her eyes gleamed. She really was a beauty, Sasha thought, like some Degas ballerina. "I suppose you'll be leaving with red Emma Goldman. Wait, don't answer. Of course you are. You were always going to leave with her one day, weren't you?"

Sasha nodded. "I suppose so, I'm sorry."

"You know, I've read those pamphlets she's started to hand out at her lectures. The ones where she prattles on about the free market system and the death of the nuclear family and the rights of women and the evils of the education system and whatever else happens to be stuck in her craw. The tyranny of monogamy, my ass—I've got news for you, Sasha. You and Miss Emma might be far more monogamous than you might think."

"You're funny," he said.

"You know what you should do? Leave in the middle of the night, like desperadoes, your rent unpaid, your things discarded, whooping with the sad mad potent glee of it all."

"I'll miss you. I really will."

"Good."

"I'll miss *fucking* you."

"Same. Now kiss me, and get out."

He rose from the bathtub, dripping water over the kitchen floor as he hunted for a towel. While he bent to kiss her, she asked him to add another bucket of hot water to her bath before he left. He obliged, and then stood over her, watching, counting seconds, memorizing the way she looked, reclined in murky water, eyes closed, in repose.

fifteen

SASHA SPENT THE RIDE hanging off the caboose, smoking like an inferno, watching the city grow smaller and smaller till it looked like nothing more than a train set model. As with Modska and Emma, he was leaving with sadness in his heart, an acknowledgement that, throughout his time in the city, he'd been too distracted by all the noise and pain for any genuine accomplishment.

They arrived in sun and cool air and took the first apartment they could find, a one-bedroom above a pharmacy, the plan being that Modska would sleep on a fold-out sofa in the living room, while Emma and Sasha would take the bedroom. At night, they all found it difficult to sleep without the clanging madness of New York City outside their window. In its place was a hollow, humid silence, punctuated only by crickets and the occasional squalling of cats.

Modska now spent his days reproducing snapshots, his medium a sheet of foolscap and a fistful of crayons. It was a popular money-maker, enlarging photographs by drawing them, and Modska excelled at it. He drew families, children, pets, newlyweds, high-school graduates and grandparents that had since departed to the great beyond. His employer, a man named Charles Caswell, said it wasn't Modska's artistic talent that kept him knee-deep in customers. Rather, it was his personality—"*Modska,*" he'd say, "a million people can make doodles. They come here because they like talking to you. You're a refreshing break from the state of the world. And if they want to spend their dollars on a drawing of their family? Well, who are we to dissuade them?"

Emma started working for Caswell as well, her job to process orders. Sasha, meanwhile, spent his time wandering the streets and parks of Springfield. It was such a foreign, unnerving place: parents cheering at baseball games, pedestrians engaging in friendly banter, shop owners giving candy to children, the scent of distant fields wafting in on slow, lazy breezes. All of this sparked feelings of dislocation and uselessness—though he took care of the apartment, and cooked elementary meals for his roommates, he found these chores dull, and emblematic of the way in which he had yet to find his true purpose. One night, with Emma curled beside him, an arm over his side, her stomach contouring his back, she murmured, "Modska and I are quitting. We know the business, and we're tired of Caswell making money from our labours. We're going to start our own shop. Caswell's a nice man, but that doesn't mean he's above exploiting our efforts."

Sasha remained silent; starting a business meant participating in the very economic system that they had sworn to overthrow. And while working for someone else could be rationalized as a necessary evil—as a way to survive before the revolution came—to open your own business, in the mind of Sasha Berkman, reeked of barbarism.

"Fishie," Emma said after a moment. "Can you hear that?"

"What?"

"Listen. Listen hard."

"I don't hear anything."

"It's your thoughts. They're as loud as my own. Don't worry, comrade. I've already discussed this with Modska, we won't hire anyone else, and any money we make, above and beyond what might provide a basic lifestyle for the three of us, will go to anarchist charities."

* * *

Modska, his ear to the metaphoric ground, discovered that the town of Worcester, about fifty miles east of Springfield, didn't have a single professional photographer. He and Emma gave a week's notice. Caswell offered to raise their salary and, when this didn't work, became tearful. "Oh well, I guess I was just being foolish, thinking I could hold on to a man as plucky as you. Good luck to you, Modska. You as well, Miss Goldman. I hope everything works out for both of you."

Sasha travelled ahead while his comrades finished their notice. On his first day in Worcester, he rented a storefront with an apartment on top, and told the landlord that he'd be living there with his wife and her brother. He slept that night on the floor, and spent the rest of the week gathering used furniture. Emma and Modska came on the weekend. They called the shop the French Art Studio, a name reflecting Modska's desire to be thought of in the same vein as the great Impressionists of Europe. Emma managed the office while Sasha tacked together picture frames. Yet the trio had a lot to learn about the perils of free enterprise: no one, other than themselves, crossed the shop's threshold. Each day was a re-creation of the day previous, in which they woke, made coffee, ate porridge, opened the shop, and waited. Their only respite was to take long walks along the country roads leading away from Worcester; on such outings, well away from the fresh-faced Yankees living in town, the three were reminded of the sights and smells of rural Lithuania, such that it felt as though they had travelled far away, over an ocean, to the place where their childhoods had transpired. But then, there came a point, usually late in the day, the sun low and orange on the horizon, when they knew they had to turn around and cross a bridge back toward their lives in town. They did this with a sinking feeling; often, they would stop in the middle of a country lane and look out over fields and meadows, putting off the moment in which they had to trudge back to their failing, humiliating enterprise.

During one such outing, Emma stamped her foot and said, "You know where we should be? Russia. We should be in *Russia*. Have you read the news? The students are quitting the universities and heading for the countryside. They say they're helping the poor and needy but I know better: it's called rallying the troops. It's called mounting an attack. That's where the real discontent lives, you know: in the small towns, far from the cities, where there are no jobs, no future, no prospects, I could go on and on. You think *we're* pissed off? At least we were treated to an education! At least we had access to doctors and decent food! Oh no, we should be back *home*, and I'm not talking about fucking New York City."

"You're forgetting one thing," said Modska.

"What's that?"

"We don't have any money."

"Money! It's always money with you, Modska. All right, we don't have two cents to rub together, so what, we'll get some, we'll steal it if we have to. We'll kidnap someone. Isn't there a bank we could rob?"

This went on for weeks, the three caught in a dispiriting limbo, until one of their neighbours, a tobacconist who had grown up in the area, and understood the sensitivities of its people, approached Modska and said, "A word of advice, my friend?"

"Please."

"I just hate to see nice people like yourselves get thrown into the drink 'cause they don't understand how folks think around here."

"I'm all ears."

"You got *French* in your name. Makes people think you're up to something fishy."

"Really?"

"There's also that drawing you got there."

Suddenly, Modska understood that what might work in a place like New York City could have the opposite effect in a provincial locale such as Worcester: as proof of his talent, he'd placed an old drawing of Emma in the front window. It was a wonderful rendering, one of Modska's finest, in that it captured her defiance, her energy, her bold intelligence, her fiery and sensual gravitas. Yet she was also half dressed, her naked (if exquisitely drawn) breasts suggesting that this place of business, this French Art Studio, was a refuge for degenerates. They took down the drawing and changed the name of the business to Worcester Photo, even if it meant that the money they'd spent on the previous sign had been a complete waste. Emma sewed lace curtains, thinking they gave the shop a cozy feel, as did the knick-knacks they put in the window—an old cowbell, an oil lamp, a porcelain doll, a stuffed bear, all collected for next to nothing at local yard sales, which the citizens of Worcester reliably held each Saturday morning.

Customers still refused to walk through the door. Modska, after giving it some thought, came up with yet another theory: they needed to forge the sort of community inroads that Caswell, having been in business for more than thirty years, had enjoyed.

"It'll never work," Emma said.

"Why would you say that?" Modska asked.

"Because we have *accents*, you dope. Small-town America is ruled by xenophobes. It's pointless. We should go back to New York."

"Bah, you just wait. I've an idea or two up my sleeve."

He began contributing to the *Worcester Commercial*, the paper publishing his funny little drawings of the day's news events: cats stuck in trees, Mr. Smith's barn dance, a ribbon-cutting at the new city hall. Sasha, not to be outdone, rented a horse and wagon and took to the roads surrounding Worcester. Emma, after some cajoling, went with him, their mission a simple one: they would visit the region's farmers, and attempt to convince them that the only way to keep their memories alive was to commit them to artful reproduction. It didn't work; they hadn't the charm, and the fact that Sasha could only speak English in the present tense didn't help.

They moved from the apartment to the single room behind the studio. They were now living cheek by jowl, sleeping like eunuchs on a single mattress, the floor covered with their scattered possessions. They cooked over a kerosene stove, opening a window at the rear of the office so that they wouldn't succumb to the fumes. The neighbours complained, and they moved to a small apartment in the Jewish section of town, where things were considerably cheaper. Their landlord, a grocer named Benjamin Sapiro, lived above them. A lonely widower, he'd sometimes come down from his apartment and have a cup of tea with his latest tenants; in so doing, he learned of their failing business, their lack of money, and their fears regarding insolvency. "You know what you should do?" he said. "You should open a lunchroom. We don't have one in our part of town— we have to walk all the way to the goy half, where you can't get rye bread if your life depends upon it."

He then offered to lend them a hundred and fifty dollars as seed money. They accepted his investment with profuse thanks; Emma even threw her arms around him and kissed him on his reddening cheek. They promptly closed the photography shop, sold their equipment for cents on the dollar, and opened a little food counter on Winter Street, a vacant store that they outfitted with a second-hand stove, a refrigerator and a couple of tables and chairs. Here, they sold rye-bread sandwiches, coffee and desserts. They purchased a soda fountain and colourful dishes. Even Modska abandoned his artwork to help at the café.

They were full each day, and they quickly repaid Sapiro's loan. They worked hard, their goal to make enough money to return to Russia. Occasionally, one would take a trip to New York and stay overnight with friends, leaving the other two to watch the business. Modska, for example, liked to visit the museums and art galleries.

Sasha attended a march in support of starving Russian peasants. Emma appeared at a rally in Union Square, her breath condensing in the chilly air, her audience looking a little worse for wear. These little sojourns caused time to lurch forward in a way that was a little less agonizing, for with every passing month, week and day, it seemed more and more as though this stop-gap measure, this running a diner in the wilds of New England, was becoming the entirety of their lives. The cold weather gave way to spring.

One day toward the end of June, a customer came into the café for ice cream. Emma was alone in the store. As she set the dish upon the man's table, she looked over his shoulder at the newspaper he was reading. The man took a mouthful. She didn't move away, her eyes shifting from side to side as she read, her heart rate accelerating, blood rushing to the surface of her skin. A tremor came to her fingertips.

"Are you all right?" asked the customer.

"Give me your newspaper!"

"I'm sorry?"

"Your newspaper. I need your newspaper. You don't have to pay for your ice cream. But I need your newspaper!"

He gave her the paper, and she hustled him out of the café, dish still in hand, before locking the door. Then, she sped to the apartment. "Look!" she cried. "Look what's happening in Pittsburgh!"

She handed Sasha the paper, his eyes narrowing as he read.

"What is it?" asked Modska. "What's going on?"

"There's a strike at the Carnegie steel plant," Emma said. "You know, in Pennsylvania? The town of Homestead? The president, one Henry C. Frick, started evicting families from company housing who'd fallen behind in their rent, even though they couldn't pay their rent for the simple reason that he didn't pay them enough in the first place! Of course, now he's hired scabs to replace the strikers."

"What a prick," Modska snorted. "What a contemptible ass."

Sasha looked up from the paper. "You know what I think? I think the movement needs us."

They had their final shift that night at the restaurant, their minds on Pennsylvania and steel and the venality embodied by the Henry Fricks of the world. It was their best night ever, seventy-five dollars in sales, enough that Modska, who held the night's take in his hands, said, "You know, maybe we shouldn't leave the café. We could use it to raise money for the cause."

A change in plans, then: Modska would stay behind, so that he could sell the business, but only when the time was right, after which he'd pack up the apartment and join Sasha and Emma in Manhattan. The next morning, Emma and Sasha took the first train to New York. They fell asleep on the way, having exhausted themselves with the urgency of the past day or two, waking just as the train was pulling into Grand Central Depot. After deboarding, they looked at each other, and, in doing so, were reminded that their first task would be to find a place to stay. Not wishing to spend precious time combing the streets, petitioning landlords, Emma voiced a better idea: the pair took a ride to Orchard Street and trudged up to the Pioneers headquarters. It was a slow day, the middle of an afternoon in the city, comrades at a half dozen of the tables. They all looked over with a measure of surprise, having heard that Sasha and Emma had fled New York for some job in... where was it now?... Massachusetts? Was that it?

"Sasha and I are back to deal with this Homestead atrocity," she announced to one and all. "We have money, free time, and a fury that will not be contained. What we don't have is a place to live. Which of you will take us in?"

"I will," said a tall, lanky man in the corner. He rose to his feet and, upon approaching, revealed himself to be Franz Mollock, a baker from Austria who lived a block away. Emma and Sasha had been to his apartment once before, and while they were a little foggy on the circumstances, they knew that, owing to a tragic situation with a child, Mollock had a spare room. They left; Mollock carried Emma's suitcase. At the apartment, they met Mollock's wife, a sullen, dark-haired comrade named Vera.

"I have to go out for a little bit," Mollock said. "Make yourselves at home."

"So," Vera said. "You'll be here for a while."

"Oh no," said Emma. "We just need a few days in order to find a place."

"I see. The room is this way."

Sasha and Emma followed her down a narrow corridor. There were pictures of cowboys and baseball players, cut out from newspapers, taped to the walls of the room. Vera turned and left them, Sasha and Emma looking at one another, feeling as though they were intruding. After unpacking, they heard Mollock burst back into the apartment. "Sasha! Emma!" he bellowed. "Come on out, I've a few people for you to meet."

They emerged, and saw that Mollock had left to collect three men. Two were identical twins, the other a tall, well-possessed man who wore wire-frame glasses. Mollock introduced this man first. "Alexander Berkman, Emma Goldman, please meet Claus Timmermann. Perhaps you've heard of him?"

"Yes!" said Emma. "You publish that new paper, *Der Anarchist*?"

"At your service."

"I used to read every issue, you know. It's been difficult of late, Sasha and I have been out of the city, but I do love it. It's a great antidote to *Freiheit*, which is starting to get a little, er, academic."

"Ah well, I do my best. But thank you."

"And these two," said Mollock, "are the noted journalists Fritz and Sepp Oerter. Back in Germany, they were card-carrying members of the Independent Social Democratic Party, but we'll try not to hold it against them."

The brothers, who both seemed taciturn, nodded. One of them said, "We've become more anarchist in our perspective of late."

"Claus," said Mollock, "tell our new guests what we were thinking."

"Ah well. It's called making a virtue of necessity, isn't it? Of making do with what we've got? The fact is, the brave employees at Homestead are continuing to strike, despite all of the intimidation facing them."

"Our fear," said Mollock, "is that, at a certain point, their stamina will wane."

"I have a printing press at my disposal," Timmermann continued. "We were imagining a pamphlet, distributed to the strikers, reminding them how important their action is to the movement as a whole. In my experience, people can move mountains when they feel as though they're connected to something bigger than themselves."

"Yes," said Emma. "I agree."

"Well then," said Mollock, "let's get to it."

* * *

With six people working on a single piece of writing, there were endless negotiations, each reflecting personal bias. Emma wanted to include an address to the wives, daughters and sisters of the strikers. Timmermann, as a devoted Autonomist, wanted to encourage the workers to arm themselves. The Oerter brothers argued for a more scholastic tone, in which parallels were drawn between Homestead and recent labour stoppages in western Europe. On and on it went, every sentence a negotiation, every word the product of barter. Fortunately, they all agreed that their words must heat the blood of the strikers, a common goal that kept them working until the small hours. Vera brought them sandwiches and glasses of beer, yawning as she placed the food in front of them. This way, they were able to keep going. Occasionally, they would flag, the room would go quiet, and they'd agree to a fifteen-minute break. Other times, they'd all be talking so loudly, and so excitedly, that no one could make his or her point known. Meanwhile, the room grew cloudy with cigarette smoke.

It was dawn before they all agreed upon the text. The title would be *LABOR AWAKENS!* and the pamphlet would read, in part: *Brave protesters of Homestead! Courageous battlers of the oppressive forces of management! Please, do not be intimidated by their bullying tactics! Do not wilt in the face of strong-arm management! Do not put down your signs, your placards, your megaphones! Your struggle is far more than your struggle alone, as it represents the same struggle that workers the world over are enduring. Oh yes, it is true, when word of your efforts travels, it will awaken the labor movements of the world. So have trust in yourselves, comrades. Have faith that your efforts are beautiful, and noble, and true. Be emboldened by the knowledge that your labor stoppage is far more than a single action. Rather, it represents one of the many steps that will spawn the collapse of the capitalist order, and usher in an era of equality, peace and prosperity for all!*

Following a celebratory schnapps, Timmermann and the Oerters left, while the others went to bed. After an hour or two of sleep, Emma and Sasha left the apartment to make travel arrangements: their plan was to descend upon Homestead like a rescuing cavalry. Yet as they walked toward the ticket office in Grand Central Depot, they passed a young boy selling newspapers on a soapbox. "Extra! Extra!" he cried. "Pinkertons open fire on Homestead protestors! Read all about it! Pinkertons open fire!"

They bought a copy and read it at the corner of Second and Seventh. The day before, Henry Frick had hired Pinkerton agents to intimidate the strikers, which they'd accomplished by shooting them. Nine strikers were dead. Nine families were now destitute, and in mourning. No arrests had been made and none were pending. Sasha read over Emma's shoulder, even though it was difficult, as the newspaper was shaking in her hands. The photograph of

Frick had been taken a year earlier, when the Pittsburgh chamber of commerce had given him some sort of businessman's award. In the photograph, he was accepting a plaque, facing the camera, a grin stretched across his bearded face. It was this expression—this wrinkled, smug, self-congratulatory *smirk*—that caused Sasha to finally envision his role in history. He closed his eyes, picturing not only the future of anarchism, but his role in its activation—it was staring him in the face, daring him, enticing him, *taunting* him. He stabbed the picture of Frick with his finger. Emma looked up at him, her round face flushed.

"I'm going to kill that man," he said.

"I know," she said, nodding. "I know that, my darling."

sixteen

FINALLY, IT HAD COME—that revolutionary spark, that moment in time, that tossing away of reason and self-consciousness, the arrival of the *deed*. But first, their intent was celebration; they ran, gleefully, Emma snorting with determination, Sasha struggling to keep up, their first stop the chicken man, with his ramshackle bungalow on Water Street, a big jovial pink-faced fellow who, upon selecting a white-feathered bird with meaty legs, snapped its neck with a deft twist, the bird flapping before coming to a rest. Then, it was on to Helga, the vegetable lady, everybody in the neighbourhood knew that she had the best carrots, the best potatoes, the best onions and cauliflower and zucchini, all grown on some farm in upstate New York by her doting son, and if you wanted to waste an entire day all you had to do was ask her how her boy was doing.

"We need strudel!" Emma proclaimed. "And not just any old strudel, my fishiest of fish-faces, but the best strudel in all of New York City!" This meant Gertrude's, in the middle of delicatessen row on Houston Street, where, just minutes later, they had to decide between apple or cherry, cherry or apple, until they threw up their hands and figured that, on such a propitious occasion, they deserved both.

They found Timmermann in his flat on Avenue A, which he shared with a pair of men who'd suffered exile in Siberia, humble ex-academics with sweat-stained undershirts and bent-to-one-side noses. Then it was the cold-water room shared by the Oerter brothers, at the bottom end of Delancey Street, in a tenement slated for destruction to make room for a roadway servicing the East River Bridge—they had no kitchen, no heat, no fresh air, no real light, just a flea-buzzing mongrel named Mikki, all of which seemed to suit them fine. "Yes!" they crowed. "We'll come! When would you like us? Six? Seven? You name it and we'll be there, bells on, what can we bring? A jug of wine or two? How's about cigarettes? How are you fixed up for cigarettes?"

Back at the apartment, Emma plucked the chicken and chopped the vegetables and put them all in a great big cast iron cooking pot. Mollock's wife came home and, looking at the state of her kitchen, sighed. Mollock returned a little after that, Emma telling him the same thing she'd told his wife: "We're cooking a special dinner!"

"Really?" he said. "What's the occasion?"

"You'll see, you'll see."

Sasha boiled peas and made gravy. Timmermann and the Oerter brothers arrived, along with their companions, ardent young women whom Sasha recognized from various actions. Wine was poured into juice glasses, coffee mugs, beer steins, egg cups, whatever the Mollocks had lying around. They all sat down to eat, everyone famished, people laughing and smoking and arguing while Sasha watched them, his new comrades, enjoying the moment, nobility written upon their glowing-bright faces. When there was no food left on the table, save for chicken bones and a few half-eaten knishes, Mollock turned drunkenly to Sasha and Emma.

"Okay you two, time to put us out of our misery. What have we done to deserve this beneficence?"

"Well go ahead," Emma said to Sasha. "It's your news."

And yes, everyone turned to Sasha, thinking *could it be that he's gotten a new job, one that pays a few pennies more than his old one? Or maybe Emma is with child, despite all of the problems she has in that particular department?* Sasha, savouring the moment, kept them in suspense. He touched his fingertips together, like some opining cleric, and gazed downward, at the surface of the table, before lifting his chin into the air, a gesture indicating that he was choosing his words carefully, so as to accurately convey the significance of what he had to say. (Meanwhile, Emma reached a hand up his leg, the tablecloth hiding the reach of her fingertips, and when Emma reached the top of his thigh, her hand travelled inward, to that spot separating left leg from right.)

"As we all know," Sasha started, "anarchism is a peaceful belief system, one that does not believe in wars, or conflict, or oppression. In fact, the very *goal* of anarchism is peace. And yet, we also know that the true anarchist, when called upon, has a duty to combat force with force. Naturally, I am talking of the *attentat*, which should never be confused with violence. To me, they are opposite terms. To remove a tyrant is an act of liberation, the giving of life to the oppressed."

"Sasha," asked Timmermann. "Is this about Homestead?"

"Yes. The target will be Henry C. Frick."

He paused, and let the others digest this news. They did so with shocked expressions, and then, after a few seconds, yelps of enthusiasm.

"I will commit the deed," he continued. "Emma will be the propagandist. She has the people's ear, particularly now that Johann Most has run off to Salinas. She will use Frick's assassination to enthrall the populace. She will inspire them to rise up and take what is rightfully theirs. As for Frick, I have no *personal* grievance against the man. He is, however, the most pungent and egregious symbol of the shameful injustice that is capitalism. As well, he's personally responsible for the murder of nine workers, his henchmen gunning them down like turkeys in a shoot. So my *attentat* will be directed not against Frick as a man, but as an avowed enemy of the working class. Emma, meanwhile, will remain behind to spread the meaning of this deed throughout the country."

Timmermann rose to his feet, a wine-filled tumbler in his hand. He looked wobbly and solemn. "A toast for Alexander Berkman!"

"Hear, hear," said the others. "A toast for our Sasha!"

Everyone downed their glasses. The Oerters went out and came back with growlers looped through their fingers, each one filled with inky red wine. The Mollocks had a cylinder player and soon there was dancing; at one point, Sasha found himself holding on to Mollock's wife, who had lost her sullen, worried disposition. She whispered in his ear, her breath liquid and hot. "If you and Emma would ever like to trade with us, it would be my pleasure, Alexander, I've always wanted to be with an actual revolutionary man. But you can't turn back now. That's the deal. This can't be something you're just *talking* about. If that's the case, the offer's off the table, I've had enough wishy-washiness from the movement, you hear me?"

"I understand," he murmured, for he'd never noticed how desirable was this saddened woman, this mourning and shapely Vera Mollock, and as he looked about the room, he realized he'd never witnessed such beauty in a single place, all of these pale-skinned revolutionists, with their moth-chewed sweaters and towering cheekbones, he'd fuck them all, male or female, why should he care? He was just about to kiss Vera Mollock—kiss her hotly and damply and with the intensity of a bursting sun—when he turned his head and saw one of the Oerter brothers approaching—he could never remember which one was which.

"Sasha," he said.

"What is it?"

"We have a connection in Pittsburgh. His name is Carl Nold. He's a printer. He makes almost all of the movement pamphlets down there. He'll help you. He'll provide all the support you need."

"Thank you. I mean it, thank you, but we can talk about this later, okay?"

Sasha turned, somewhat rudely, only to discover that Vera had stumbled off, the moment lost, most likely forever. But really, it hardly mattered. Emma was dancing frenziedly, and when she spotted him she came over and kissed him on the mouth, her voice loud and wine-infused, "You know what, fishlips? You're an angel, you're a devil, you're a vicious son-of-a-bitch." She fell, landing with a thump on the pinewood floor. The cylinder skipped. She managed to sit up, legs out in front of her, holding her forehead, saying, "Uh-oh, I might have had a little too much wine."

Sasha helped her up and supported her as they walked back to the room in which they were staying. The party continued on the other side of a stick-thin wall. They both lay down.

"Are you going to be sick?" Sasha asked.

"Yes. Just not yet."

"You'll give me some warning?"

"I'll try. Oh fishie, it's quite a life we lead, isn't it?"

"It is."

"Would you trade it? For anything in this world?"

"No, not a thing, I couldn't."

"Good. Neither would I. Some things *should* be difficult."

"By which you mean life."

"By which I mean life and love and work and everything else besides. It's the Russian in us, isn't it? Cherishing tribulation over all else? It's no wonder we're ruled by a heartless tsar. Deep down, we wouldn't have it any other way."

There was a crash of glasses in the other room. This was followed by laughter. Emma cuddled against Sasha. "Tell me, lover. Tell me everything. How will you do it, how will it happen, spare no detail."

"I'll use a bomb."

"Good."

"I'll blow the bastard to smithereens."

"Yes!"

"I'll teach the prick a fucking lesson."

"That's the spirit!"

"I'll show him a god damn thing or two."

"Oh fishie, I can feel your energy, you're bursting with it, it's filling me up. Why do I find you irresistible, all of a sudden. God damn it, fishie, it's like I'm falling in love with you all over again."

She was removing him from his corduroy trousers when she went pale and ran from the room, seeking the toilet, which in the Mollocks' building was at the end of the hallway. Sasha joined the others. It was very, very late. The guests, having seen Emma's condition, decided that maybe it was a good time to depart; they all said goodbye to Sasha, kissing him twice on each cheek. Mollock then embraced Sasha and went to his room, where he joined his wife, who, toward the end of the evening, had started to cry. This left Sasha in the living room, mess everywhere, Emma vomiting at the end of the hallway, the sun preparing to rise, and the only thing to be done was to gaze out of the living-room window and watch as the city began to awaken—there were buckets of water hitting sidewalks, rooftop roosters turning vocal, the crank of metal shopfronts, the first calls of newspaper vendors, how happy Sasha was to be home.

* * *

The next day, he visited Justus Schwab at his watering hole on First Street; even in mid-day, it was all gloom, dust motes floating in whatever light managed to brighten the front window. A few men sat at roughly hewn tables, talking quietly, drinking from lager steins or shot glasses filled with vodka. Schwab himself was behind the wide-plank bar, wiping the inside of a glass with a cloth.

"Comrade?" Sasha said. "A word?" Schwab nodded and Sasha leaned in. "I need dynamite," he said in a low, urgent voice.

Schwab stopped rubbing the glass and held it up to the light. "That's what I hear," he said. He glanced at a table of men speaking Russian in the corner, as though worried that they might be eavesdropping. He then reached beneath his rudimentary bar and pulled out a pad of paper. Using the pencil he kept behind his ear, he wrote something on the topmost page and tore it off. He handed it to Sasha. "Go alone," he said.

Sasha thanked Schwab and left, his heart beating quickly, his skin hot, for he knew where he was going: he'd heard all the stories, the name was Panofsky, and you never saw him since he hated parties and rallies and speeches and gatherings of any kind, in fact he rarely left his apartment, or so went the story, there being times in which Sasha, a born skeptic, had to wonder whether these rumours masked the fact that the man didn't actually exist. But now he knew: Panofsky was real and he lived in a Spring Street tenement as decrepit as any Sasha had ever seen, the halls reeking of garbage, the landings covered with oily soot, the walls a crumbling mess. As he climbed, he could hear a man weeping and a woman yelling and, during lulls in their argument, the scurrying of vermin. He was about to knock on Panofsky's door when he noticed a lump, about halfway down the unlit hallway: it was grey and glistening and wriggling, a live octopus, slithering toward him, as if seeking assistance in its escape. Just then, a child came running into the hallway. She looked to be about ten years of age, though one could never really tell with a tenement child: likely she was older. She ran up to the octopus, which was huge, the size of a piglet with arms, and was about to pick it up when she noticed Sasha and stopped. She was wearing a stained blue dress and torn canvas slippers. Her skin was dark olive. She looked at him blankly; then, with a furtive motion, she picked up the creature and held it away from herself, its tentacles leaving a trail of moisture as they dragged along the hallway.

Panofsky must have heard the ruckus—the door to an apartment opened, as if on cue, affording Sasha's first glimpse at the mythical revolutionist. He was little more than five feet tall, wearing a grey undershirt and drooping pants, bald but for a ring of hair around the side of his head, his ears strangely pink, his nose bulbous and run through with purple. The third, fourth and fifth fingers of his right hand were missing. "I'm Berkman," Sasha said. Panofsky grunted and beckoned Sasha inside. He walked toward a doorless closet and selected a jute bag filled with dynamite powder—it was stamped with the words "potting soil"—and deposited it carefully on his kitchen table, next to a plate covered in dried egg yolk. He then went to a filing cabinet near a filmy window. He rummaged inside; when he turned, a half dozen blasting caps, already connected to fuses, dangled from his remaining fingers. He stepped toward Sasha and deposited them next to the bag of dynamite. His voice was scratchy.

"The pipes you can get in a hardware store. Get ones, oh, about two inches in diameter."

"What do I owe you?"

"You don't pay me. You'll never pay me. I don't receive payment, I never take any money, do you understand that?"

Sasha nodded, and looked at the explosives.

"You don't have to worry," Panofsky said. "Dynamite is inert unless it's exposed to an explosion itself. That's why it was invented—nitroglycerine was too unstable. I should know." He held up his right hand. "But when you mix nitro with sawdust and a splash of sodium nitrate, you can control it. Then again, you never know. You could throw this bag off a table ninety-nine times and nothing would happen. But the hundredth time? *Kaboomski*. So don't worry about dropping it. At the same time, don't drop it."

"Thank you," said Sasha.

"You're welcome," said Panofsky.

Sasha packed his pockets with the blasting caps and walked back to the Mollocks', the bag of dynamite cradled in his arms. Later, he went to a hardware store and bought two lengths of hollow pipe.

Later still, after a supper afflicted by a notable silence, Mollock finally spoke up. "You can use the table," he said, a statement that apparently upset his wife, who excused herself and went to the bedroom. "Don't mind her," Mollock said. "The stress of all this. It gets to her. We've been through a lot. But she knows what needs to be done."

"Thank you."

Mollock lowered his voice to a whisper. "You *do* know what you're doing, don't you?"

"I do," Sasha lied.

In his room, Sasha retrieved an instructional manual that Johann Most had published in English several years earlier. It was entitled *The Science of Revolutionary War: A Little Handbook of Instruction in the Use and Preparation of Nitroglycerine, Dynamite, Gun-Cotton, Fulminating Mercury, Bombs, Fuses, Poisons, etc., etc.* Sasha's copy, which he'd lifted from the offices of *Freiheit*, had been reproduced so many times that the ink had smudged, the illustrations like splotches of mud. He showed it to Mollock.

"Ahh," said Mollock. "Most's primer on bomb making. Is it any good?"

"I suppose we'll find out."

Sasha laid out his equipment—dynamite, metal pipes, the wired blasting caps. His only problem was the booklet itself; as Sasha flipped through it, he had to wonder whether it was the process of translation that had robbed it of all clarity: *Introduce the fuse into the open end "A" in such a way that it rests directly on the filling "C" at which point you crimp the rim at the open end tightly, so that the fuse is held firmly, and can no longer slip out, for which you can use a pair of pliers or, if need dictates, your teeth.* Sasha persisted, his interpretation of Most's instruction guided by the principles of bomb making: you obtained a pipe, you filled it with dynamite, you attached a blasting cap and fuse. The most difficult part, he soon discovered, was fitting the cap and fuse to the tube in such a way that the explosive powder didn't spill out, a technique that Most described as such: *To fix the outer end of the blasting cap, fix in the hole in the casing as firmly as possible, either with tiny wooden wedges or by wrapping thread around it, so that it is jammed firmly in position.* Sasha's hands shook as he tinkered. There was a clock in the room, and its ticking put him on edge. Emma, meanwhile, worked in the kitchen, washing and rewashing the dishes; Sasha could sense her, looking over from time to time, a nervous expression on her small, round face. He could also hear Mollock and his wife whispering angrily in their bedroom, Vera's voice occasionally veering toward the shrill. At one point, Mollock came out and stood behind Sasha, attempting to divine how he was doing.

"Almost there," Sasha told him.

"Of course, comrade, no one's worried, no one at all."

Sasha kept working. He tapped and fitted and jiggled, knowing that if he erred, he wouldn't be the first anarchist to blow up his own lodgings. "I'm done," he announced.

In front of him, on the kitchen table, was a pair of pipe bombs. Emma came over and grinned.

"Well done," said Mollock.

Even Vera came out, her face flushed with relief. "Will they work?" she asked.

"I figure I can test one. If it explodes, I'll use the other to get Frick."

"Good thinking," said Mollock.

Sasha went outside to smoke on the building's stoop. It was three o'clock in the morning. He held in the smoke until his lungs felt scorched. Across the street was a park; in its centre was a small fire that'd been set by homeless men. They sat around it, looking like hooded gnomes. Someone far away started yelling in a language that Sasha didn't know; slowly, these ravings faded, and then there was silence but for the crackling of the fire across the street. Sasha's cigarette was helping. The air began to spark with promise, so he smoked another, exhaling long plumes of dense blue-grey smoke. By the time he'd smoked his third, his fingertips shook and he felt giddy. He joined Emma in the Mollocks' spare room. Sasha couldn't sleep. Emma was awake as well; he could see her, eyes open, in the near darkness. She rolled on top of him, and whispered endearments in his ear. Sasha filled his hands with her hair and said, "Think of it, sailor girl, think of what we're going to accomplish."

"Don't move," she purred.

"I won't."

"I mean it, not a muscle."

"I won't."

"Is there anything better than stillness?"

"No, not a thing."

"I love it, sometimes, not moving. Not feeling the *impulse* to move."

"It's rare but yes, it happens."

"And I don't mean being too exhausted and weak too move. That's something else altogether. I mean feeling as though it's *okay* not to move. That the universe, for whatever reason, has chosen that *moment* to let you be still."

"It happens, but, as I say, not very often."

"This is one of those times, isn't it?"

"Yes," he said. "It is."

*   *   *

Having wrapped one of the bombs inside a sweater and a light jacket, Emma placed it in a large jute sack with sandwiches wrapped in newspaper on top, so that it would look as though they were just a young couple on their way to a picnic, happy for a reprieve from the demands of the city. The ferry, at that time of day, was mostly empty, with traffic heading toward Manhattan and not away from it. Though there were a couple of people out on deck, enjoying the breeze, Emma and Sasha sat inside, holding hands, in desperate love. Everything smelled of wood and seafoam. At the Staten Island docks, they hired a carriage to take them to the dunes; the driver's dark hands were covered with pink splotches and little scars. As they rode along, the horse made clopping sounds against the packed sand roadway; Emma turned her face toward the ocean and let the breeze cool her skin. With time, the white clapboard houses began to thin, and they came to a weedy beach sided by a marsh. Sasha called to the driver. He stopped and his passengers climbed down, the lunch bag held tightly in Emma's hands. Sasha paid, the driver tucking the money into his shirt pocket. He looked around, his eyes narrowing. "Can't remember the last time I been this far out. You want me to wait?"

"No," said Emma. "Thank you, though."

"I don't know how you gonna get back. You be all alone out here."

"We'll be fine."

He made a noise that was halfway between a whistle and the chirrup of a cricket. This triggered his horse, who came about-face and started trotting off in the direction from which they had come. Emma and Sasha watched the horse and rider slowly recede into the distance, the two now alone on a pleasing and expansive shoreline; they could hear cawing seagulls and waves rolling onto shore.

Sasha unpacked the picnic bag, slowly removing the layers of clothing and newspaper. He set the device a little way off, such that it was poking, fuse side up, from the surface of the beach. Sasha then pulled a box of matches from his pocket and was about to light the fuse when Emma said, "Wait." She kissed him. "There," she said, "that was for good luck." He nodded and lit the fuse, the two taking cover behind a sand dune about fifty feet away. From there, they watched the fuse burn down, their ears plugged, their teeth gritted, even though there was nothing beyond the rustle of tall grass and the restful sound of water washing upon the shore.

"What's happening?" Emma whispered.

"I don't know."

"Shouldn't it have gone off by now?"

"Yes," Sasha said, unsure of what to do—a damp fuse, dynamite packed too hard, unfavourable winds, a misplaced blasting cap, all could cause delays. Really, there were so many opportunities for failure: perhaps he'd introduced the fuse into open end "B" instead of open end "A"; perhaps he had tightened with thread where he should've fastened it with wire; perhaps Panofsky had given him faulty caps, you never knew. Sasha continued to gaze out over the sand, his eyes fixed on the length of pipe, willing it to explode. A minute went by, and another. Still the pipe stood upright in the sand, like a soldier awaiting instruction. "Damn," he muttered. "Damn damn damn damn." After another minute or so, he approached the bomb, and saw that the problem wasn't the fuse, which had ably burned its way into the blasting caps: obviously, the connection had failed somehow. No longer afraid, he picked up the pipe and threw it as far as he was able, thinking it might at least have the grace to explode when it touched down. The pipe landed, kicking up the tiniest funnel of sand. He waited a few seconds, still hoping for some sign of the bomb's potential, before muttering, "Shit, shit, shit." He then retrieved it and tossed it into the ocean, concerned that children at play might come across it.

* * *

They ate their sandwiches as they walked. After ten minutes or so, just as they were approaching a bend in the roadway, they heard a· horse whinny. The driver appeared, and asked if they wanted a ride back. They thanked him and climbed up, salmon salad at the corners of their mouths. The driver then made that funny chirruping noise, which set the horse trotting off in the direction of the docks. Aboard the ferry, Sasha and Emma clung to the railings and caught their breath.

"I'll go to Pittsburgh and get a handgun. We have comrades there. That fellow Nold will put me up. Maybe he'll know someone."

"Are you a good shot?"

"No. I'll have to get close."

"Yes," she said, picturing the moment. "You will."

When the two re-entered the apartment, Mollock was waiting for them.

"How did it go?" he asked, the answer provided by Sasha's wounded expression. This was only confirmed when Sasha took Most's bomb-building manual and set it on fire over the kitchen sink, the ashes catching in an updraft caused by an open window, such that they fluttered into the alley separating Mollock's tenement from the one next door.

"Is there a plan B?" asked Mollock.

"There is," said Sasha, briefly forming a little pistol with his thumb and forefinger.

Mollock lowered his voice. "What about the other bomb? Vera will lose her mind if it hangs around here much longer."

"Don't worry," Emma said. "We'll throw it in the East River."

Over the next week, Sasha and Emma spent a lot of time together, walking hand in hand through parks, along boardwalks, across bridges, and through neighbourhoods they'd always said they'd wanted to visit. In some ways, it was a lovely time, for neither of them had jobs to distract them, and they were able to remind themselves why they were so devoted to the city. These outings were also tinged with the bittersweet, for while they were both excited by their plan regarding Frick, they knew that there were inherent risks, and that there was a decent chance that Sasha might never enjoy these sites again. This struck Emma as cruelly ironic: now that Sasha had finally grown into the man she'd always suspected was hidden deep within him, there was a very real chance that she might lose him.

Mollock, despite his wife's reticence, threw a going-away party for Sasha. There was Timmermann and the Oerters, along with Solotaroff and the Minkin sisters. As the night wore on, others arrived whom Sasha and Emma knew by reputation only. There was little Annie Netter, who, along with her father, operated a grocery store at 16 Suffolk Street—it was here that the anarchist community shopped, and where, on any given day, one could watch a pair of comrades argue over the necessity of a revolutionary vanguard while picking through rutabagas. There was Jacob Maryson, a stalwart physician known for treating strikers who had met with a truncheon to the forehead. There was Moshe Katz, a man who, in addition to the usual languages spoken on the Lower East Side, knew French, English, Spanish, Czech, Greek, Ukrainian, Finnish, Turkish, Italian and a smattering of Norse; as such, he scratched out a living as a translator, charging next to nothing as long as the text promoted the toppling of the free market system. Yet there were two obvious absentees, the first being Sofia; Sasha couldn't help but wonder if she'd finally managed to find her way back to Tallinn. (He'd have to ask Mollock if he'd thought to invite her.) The other was the poet Edelstadt, who, after a few drinks, would have been standing on the coffee table, a drink in hand, spouting revolutionary verse, while eyeing the more comely of the female comrades in attendance; more than one toast was made in honour of his memory, the party-goers turning quietly solemn as they downed a measure of beer, wine or spirits.

Of course, they were all eager to hear about the progression of Sasha's plan, with many asking if the device he'd made in this very apartment was still the weapon of choice. Each time, Sasha laughed, as if the failure of his bomb was nothing but the most minor of inconveniences. He then assured them that everything was marvellous, everything was grand, *okay, okay, it's true, the test bomb didn't go off, or at least it didn't go off the way we might have liked it to, that much is true, but otherwise everything is all set, it's off to*

Pittsburgh tomorrow, and it won't be long before Frick gets what's coming to him.

Someone handed Emma a measure of vodka, which she downed in a single, searing gulp. She gasped, laughed, and wiped tears out of her eyes. Others were arriving, now, most of them from the old crowd; there was Faltzblatt and Bernstein and Strashunsky, Yedelvich and Lewis and Yanovsky, all of them patting Sasha on the back and saying how proud they were that they had a comrade with his mettle. *Believe me, Sasha*, was the refrain, *we knew we had it in you, we knew it all along, Emma always said so, I wish I had a woman who knew me that well...* During one of the interminable toasts, Sasha happened to look toward the front door of the apartment and saw Modska, returned from small-town Massachusetts. Sasha pushed his way through the crowd and hugged him, the cousins then stepping into the relative quiet of the hallway.

"When did you get back?" Sasha asked.

"As soon as I heard."

"Did you sell the café?"

Modska looked baleful. "It turns out there wasn't much to sell."

"So we're broke."

"More or less. I'm sorry."

"Ah well," Sasha said with a shrug. "I'm so used to it by now it hardly makes a difference. A bit of money would've helped, though."

The tenor of their reunion changed, Sasha growing stiff and Modska's expression losing its usual bonhomie. "Sasha," Modska finally said, "please, are you sure about this?"

"Yes," Sasha said, nodding. "I'm sure."

"It's just that, you know, what could happen..."

"I know, Modska, I know."

"But really? Cousin? You're sure about this? Emma's okay about this? About *all* of this?"

Back inside, it was loud and chaotic and someone had put food out on the kitchen table, lox and salami and dark bread and pots of mustard and sauerkraut and boiled potatoes, the apartment filling with the smell of dill and sour cream, of boiled meat and raw onions, of knishes and lox. More people arrived, Zum Groben Michel types, hard men with scars and prison records, and even though they didn't know Sasha personally, they went up to him and shook his hand and they all said more or less the same thing, *I wish it was me, comrade, I wish to hell it was me.* The apartment was so crowded that Sasha started to suspect that his *attentat* was merely an excuse to have yet another party, one in which everyone would drink themselves into a stupor and couple with another comrade, only to awaken in the morning with a blinding headache, a sour stomach, and hair smelling of tobacco. With this thought, he couldn't breathe: the floor tilted, his legs trembled, he closed his eyes and forced himself to take a breath. It was the drink that was to blame; despite the temperature in the room, he felt cold and weak.

A warm hand slipped into his. Emma led him through the apartment. They stepped into their room and closed the door behind them. The drop in volume helped. Emma held Sasha to her and said, "Oh fishie, it's all catching up with you, isn't it?"

They lay down, Emma's head on his shoulder, an arm over his chest.

"Emma," he whispered.

"Shhhhh," she said.

"I'm afraid."

"Shhhhhhhhhh."

She helped him off with his shirt and trousers. In the background, they could hear laughter and singing and breaking glasses. Emma undressed and they crawled beneath the covers, their intimacy tinged with the knowledge that this might be the last time they ever saw each other in the planetary world. There was no talking, no crude movements, and no cries of exultation, just a silent transfer of essence, both Sasha and Emma making a sojourn to a different world that night, where they both glimpsed what they'd suspected all along, that every human alive was far more than a single physical shell, and that life, real life, was not corporeal, but a magnificent and infinite glimmer.

They didn't sleep. At seven o'clock in the morning, they skipped breakfast and rushed to the station, only to discover that there were no seats left on the train to Pittsburgh. There was, however, room on the train to Washington, which would then connect on to Pittsburgh. It was a circuitous route, but after last night's festivities— after all the toasts and well-wishing and high expectations—Sasha was determined to leave the city that day.

Mollock and his wife were with them; Mollock was beaming, while Vera looked uncomfortable. A bearded conductor walked up and down the platform. "All aboard," he called out. Sasha shook Mollock's hand. "Thank you for everything," he said. "You're a fine comrade, you really are." He then turned and kissed Vera on the cheek. "I'm sorry," he said. "I was a huge inconvenience. I know this and I'm sorry."

Emma wept into the lapels of Sasha's old, worn jacket. This went on and on; it was Mollock who finally pulled her away. Sasha boarded the train and took his seat and looked out of the window at Emma, who was crying and coughing and giggling at the intensity of it all. She waved and he waved and she called out that she loved him and what could he do but call, "Yes, yes, my love, I do too" through a warped pane of glass. A whistle blew and the train shunted forward and Sasha was gleeful, he really was, as the locomotive gathered momentum, moving faster and faster, the wheels shrieking, plumes of coal smoke chugging thick and black into the atmosphere, the train carrying Sasha not to Pittsburgh, nor Frick, but to his permanent and glorious forever.

seventeen

THE CITY GAVE WAY to fields and forests, to small towns and far-off hills and looming, cracked-wall factories. Sasha kept drifting off, only to come awake with the next screeching turn, after which he'd fall, once more, into the depths of a recollecting dream—there he was, a small boy, picking blueberries near the family dacha, by himself, the sun blazing overhead. Or there, over there, in Kovno, Modska helping him hang a knotted rope from a tree branch that reached out over the water, and they're taking turns, flinging themselves off the rope, seeing who can fly through the air the farthest. And is that really Rosa, with her wondrously sullen expression and *matryoshka*-like body, bathing in the river with her pretty and laughing friend Justina, while he and Modska hide behind a stand of wild shrubs? The train shuddered and he came awake, though only for the briefest of moments, just long enough to be mesmerized by the flicker of light through the trees, and then he was in Café Sachs, eating a steak drowned in salty gravy, and who should come in but Emma, his beautiful Emma, wearing that sailor's blouse, her eyes a blaze of understanding and warmth.

The smell of food roused him. A man in a business suit was seated beside him, eating lunch: beef, potatoes, carrots, black coffee. He was chewing methodically, resting his cutlery between each bite. Sasha struggled to fall back asleep, and failed. How funny, he thought, that he should be visited with such wondrous visions, when he'd always considered his boyhood to be one of difficulty. That was when he realized what was happening: his dreams were his psyche, struggling to be saved, for everyone had a life force, the Austrians spoke of it, and Sasha's was trying to convince him that his existence was too valuable to sacrifice. This, he now understood, was the reason why only the rarest of beings actually went through with an *attentat*. It wasn't the certainty of arrest, trial and execution—the real opponent was recollection. It was that elemental self, a megaphone to its terrified lips, calling, "Comrade, comrade, look at your lovely and important life, you'd really give all of this up?"

"Stop it!" Sasha said out loud, slapping the top of his right leg. This drew the attention of the businessman. He looked over. His plate was empty, save for a residue of sauce.

"Is something the matter?" he asked.

Sasha muttered that an insect was bothering him. The businessman relaxed noticeably and said, "Oh yes, yes, these trains can be real flytraps, I'd hate to think what the kitchen is like. I say, I hope it wasn't my lunch that was attracting the damn thing."

"No, no," Sasha said.

"At any rate, the little bugger seems to be gone now."

* * *

The train chugged into Washington, where Sasha had a three-hour layover. To kill time, he checked his luggage and took a walk around Capitol Hill, trying to imagine what would become of it during the revolution: likely, it would be burned to the ground by an angry mob, aware of the symbolic value of such a conflagration. Sasha, however, hoped that wouldn't happen—with a bit of effort, it could be converted into a palace for the people, a complex with theatres, an opera hall, an indoor gymnasium and a few dozen bowling lanes. The lawn would be a playground, the kitchen a communal dining area, the ballroom a games court (or two). This thought sparked Sasha's appetite, so he purchased lunch from a sausage vendor. As he ate, he quenched his thirst by taking sips from a bottle of Hires, which he really did enjoy, and, as such, it cued a reoccurrence of that maddening desire to remain alive—to eat an infinite amount of sausages and drink an infinite quantity of root beer and sit in an infinite number of quiet, green, leafy parks. To hush these thoughts, and further rekindle his sense of purpose, he walked over to the White House—apparently, the paintings hanging on its walls were worth enough to feed every malnourished infant in New York City, Chicago and Detroit for a year. Sasha lit a cigarette. Where did he get that statistic about the paintings? Was it a Most speech? Something Emma once said? He couldn't remember. It didn't matter. The idyllic moments of his boyhood were no longer popping up before him, so he smoked another cigarette while thinking about martyrdom.

He walked around for another hour or so, which gave him plenty of time to retrieve his bag and board the train to Pittsburgh. This time, his seatmate was an elderly woman with a ruddy complexion, her face etched with years gone by; she spent her time knitting and humming to herself. The train pulled into the station with a series of jolts. When it finally stopped, Sasha deboarded and looked around the crowded salon. The crowds thinned, slowly, and he spotted a man who had to be his contact, for he not only looked like an anarchist—the pale skin, the thin frame, the suit coming apart at the seams—but he was peering in every direction. He caught sight of Sasha and grinned. He came over.

"Alexander Berkman?"

"Please, call me Sasha. I take it you're Mr. Nold?"

"Yes, but it's Carl, please, call me Carl."

He reached out a hand; Sasha took it. "Thank you for helping me."

"Not at all. It's a wonderful thing you're doing. Finally, some movement in the movement! But please, allow me to take your bag."

"No, really, I'm fine."

"I insist. You've had a long trip. I understand you came via Washington?"

"It couldn't be helped."

"Please, please, let me take it, it would be an honour."

Sasha nodded and followed Nold outside, where they boarded a carriage filled with commuters. They rumbled along, their progress slowed at first by city traffic, and then by ruts and furrows in the roadway. After a half hour or so, they reached Allegheny; while Nold described it as its own city, it appeared to Sasha as an extension of Pittsburgh itself.

"We're here," Nold said at one of the stops. The two walked along a packed-earth street, Nold still carrying Sasha's suitcase, saying, "I tell you, everyone is SO thrilled to meet you. While the community is small here, I dare say we're every bit as committed as our New York City comrades, and when they all heard what was afoot—well, you can imagine their excitement."

They reached a dilapidated little house that was no better, or worse, than the neighbouring homes—Allegheny, Sasha concluded, must be the Lower East Side of Pittsburgh, for the porch of Nold's house was slanted, and the paint was coming off in jagged chips, and a portion of the chimney had collapsed, littering bricks on his poorly shingled roof. "Come in, come in," Nold said, and Sasha followed him into a front vestibule, where a pair of doors led to separate apartments. Nold pushed open the second door, which hung slightly askew in its frame: Sasha doubted he could have locked it even if he'd cared to. They walked up a flight of narrow steps and entered a dingy room. There was a sofa patched with adhesive tape and a card table where, Sasha suspected, Nold ate his meals. "Home sweet home," he said. "My room's down the hallway. You'll sleep there."

"No!" Sasha protested. "You've already done more than enough. I will not put you out of your room."

"Oh yes you will. You need to be well rested."

"But I'd feel terrible."

They argued for a bit more, eventually settling the matter with a coin toss—Sasha won, meaning that he was entitled to choose, so he moved his bag next to the sofa and sat. Nold chopped vegetables. Dinner was a watery stew with slices of firm black bread and butter. There was a jar of homemade pickles and, after the meal, tumblers filled with schnapps. Not long afterward, Sasha collapsed on Nold's lumpy sofa, where he slept fitfully, his thoughts populated by people he'd long forgotten.

* * *

After a breakfast of warm oatmeal and coffee, Nold insisted that they take a carriage back into Pittsburgh. "Tell me," he said as they jostled along. "Do you know of a comrade named Max Metzkow?"

"No. Should I?"

"Of course. He's the grandfather of the Pittsburgh anarchist community. He used to be Johann Most's printer in Berlin. After some jail time there, he fled to London, where he colluded with none other than Pyotr Kropotkin."

"Really? He knew Kropotkin?"

"Oh yes. I tell you, Metzkow is a real leading light here. Still. He's getting on, and needs help getting around."

It was a short walk from the carriage depot to the men's shelter where Metzkow resided.

When Nold knocked on Metzkow's door, a bony old man wearing shorts and a stained undershirt answered. He was smoking a cigarette, and his clavicle pushed through papery, purple-veined skin. The room behind him was dark and cluttered with bottles. Snow-white whiskers speckled his face.

"Berkman, is it?"

"It's an honour."

"Oh cut the crap. I'll be with you in a minute."

He closed the door. Nold grinned, and said, "He's a bit of a character."

When Metzkow emerged, he was dressed in sagging pants and an old frayed shirt. He also had a vodka bottle in his rear pocket, which he drank from as they all rode back to Allegheny. "You know we're living in a police state, don'tcha Berkman? Forget all this bullshit about home of the free."

"Shhhh," Nold said, "not so loud."

"See this?" Metzkow asked while holding up a thin, crooked arm. "Look! Look at what those fascists did to me! And for what? Holding a placard? Try having three beefy constables jumping up and down on you and see how *you* make out. I'd been here... what? A week? A week and a half? That's the truth of it, Berkman. Just look at my fucked-up arm. Things are no better here than they were back in Germany. Spies everywhere, stooges galore, everyone on the take, money money money, the American way, bullshit bullshit bullshit. And now *you* come along! Ha! What timing! They'll shit themselves when you plug that son-of-a-bitch Frick."

"Metzkow! Please!"

"I'll tell you something, Berkman. I wouldn't want to be you afterward. When you think about what they're going to *do* to you? My guess is you don't even care. You know what causes bravery, don'tcha Berkman? It comes from having had enough of life. That's what I figure about you—even though you're young, you look like maybe you've had enough of it, am I right? Hell yeah, I bet you were *born* having had enough."

They reached their stop and started walking back to Nold's house. It was late afternoon, the air a summery musk, Nold's neighbours having taken to their sagging porches to drink beer and talk. Mostly, they spoke in Polish and Italian; the men had pot-bellies, the women looked tired, their children were dirty-faced and small. Sasha could smell roasted tomatoes and grilled meat. He felt depleted, all of a sudden, yet as they passed Nold's house, Nold explained that Sasha's official welcome dinner was at the home of another comrade—"You'll like them, you'll like them all just fine, they're a good bunch of revolutionists, they can't wait to meet you." They walked a few more blocks, Metzkow complaining that his feet were hurting and the weather was too hot and one of his teeth was bothering him—"You think I got money to see a dentist? Well do ya, Berkman? If you do you're a whole lot dumber than you look."

They reached yet another decrepit bungalow and, in short order, were joined by fellow anarchists—one had a right leg much shorter than the left, and had to wear a platform boot to compensate, while another had lost a portion of his right ear in a dog attack. They ate roasted chicken and potatoes dripping with grease; by midnight, they'd all started singing Bavarian worker songs while waving Pilsner steins in the air. Sasha slipped away and trudged back to Nold's house, where he dreamt of Emma and glory and beauty and death, only to awake feeling refreshed for the first time in days.

That morning, he travelled to a section of woods about a half hour outside of the city; here, Frick lived on a grand street lined with mansions. One glance, and Sasha felt all the more justified in his decision—Frick's home was an entire compound, comprised of an enormous main house, a stable, a kennel, a greenhouse, a garage, a tennis court, a bowling lawn, marble gazebos, a children's play-house and a petting zoo. His neighbours had similar residences, if slightly less ostentatious, and as Sasha strolled along, attempting to appear as casual as possible, he felt almost sickened: these houses, these testaments to avarice and corruption, were the very reason that upheavals occurred. Oh yes, Sasha thought, there'd be no more fitting a place to kill the man, right in his own den of excess. And yet, there were obstacles, namely the security guards, a twelve-foot wrought-iron fence, and a pair of German shepherds who patrolled the fence line, barking at everything that moved.

The next day, Sasha visited Frick's workplace, which occupied several floors of the Chronicle Telegraph building in downtown Pittsburgh. He stood and watched for an hour, camouflaged by passersby; in that time, more than a hundred people either left or entered the building. This presented Sasha with an idea: if he could employ some ruse that would allow him to *become* one of those people, he might be able to gain access to Frick's office. Though Sasha had never considered himself to be particularly imaginative, and was not duplicitous in any way, the ideas nonetheless came like rain: he could pass himself off as a developer, a union buster, a fellow Mason, a charity director, or a representative from city hall, wishing to discuss some civic award or another.

Later, he sat with Nold: "I'll infiltrate Frick's offices, and do it there. It's either that or his house, but his house is too well protected."

"Yes, yes, good idea."

"There's one problem."

"Yes?"

"I need money. For a suit, a decent hat, a necktie, a pair of leather shoes, professionally made business cards and, most of all, a revolver."

"Oh."

"I was hoping that the local anarchist community could provide the funds."

"Of course, of course, consider it done, my friend. The one slight problem is that nobody seems to have any money these days. But don't worry! I'll tell you what. At the end of the month, there's a committee meeting of the local Pioneers chapter, and I'll add your fundraising plea to the agenda. It's a fun event, actually; there's usually an oompah band and dancing. I'm sure we'll be able to fig-ure something out. A bake sale, perhaps?"

That night, Alexander Berkman wired Emma Goldman and told her of his predicament. A day later, he received her reply:

```
I understand stop will send funds soon
stop I love you stop your sailor girl
```

* * *

The *distress* that Emma Goldman felt upon receiving Sasha's telegram—she had no money, no work, no prospects and, to make matters worse, was starting to rub Vera Mollock the wrong way. Despite it all, she'd told Sasha not to worry, that the money was on the way.

Again: how? How, in a city so penniless that the mayor himself, one Hugh J. Grant, had taken to giving speeches on the steps of Tammany Hall, where he urged his fellow New Yorkers to please, please, be generous with one another? Yet Emma's anguish did not stem from the impossibility of her task. If Emma Goldman felt distraught, it was because she knew *exactly* how a woman of her tender age could acquire fast, easy money. As such, she embarked on the process of talking herself into it: You, Emma, are not only a woman, but a *young* woman, and you happen to believe that nothing to do with the body is dirty, or sinful, or lurid, and if it came down to the commodification of said body, wouldn't that be a commentary on the way in which capitalism exploited the more vulnerable members of society? She even had a literary inspiration, Sonya, her favourite character in *Crime and Punishment*, the comely daughter of Marmeladov, who peddles her body in order to feed her younger siblings and her tubercular, bed-bound mother.

Just as Sonya had lain on her little cot, shaking with trepidation before her first outing, Emma was possessed by a sickening dread, for the thought of rubbing her flesh against an absolute stranger, with neither love nor attraction nor lust to inflame her, was appalling. *You weakling*, she berated herself. *You absolute coward, Sasha is giving away his life for the cause, and you shrink from giving up your body?* She was ashamed of her shame, disgusted by her disgust. This went on for hours, Emma accusing herself of being a spoiled child, a prevaricating brat, a self-obsessed poseur, a listless jellyfish, a mawkish dilettante and, above all else, a coward. Finally, she felt too tired, and too bludgeoned by self-recrimination, to muster any more resistance.

I have to do this, she thought.

I just do.

* * *

There was a standing mirror in the Mollocks' guest room, a silvery hand-me-down that had been in the family for so long that its surface undulated slightly, making Emma look long in places where she was short, and short in places where she was long, and fat in places where she was thin, and thin in places where she was fat. Still, it would have to do; Emma removed her clothes and took stock. At least she was still in her physical prime, just twenty-one years of age, and while she looked tired, her complexion had, for the most part, survived the ravages of the Lower East Side. She also had blond hair and blue eyes (and how *was* it that she, a Jewish girl from the Pale, ever acquired her colouring? How, when everyone else in her family had black hair, dark eyes and the skin tone of an Andalusian farmer?) The real problem, Emma thought, was her midsection: she was shaped like one of those wooden toys for children, the ones so weighted in the centre that they pop up every time the child pushes them over. There was no denying it—if she was to snare a customer or two, she'd have to wear a corset, and elongate her legs with heels. While she had a dress she could wear, she still needed evening shoes and decent underwear. Fortunately, she happened to own an old white-linen cloth, trimmed with embroidery, that she no longer used, having spilled food on it during some all-night vodka klatch. With a pair of scissors and a little ingenuity, she quickly fashioned an unstained portion of the material into a pair of undergarments that, she hoped, might pass in low light. As for the shoes and the corset, there were stores on Houston Street that sold such items at an attractive price, as long as you were willing to sort through the massive bins that the store owners set out on the sidewalks.

It was a short walk from Fifth Street. She fought off elbows belonging to aggressive *babushkas*, all of whom seemed to be on the hunt for a bargain that day; before the hour was out, she'd found the items she needed. Back in the apartment, she dressed in her uniform and, once again, regarded herself in the mirror. This time, she saw an imposter. *Good*, she thought, *that's what I want, I want to be someone completely different.* She pinched her cheeks and smeared herself with a cheap lipstick that smelled like candle wax.

It was a beautiful Saturday night. She walked up to Fourteenth Street, where the litter-strewn blocks stretching east from First Avenue served as an open-air workplace for desperate women— some opium addicts, some single mothers, some under the thumbs of alcoholic husbands, some needing medicine for ailing parents, some addicted to the twin intoxicants of danger and money, and some, for reasons too varied to consider, having chosen to give up not only on themselves, but on life altogether. Meanwhile, Fourteenth Street west of First Avenue was a picture of gentility and upper class majesty; it was a case, Emma thought, of the market situating itself next to the marketplace.

She tottered up and down, feeling sick to her stomach. So many of the women were thin, with bloodshot eyes and skin rendered pallid with anemia—a draft of laudanum would've bolstered her courage as well. Still, she strolled, she rotated her hips, she cast come-hither glances at passing gentlemen. And then, there he was, strolling toward her, a businessman with mutton chops and a bowler hat, a walking stick in hand, one thing and one thing only on his mind, yet when he lifted his hat to greet her, she frowned and scurried past him. For a minute or so she secreted herself in an alcove, telling herself not to worry, she was new at this, it was bound to happen, just a minor attack of nerves, she would engage with the next one. She stepped back out on the street just in time to see the bowler-hat man leave with another young woman on his arm, this one thin and chatty and waving her narrow hands in the air as she talked.

Emma resumed her prowling, soon catching the attention of a ginger-haired burgher in spats. Really, she thought, she'd never seen anyone so orange—his freckles were orange, his eyelashes were orange, his skin tone was orange, even his lips were so light as to create the impression that they, too, were orange. He smiled at her. She knew she was supposed to grin back, flutter her eyes and lean suggestively forward, so as to narrow the distance between them, her voice soft and suggestive when she said something along the lines of *how 'bout a bit of company this evening, sir?* Yet she didn't. She suddenly felt dizzy and nauseated, and acutely aware of the touch of her feet against the pavement. She scowled at the man and moved around him, as though he'd committed some unpardonable offence (which, she couldn't help thinking, he had).

This became a pattern. Every time a man indicated interest, she'd make eye contact, smile like a coquette, and then scurry away, at which point she'd take a breath, berate herself, and try again. Soon, this process—seduction, attraction, withdrawal... seduction, attraction, withdrawal—started to feel like something immutable, like something that she, herself, could not control. It was eleven in the evening; already, she was tearful and exhausted. She would go with the next man who approached her. That was all there was to it—he could be a fiend or a friar, a brute or a barrister, she didn't care. She wandered close to Fourth Avenue, where she stopped and loitered suggestively next to an edifice that, during daylight hours, served as a bank. Here, a handsome older man with a white beard and a topcoat came toward her. Funny, he didn't have that look of conquering intent in his eyes that the others did; for a moment, she thought he might just be in need of directions. She commanded her feet to remain planted, and managed a weak, cautious grin.

"Good evening," he said.

"Hello."

"Would you care to have a drink?"

She nodded and followed him, not to one of the seedy hotels encircling Washington Square Park, where rooms could be rented by the hour, no questions asked and no answers expected, but to a posh restaurant in the direction of Union Square. Was this common? A client wishing for a beverage before engaging in carnality? Also, would she be expected to pay for her own? She didn't know; she hated her own ignorance. They took a seat. The man wasn't smiling. Again, there was none of that lustful entitlement written across his features. Emma ordered a Pilsner, the man asking for a glass of something with a French name, which the waiter seemed to understand, as he nodded his head and said, "Of course, sir, right away, sir."

Meanwhile, the man was scanning her—face, body, hair—and she found herself almost looking forward to the moment in which he turned vulgar, for at least that would be behaviour she understood. Instead, he leaned forward and said, "You're new to this business, aren't you?"

She blinked. What should she say? If she denied it, he probably wouldn't believe her. He might have even chosen her simply because he wanted a novice, in the same way that some men are aroused by the despoiling of innocence. "Yes," she said. "How did you know?"

"I was watching you. I saw the look of distress every time a potential customer approached you. I saw how you practically fled, each time."

"Oh."

"I assume it is some matter of economic necessity that took you to Fourteenth Street."

"Yes, you see..." and she was about to make up a story, some malarkey about a dead husband and hungry children at home, when the man lifted his hand and stopped her.

"I don't need to know your reasons. I'm sure they're tragic. Everyone has tragedy in their lives. I happen to as well. My point is: you haven't the aptitude for this line of work, and that's all there is to it. Here." He reached into the inside pocket of his coat, and pulled out a wallet. He extracted a ten-dollar bill and put it on the surface of the table. "Take this and go home."

She looked at the money, and she looked at the man's face. He seemed annoyed.

"Why would you give me this?"

"Your dress is worn, and it doesn't go with your cheap shoes and stockings. Also, the brooch you're wearing is tawdry. Plus, I hate having to see fear. It's unbecoming. It makes me hate myself for the things I do. We are all born into loneliness, you know. Don't ever make the mistake of thinking you're the only one. Good evening to you."

He stood and left, though not before settling the bill with the waiter. Emma now sat before a glass of beer and the man's untouched wine. She drank the beer (as well as the wine) and went home feeling as though, in some small and indefinable way, she'd still been violated.

The next morning, she awoke feeling as she often did, that the job she had given herself—to replace the old world with a better one—was too difficult, not just for her but for anyone, and the day in which she admitted this to herself would be the day in which she was finally free. She had ten dollars, it was true, though ten dollars would likely not be enough. A stiffness invaded her body. Her arms, legs, trunk—they all felt weighted, as if filled by sand. There was no question: this would be a day spent in bed, a day that might turn into a week of headaches, of burning sadness, of cramps and joint pain and dizziness every time she stood. She closed her eyes and tried to sleep. She awoke, and made black Russian tea, just as her mother had done whenever Emma was sick as a child. At ten o'clock, she received a letter from her sister in Rochester. Inside was a note saying, *Emma. I know your birthday is coming up, so I wanted to send you a little something. Be happy! Your loving sister, Helena.* Accompanying the letter were a ten-dollar bill and a five-dollar bill. Emma couldn't believe it; it was as though the universe had been listening, and had staged an immediate rescue.

She kept five dollars to live on, and wired the rest to Sasha.

* * *

Sasha now had a location, financial backing, and a plan that grew more distinct on a night in which he accidentally cut the top of his hand while struggling with a tin of sardines in Nold's dimly lit kitchen. The wound healed quickly, spawning both a scab and a moment of inspiration: Sasha would become "Simon Bachman," head of the brand new "Bachman Employment Agency," an operation that provided workers, be they permanent or temporary, to employers who, through no fault of their own, had found themselves faced with sudden labour stoppages.

He then went to a clothier and, with the help of a salesman whose behaviour bordered on the unctuous, selected a staid grey suit with narrow stripes, a white shirt and a necktie. "You look very handsome," the clothier said while squaring the suit on his customer's shoulders. Sasha stared at himself in the full-length mirror. While this was something he normally would have abhorred, as he suffered from a profound aversion to his own appearance, on this occasion it didn't, for he wasn't looking at Alexander Berkman, but at the employment agent Simon Bachman, and who cared if Bachman had rotund lips, and large ears, and a widow's peak?

Sasha even practised smiling—he suspected that an amoral profiteer like Bachman would do so readily, and easily.

"Ahhhh," said the salesman, "I can see you're pleased."

"I am," said Sasha, for there they were, a pair of dimples bookending his smile. While Emma had always told him that he was handsome, that his was a sort of rugged attractiveness, he'd never believed her. And yet, staring at this new person, this Simon Bachman, Sasha was visited with the feeling that maybe, just maybe, he wasn't as homely a man as he'd always considered himself to be. "Thank you," he said. "This will do just fine."

He walked out with a Kaufmann Brothers box tucked beneath his arm, confident that the last piece of the puzzle would be fitted when he met with Metzkow in his filthy room. This happened the next day, Metzkow greeting Sasha at the door. Sasha's nostrils filled with the reek of tomato soup and unwashed sheets. Waiting in the room was a large, bald-headed man with a beard.

"Berkman," said Metzkow.

"Metzkow."

"I haven't done those business cards yet. But I'll get to them soon. I've been busy. I'm a busy son-of-a-bitch."

"All right."

"But don't worry, they'll be done soon. This is Tekin, by the way."

The man nodded and said nothing. Next to the window was a wide, narrow table. Here, Tekin had arranged a collection of handguns. He pointed them out, one by one, speaking in a strangely accented English. "This, Colt 45. This one, Beretta. This one, Smith & Wesson. This one, Luger."

Sasha's mouth went dry; seeing the guns, laid out like a collection of bread knives, made his *attentat* seem so close. He took a moment to curse his genteel upbringing, for without it, this would've all been so much easier. Meanwhile, Tekin looked impatient. "Which one you wanting, then?"

Sasha told him how much money he'd put aside for a weapon.

"Hmmmm," he said. "Is not a lot." He pointed a fat finger at the smallest pistol on the table. "In that case, maybe this one."

"What is it?"

He picked it up: ".38 calibre, snub-nose, made in Britain, we calling it 'Bull Dog' special. Is very interesting. Look..."

He made a snapping motion with his hand, which caused the cylinder to fall away from the body of the pistol.

"It take five bullets. Very unusual."

"It is?"

"Yes. The gun is small. Very... uh... simple to conceal. Perhaps what you needing. You want?"

That night, Sasha and Nold visited a deserted stockyard near a lonely turn in the river. They had a lantern and some tin cans. A little way off in the distance, there were abandoned, wood-sided warehouses; many of the planks had rotted and fallen away, giving the buildings the look of a child with missing teeth. Closer to the riverbank, they found an old tree with a branch that extended sideways at more or less the height of an average man's chest. They lined up the cans. Sasha took eight or nine steps backward, thinking that this would be the distance separating himself from Frick when he opened fire.

"Do you know what you're doing?" Nold asked.

"I don't."

"I wish I could help."

"I wish you could too."

"The only thing I know is you're supposed to aim with both eyes open."

"Really?"

"Yes. I'm pretty sure I heard that somewhere."

Sasha took aim and squeezed the trigger. There was a retort and the smell of gunpowder, the gun propelling from his hand and landing in the dirt. He shook away the pain in his wrist.

"Maybe use two hands."

This time the gun stayed in Sasha's grip, though he came no closer to hitting the target, the bullet pinging off one of the stockyard walls.

"Sasha," Nold said. "How much did you pay for this gun?"

"Not a lot."

"Wait... you didn't buy it from that friend of Metzkow's, did you?"

"Yes."

"That rat bastard Tekin?"

"Yes, that's the one."

"Oh for the love of... I can't believe Metzkow let you buy a pistol from that thief. He's not even a real anarchist. He'll sell a gun to anybody and that includes fascists. Damn it! I'm going to talk to Metzkow, that old buzzard. He's quickly outgrowing his usefulness. I can tell you this, Sasha. I'm mighty steamed." He nodded his head in a gesture of aggravation. "Now, try aiming beneath the target."

Sasha aimed and fired. Again there was that distant ping.

"Okay, okay, now try shooting *above* the target."

One of the cans went down. Sasha whooped and Nold said, "Well there you *go*."

The next time Sasha fired, he missed again. He reloaded and squeezed the trigger, again aiming just above his target, the can spinning in the air before landing in a puff of dirt. While he reloaded, Nold reset the fallen cans; they were crumpled, with small apertures allowing the passage of moonlight. Sasha fired a few more times and, though he mostly hit what he was trying to hit, there were times when he did not. Dispirited, he handed the pistol to Nold, and advised how high he should aim. Nold missed a few times, and then found his range, whooping with glee when his targets started to fall. He handed the gun back to Sasha and said, with a wink, "Enough fooling around, *you're* the one who needs good aim." Sasha nodded and took aim and knocked down several more, Nold resetting the targets and Sasha firing again, and again, until the box of ammunition was empty, and his right wrist was in agony, and he was beset by a feeling of helpless inevitability.

eighteen

HE STARTED HIS DAY by dressing in his new suit and looking in the mirror, thinking, *yes, yes, I am that man, I'm Bachman through and through, just look at me now!* He drank coffee and smoked cigarettes, just as he always did, though he refused Nold's offer of breakfast, his stomach too afflicted with nerves. When he was done his coffee, he stood and donned his new hat and tucked his pistol into the waistband of his trousers, such that he could feel the handle protruding into his lower back. In the jacket's breast pocket, he carried a sharpened file set into a wooden handle, a rudimentary knife that he'd constructed back in New York, during the days when he was walking Emma home from her speaking engagements late at night and reasoned he might need some sort of protection. In one of the trouser pockets he put a dozen or so business cards, acquired just the day before from old Metzkow.

In downtown Allegheny, he boarded a carriage. A half hour later, he arrived at the Chronicle Telegraph building in downtown Pittsburgh. The fifth-floor receptionist was a young woman; she wore a light blouse and red lipstick and, as Sasha looked at her, he wondered if she might be that last beautiful person he would ever see.

"May I help you?"

"Yes. I'm here to see Mr. Frick."

"And you have an appointment?"

"I do."

"Mr. Frick's office is on the second floor, actually."

"Wonderful, thank you so much."

He tromped down, conscious of his pounding heart and the weapons on his person, and entered the appropriate office; here, he encountered a young male attendant who wore a moustache so thin that it looked like a line of gunpowder.

"May I help you?"

"I'm here to see Mr. Frick."

"And you are?"

"My name is Mr. Bachman. Simon Bachman. I'm with the Bachman Employment Agency. Actually, I'm head of the Bachman Employment Agency."

Sasha handed the man a business card.

"When is your appointment?"

"I don't have an appointment, per se, but I was speaking with Mr. Frick last week about his, er, employment needs at the Homestead plant—in light of everything that's going on down there—and he told me he'd very much like to speak with me, and that if I was in the neighbourhood I should drop in. Our headquarters are in Philadelphia, you see, but this morning I found myself here, in Pittsburgh, making calls to various other companies, and I figured I'd make good on my promise. I called earlier. A young woman said it would be fine if I came by."

"A young woman?" he asked, eyebrows lifted.

"Yes."

"What was her name?"

"I don't know. She told me, but I've had a very busy morning, and I can't say that I remember. She's up on the fifth floor, I believe."

"Caroline?"

"Yes, that's it."

"Well, I'm sorry. Mr. Frick is very busy, and he can't see you this morning. You'll just have to come back."

"I see."

"Perhaps some other time?"

"It's just that, well, with the head office in another city... you understand."

"Yes sir, I do understand, but Mr. Frick is just swamped this morning. It's a very busy time."

"I understand that but... are you sure he couldn't spare just five minutes?"

"I'm quite sure."

Sasha smiled, and remained rooted, unsure what to do next.

"Sir? Was there something else?"

*　*　*

He returned home, startling Nold. "Sasha! Either you're a ghost, or Frick still walks amongst us."

"I was turned away."

"What... you mean you just walked in and asked to speak to Frick?"

"Yes."

"Well no wonder you were turned away. Fat cats like Frick won't see people who've just drifted in from the street. He's an important man, Sasha. You're going to have to think of something better."

Sasha spent a long, anxious day succumbing to his own worst habits; under such circumstances, when his nerves could have used a vacation, he drank more coffee and smoked more cigarettes than ever, rendering him in such an excitable state that he could neither eat a decent amount of supper, just a few bites of rump roast and a jigger or two of vodka, nor sleep in a way that was at all restorative. The hours until morning passed slowly. He spent the following day recuperating, planning, honing his pitch, and gauging his manner in a mirror—hands just so, chin parallel to the floor, his movements infected by an ingrained smarminess.

The next morning, he awoke feeling no less jagged. He dressed and bid Nold goodbye for the second time, Nold again clapping his shoulders and saying, "Let's not make a habit of this, all right?" They walked together to the carriage stop. This time, Nold hugged him, and said, somewhat tearfully, "It'll happen this time. I know it, my friend. Your date with destiny. It's here, comrade."

Sasha nodded, a little saddened himself, for he was not a man who had had any male friendships in his life—Modska didn't count, given he was a relative—and as he climbed on board he had to wonder why. A lack of confidence, perhaps? His tendency toward the pedantic? A belief that he was not worthy? A certain distasteful pugnaciousness? If so, where had these notions come from, exactly? Who had given him this idea that he was unlovable, an idea that Emma, bless her, had worked so hard to counteract? His head whirled with thoughts, with regrets, with promises to be a different man when his spirit, having passed to the other side, was granted life again.

He walked from the carriage stop to Frick's building. Again, he encountered the sycophantic attendant. Again, he was told that Frick was too busy to see anyone without an appointment. This time, Sasha responded with testiness.

"I'm *sure* that Mr. Frick would like to see me."

"And I'm sure that he cannot. He's a very busy man. Again, I can only suggest you come back at a more propitious time."

"And when might that be?"

The man looked down at an opened agenda book, and ran a finger up and down the page.

"All right," he said. "The day after tomorrow, just before lunchtime. Say... eleven o'clock? Mr. Frick might have a few minutes, though I can't guarantee anything."

Sasha turned and left. He walked, block after block, unsure as to where he was headed, smoking cigarette after cigarette, his head spinning, his fingertips tingling, his mind bothered with the belief that everything around him—the sidewalk, the buildings, the people—was nothing but mirages, with something sinister lurking beneath. After a time, he passed a small hotel called the Mercantile. Impulsively, he walked in. The clerk wore a bellboy's cap.

"Could I have a room, please?"

"For how many nights, sir?"

"Two, please."

"Of course, sir," he said, handing Sasha the ledger.

He signed his name as "Rakhmetov," the hero of Chernyshevsky's *What Is To Be Done?* Were Emma here, she'd surely be amused. The clerk gave Sasha a key and directed him to the third floor. He entered the room and thought *This will be the last place I sleep on earth*: there was a bed, a chair, a dresser, and a small table against one wall. He wished it were more monumental, somehow. He sat on the bed and it squeaked beneath him. The window overlooked a rear laneway. He opened it and disturbed a pigeon, which had been roosting on the ledge of a building across the way. It fluttered skyward, dropping feathers as it flapped.

Sasha lay on the bed and stared upward, a black ceramic ashtray on his chest. His mind went blank. It'd been a long day and he fell asleep, awakening shortly after dawn. Having missed dinner the night before, he was hungry; thankfully, he was able to find a cheap eatery that opened early to accommodate workers with morning shifts. It was called the Maple View, its name spelled out in bright lettering over a long, thin, white-brick building. There was a counter spanning the length of the restaurant, and a row of tables for two stretching along the window. Sasha sat at the counter and treated himself to his favourite meal, the meal he was eating when he'd met Emma, in fact, steak and fried potatoes and gravy. There was a portion of a newspaper on the stool beside him. He picked it up and started reading—the news was all Frick and Homestead, Homestead and Frick, and he soon discovered that yesterday, at the very time in which Frick's pompous attendant was turning him away, Frick had been in his office, telling a reporter that he meant to rid his workforce of any so-called "radical elements," meaning that he'd be looking into the affiliations and pastimes of any man or woman who worked for him, and that any of the "wrong sort" would be quickly dealt with. While this would normally have enraged Sasha, he couldn't help but feel pleased, as the news made him glad, once again, of the destiny that had been revealed to him.

He spent the whole day walking around Pittsburgh, its factories and workhouses all tucked into a wide, arcing bend of the Allegheny River. Everything he saw on his perambulations felt important, somehow. He saw a robin feeding worms to its family, a quartet of beaks pointed upward while the chicks madly peeped. On any other day, he wouldn't have noticed, but on *this* day, he was moved by the knowledge that this would likely be the last time he'd ever see a mother robin feed her chicks: he stood and watched, the scene having an almost mythical flavour. Everything had a similar effect, that day: every child skipping rope, every shop owner sweeping his stoop, every woman adjusting her hair, every horse stopping to accept an apple from its owner—all of it, every moment, contained some vast, even cosmic, significance. With so little time, he commanded himself to think—to really *think*—about each cigarette he smoked, that rasp of smoke against the throat, that glorious taste filling his mouth, that sudden awakening of the mind and spirit and his sense of what was and was not possible. And coffee! How magnificent was this hot and dark velvet beverage! He kept stopping for a cup at small battered cafés filled with unemployed men, all of whom were finding a way to fill their day; as he sipped, he eavesdropped on the conversations occurring at the tables surrounding him. They were all laments—no jobs, no money, the wife bitter, the kids looking rough, oh for the days when the steel plants were just crying out for good people. As he listened, he struggled against the impulse to lean over and say, *psssst, listen, don't worry, everything will change, this I can promise, oh yeah, mark my god damn words.*

His eyes kept welling with tears. He saw a group of children, happily playing in a schoolyard, and he began to wonder whether he should postpone the *attentat*, so as to concoct a strategy in which he could both murder Frick *and* escape with his life and liberty intact, so that he might one day have children of his own. This impulse confused him: he had never liked children, had always found them brattish and loud, yet now it seemed that he adored them. Again, it was that life-preserving impulse, trying to cheat him out of his martyrdom. Everything moved him, that day—dogs barking, Italian men selling fresh bread, the listless motion of clouds, birdsong. All of it wondrous, all of it sublime, all of it of-this-world and of-this-world only. He was sitting on a park bench when he saw a young woman, a little ways away; she was short, glorious in the hips, with that cannonball manner of walking. His heart thumped— Emma, my Emma, what are you doing here? Did you follow me? Just to say a final goodbye? Is that it? He jumped up and hustled toward her, only to find that it wasn't his sailor girl at all, it was just a young woman walking through a park; at close range, she didn't even look that much like Emma. She asked if she could help him.

"No, no," he said. "I'm sorry. I mistook you for someone else."

She nodded and went on her way. He sat back down, tears in his eyes. It was a beautiful day, damn it. He lit yet another cigarette, tossed his head back, and let the sun warm his face. Imagine—a state of nonbeing, in which you could not experience warmth, in which you could not feel the wooden slats of a bench upon your body, in which you couldn't be charmed by a lovely young woman who happened to look a little like someone you love. He couldn't help it. His mind was a cauldron. Picturing nothingness... no, no, the *impossibility* of picturing nothingness... was causing it to boil. He walked some more, and finally succumbed to hunger: yes, another steak, his favourite meal, this one served with peas and carrots in a steamy, sawdust-floored café. He chewed with misgiving; he should've ordered something he didn't like, maybe kidneys or mutton, if only to make it all a little easier. He left with a full stomach. He could've gladly eaten more. It was one of those hot summer nights on which he could smell the plants and flowers communicating with one another, their secretions smelling like sexual desire. He even thought about acquiring the company of a courtesan—one last fuck, how this thought enticed him—though he was pretty sure he didn't have the money for such a pleasure. What did buying a woman cost in Pittsburgh? What did it cost in New York, for that matter? He decided against it, aware that purchasing sex would've made him the biggest hypocrite on earth, for wasn't he giving up his life to put an end to the sort of social conditions that forced impoverished women to sell their bodies?

He kept walking. His legs were starting to hurt. The streets were busy. Would he miss humanity? Would he miss the workings of a society? There it was, popping up again, the human inability to comprehend oblivion. It made sense, really, for the only thing he had ever understood—ever truly and irrevocably *known*—was that he had this thing called existence. He took a breath. Again, he felt tearful. To have nothing at all: in a way, it would be an act of purification, a freeing-of-himself from the need to possess, even if that possession was this maddening frenzy called life. This thought—that his *attentat* would be the highest expression of anarchism—gladdened him, slightly, and spawned a few moments of cheerful thinking. Yes, killing Frick would spawn the revolution necessary for the fair advancement of mankind. But maybe, just maybe, it would also be a gift to himself, a blow against the relentlessness of this chore called living.

He went back to the hotel and crawled into bed. He lay awake for some time, his heart speeding, anxious colours forming behind his eyelids, and when he did sleep it was in fleeting bursts. In these brief, disturbed interludes, Sasha Berkman suffered violent nightmares, in which he was shooting people who were close to him—his father, Modska, Emma—and each time he'd awaken with damp skin, along with a feeling that the heat of the room was unbearable. To calm himself, he'd light a cigarette. The curtains on the windows were far nicer than he was accustomed to, and they blocked out the street lamps so convincingly that, upon striking the match, the darkness of the room seemed to explode. After a few inhalations, he'd extinguish the cigarette, the cycle now repeating itself: lengthy wakefulness, fragmented sleep, apocalyptic visions, sudden awakening. In the last dream he had that night, a nightmare in which he literally shot himself, he bolted straight up in bed, hyperventilating. To calm down, he told himself that it was all a dream, only to suffer the sickening realization that it wasn't at all—it was a portent of what he'd do to himself in a scant few hours. To bolster his courage, he thought of other men who'd given away their lives for the sake of the revolution, key among them Louis Lingg, who'd chewed an explosive capsule rather than face charges for his role in the Haymarket riot. In so doing, he became a hero of the movement, a name that would never be forgotten, a hero for all of eternity. Perhaps Sasha would become the next Lingg? Was this really so far-fetched? He thought of Nikolai Rysakov, who had assassinated Tsar Alexander, even though the act resulted in a date with the gallows. Was it worth it? Both would have died one day anyway. Yet in choosing to die in the name of revolution, they had become legends. This, he promised himself in that clammy hotel room, would happen to him as well.

* * *

He was eating a cold bun in his room when the sun finally came up, a giant yellow eye gazing down from above. He purchased coffee from a vendor on the street. He was a small Italian man, and he wouldn't let his customers drift away from the cart for fear that he'd lose the cheap porcelain mugs he used. *Hey you*, he kept yelling at his customers, *you-a-come-back, and you, you, you-a-come-back-here-too.*

Sasha stood in a small clump of coffee drinkers, watching the street come alive. When he was finished, he dutifully returned his mug and went back to his room. He bathed, shaved his face, dressed in his grey pinstriped suit, and reached under the bed to retrieve his weapons. For some reason, he took a last look at himself in the mirror, thinking that the significance of his mission had actually changed his appearance slightly, for who wouldn't want to be handsome, really handsome, like Louis Lingg or Modska Aronstam or his brave and adventurous uncle Maxim, even? As he walked to the Chronicle Telegraph building, a curious thing happened. His anxiety, his drenching thoughts, his lifelong self-contempt—they all disappeared. In their place came a sepulchral calm. If he had any emotion at all during that walk, it was a weak, pulsing pride, and he commended himself for arriving at this place of cold rationality, as he believed that this was the only state of mind from which a revolution could spring. Oh yes, he now knew it to be true, he knew it as well as he'd ever known anything, he would go to Henry Frick's office, he would be granted his appointment, he would kill the viper and then turn the gun on himself, thereby avoiding the indignities of incarceration, unfair trial and execution. This was all that he knew. It felt wonderful, this clarity. Had you asked him his real name, he would have required a moment's thought to summon it, for his identity had changed once more—he was a dead man, out to wreak havoc; he was a crazed man, thirsting for chaos; he was a nameless man, bound for glory.

He found Frick's sycophant. "Hello," Sasha said. "I've come for my appointment."

"Your name?"

"Simon Bachman."

"Hmmmmmm."

"I came here two days ago, and a day before that."

"Oh yes... you're with the employment agency."

"That's right."

"Do you have an appointment?"

"Yes. You gave me one."

"Hmmmmmm, that's strange. I don't have you down... I'm afraid Mr. Frick won't be able to see you today."

"He won't?"

"Oh! Now I remember! I told you that if Mr. Frick had some time he *might* be able to see you today. But he's no longer in the building. He's out for an early lunch."

Sasha appraised, coolly. He'd been a fool not to see it earlier—this little pissant's sole function was to ensure that Frick was never bothered by the real world. "I understand," he said.

This equanimity disarmed the creep. He went fumbling for his ledger. "At this point, he's got a bit of time on Tuesday. Perhaps if you..."

"No, thank you," Sasha said with a gracious smile. "I have many other sales meetings to take. Please extend my regret that I could not meet the good man, and should he ever have any employment needs that are not being satisfied, well... you have my card."

"Yes, of course, I do have your card here somewhere."

"Thank you. Please, enjoy the rest of your day."

* * *

He exited the building and, for the longest time, stared at the second floor, trying to decide which window was Frick's. Was it that one? No... that one... or maybe *that* one. At the same time, he concocted alternative ruses to get inside his office. Perhaps he could acquire the clothing of an office cleaner and gain entry that way? This would be unfruitful: he suspected that the cleaning staff came in after hours, when nobody was around. Perhaps he could pretend to be an exterminator, sent by the building's owners to examine each room for vermin? Then he remembered that Frick's man-Friday knew what he looked like; he'd have to grow a moustache, remove his glasses, buy a different hat. All of this would take time. As he stood there, thoughts churning, Sasha was forced to confront a nauseating truth: his employment-agency ruse had ruined Frick's office as a place of attack, the cold truth being that he was known there now. Given that Frick's house was heavily guarded, the only place to get him would be between the two places. Sasha's heart sank; this meant more planning, more delays, more torment. It would also mean more money to live on, which he didn't have, having timed the attack down to his last dollar.

But there! There he was! Frick! The man himself! Sasha could scarcely believe his good fortune, his target stepping out of an actual, chauffeur-driven motor car. Frick strode toward his place of employment and entered. Sasha, in turn, ran toward the building, which he'd visited enough times to know that there were stairs at the rear. He took them two at a time, and reached the second floor just as Frick stepped out of the elevator. He was now two feet from the man. Had he had his wits about him, he could have fired at him right then and there, in the middle of a populated foyer, yet by the time he found the handle of his pistol, the time had passed, and Frick had entered his office.

Sasha approached the attendant and said, "Oh, hello, I realized I had some further business in the building, and I couldn't help but notice that Mr. Frick has just entered his office. If it was convenient, might I now have the quickest of words with the good man?"

"Perhaps..."

"Really, it would only take a moment, and I would be most grateful."

"You know what? Let me see."

The employee stood and walked into Frick's office, presumably to inform the boss that a fellow with one of the city's employment agencies wished to have a word *and while I normally wouldn't bother you, sir, he's been here three times, and he really has been most patient.* He walked back out. "Mr. Frick will see you now. Though I caution you, he has five minutes at the most."

"That will be most sufficient."

Sasha walked into the office of the industrialist Henry C. Frick. No—he strode into the office, for as he crossed the threshold, a rippling of energy passed through his body, the likes of which he had never known, his eyes narrowing, his skin flushed, his nostrils flared, handsome with determination, he was Rakhmetov and Lingg and Rysakov, all come to life in the skin of one man, oh yes the power welling up from within felt electric and regal and pure. Frick was seated on a floral-print sofa. Across from him was some wide-shouldered toady in a business suit and brogues. They looked up. "What is the meaning..." said Frick's associate, his voice drifting away when Sasha smiled and extracted the Bull Dog. Frick and his associate both leapt up, intending to charge, at which point Sasha took aim and fired, his gun hand steady, both eyes open, his aim sincere, and if it wasn't for the poor quality of the firearm, he would have plugged Frick in the middle of his forehead. Instead, the bullet grazed Frick's ear. The target dropped to his knees, holding the left side of his head, his mouth cratered with surprise. The other man charged and leapt upon Sasha's back. With his full weight upon him, Sasha roared and fired again, the bullet striking Frick's left shoulder. Sasha was preparing to issue a third shot when the other man reached from behind and lifted Sasha's hand. The shot hit the ceiling. Plaster rained. Sasha threw off the toady, though as soon as the man landed he jumped to his feet and charged again, hitting his target low and hard, Sasha striking the back of the man's head with the handle of his useless pistol, by which time a wounded Frick jumped upon the two of them, so that Sasha was now writhing and kicking under the weight of two men. He dropped the pistol and the damn thing fired of its own volition, the bullet pinging off a floorboard somewhere. He shouted, he roared, he worked an arm free so that he could retrieve his knife and start stabbing, the blade catching Frick in the hip, in the lower back, in the thigh. The target cried out, over and over; to Sasha this was music, like a symphony. A carpenter who was working in the building heard the ruckus and rushed in and, upon seeing the melee, struck Sasha in the head with a hammer. Sasha's vision spun but still he struggled, in fact he'd never felt more alive, the pain in his head felt majestic, and as he fought the three of them—fists landing, an elbow catching someone's nose, blood everywhere—he was soon mobbed by clerks, workmen, security guards; even Frick's supercilious attendant rushed in and slapped Sasha with an open hand. How wondrous it all felt! How ecstatic was this moment! Someone kicked him in the mouth, removing a tooth or two. A shoe met his nose, and now there was *his* blood, flowing out of him. Yet another lackey dropped hard upon him, a bent elbow smashing his ear, such that all the yelling in the office receded. All he could hear now was a high-frequency whine. He laughed as he fought back. "Do your worst!" he screamed as he kicked at the amorphous blob of arms and legs and torsos above him, all of which had no effect, so he protected his head with those big meaty hands that Emma had always loved so much, hands that had rubbed and touched and caressed every part of her body, and he made himself a hard and determined ball, a ball made of spit and iron, of hard will and liberated spirit, Sasha savouring every kick, every wonderful punch, every glorious and intractable blow.

nineteen

HIS FIRST STINT IN SOLITARY occurs just a few weeks after his conviction, when a blade is found on his person. A few months after, there's a fight in the hosiery shop, in which Sasha defends his lover, a young man named Johnny Davis, from a Wallachian goon with a flattened nose and a barbarous odour. The warden is a little confused about who started it, so he gives all three parties a week in the hole, which isn't so bad, since Berkman and Davis spend the time chatting via the plumbing leading to their respective privies.

Another year in, Sasha is caught producing an anarchist journal called *Prison Blossoms*, the paper smuggled from one of the shops: two weeks, this time, nothing to sneeze at. Sasha finds his spirit weakening, and his body losing a little of its elemental strength. (He is also grieving for Johnny Davis, who died a few months earlier from a case of meningitis that would have been easily treated outside of the prison.) Some years later, when a lunatic named Leon Czolgosz shoots and murders President McKinley, Sasha is sent down for a full month, along with every other anarchist, communist, socialist, libertarian and rabble-rouser who happens to reside there, it being the warden's feeling that, despite the fact that they all have the most rock-solid of alibis, they must somehow be guilty by association. Sasha emerges shaky and underweight, though he's still wilful enough to testify against the warden in an inquiry into prison corruption. The warden is pardoned, a natural consequence of police policing police—Emma speaks about this in her lectures, which she now gives all over North America and, yes, Europe. Sasha gets two months; he emerges trembling, with a tenuous grip on what is and isn't real.

Yet there *is* movement afoot on the outside, all of it courtesy of his sailor girl, who has caught wind of Sasha's failing constitution, and has concluded that something needs to be done—it's Emma who raises money via an organization she calls the Alexander Berkman Relief Fund; it's Emma who rents a house directly across the street from the Western Penitentiary of Pennsylvania; it's Emma who hires a pair of like-minded revolutionaries to dig a tunnel, a conveyance that will, with any luck, afford the prisoner his freedom. Unfortunately, the diggers surface under several tons of building materials, recently deposited in the prison yard to aid in a restoration project. A month later, the tunnel is discovered. Though the warden has no direct evidence, he concludes that it must be the anarchist community, trying to liberate Berkman: a full year in solitary, then. They take Berkman's glasses. They put him on a restricted diet. They fill his privy bowl, robbing him of any connection with others. Slowly, he becomes mad, Sasha Berkman learning that, when deprived of sensory stimulation and adequate nourishment, the mind becomes a kaleidoscope. He sees the countryside around his boyhood home, with its blue skies, tall green cedars and tawny wheat fields, shimmying in the breeze. He rubs his hands, for he knows what's next, Fifth Avenue, with its shops and lights and people people people, all dressed in Saturday-night finery. Other times, he hears music, trumpeting her arrival, Tchaikovsky or Mussorgsky or Handel, even. He can barely contain himself! He trembles and his mind dances and then she's there, radiant in the motionless air—his love, his Emma, his beautiful and world-famous sailor girl, dressed in low heels and a snug satin slip, her blond hair loosened, grinning mischievously, her voice a desiring husk: "Well, what are you waiting for fishie? You know how unhealthy it is to suppress physical desire..." So he yowls and leaps up, hands risen, a free man, rushing toward her, and it really is her, it's her flesh and her scent and her brazenly sexual aura, as if delivered by angels.

When guards finally descend to solitary to release him, they find him on the floor, rolled into a ball, hugging his knees as though they were a person and grinning. "She was just here," he says. "Did you see? Did you see her? Emma? My God she's beautiful."

Two weeks later, they put a broom in Sasha's hand, and he spends the rest of his sentence shambling across his assigned range, an old man in his thirties, tortured by his failures, though on days when he's at his worst, he returns to his cell and there she is, waiting for him, the other half of his being, a spectre humming, "Fishie, don't worry, you'll see, it'll all be over soon, this is nothing, a few brief moments, wrestled away from eternity, don't you worry, now kiss me you sad, mad bastard."

* * *

One afternoon, a little less than fifteen years into his twenty-two-year sentence, a guard tells Sasha that the warden wishes to see him. Sasha nods, and he follows the man to the administrative wing. Even though Sasha has a broom, which he could easily brandish as a weapon, the guard, a decent sort named Johnson, feels comfortable turning his back on the prisoner. He unlocks door after door until they reach a part of the institution that looks less like a prison and more like an office building. They proceed down a hallway, Johnson knocking at the door of the warden's office. A voice beckons them and they step inside. The new warden is at his desk, working away, his head low, the surface of his desk lit by lamplight.

"Berkman?"

"Yes sir."

"Your sentence is being commuted. Do you know what this means?"

"No sir."

"The state has decided to give prisoners time off for good behaviour. Since you've toed the line for the last five years or so, you'll be getting out shortly. Congratulations."

"Thank you, sir."

"Don't thank me. I think it's a mistake, what with your kind running wild in the streets. You're getting out because the place is getting too crowded, pure and simple. Plus, some review board deemed that you're no longer a threat to society. Judging by the look of you, I'd say they're right."

Johnson takes Sasha's arm and says, "Let's go." Sasha takes a step or two before turning back toward the warden. "When will this happen, sir?"

"You'll know soon enough."

That evening, Sasha writes Emma at the most recent address he has for her and informs her that he'll soon be a free man. He also writes Carl Nold, who is now married and living in a small house outside of Detroit. In the letter, Sasha tells him of his commutation, and asks if he and his good wife might be willing to house him for a few days upon his release. A week later, he receives a reply: *By all means! Come! Stay with us! Restore your equilibrium in our humble abode! It will be an absolute honour to house you, my friend. Things have changed greatly since you've been gone. But tell me—what is your release date? If you forward it to me, I shall endeavour to have a few comrades waiting at the gates of the prison on the day in which your liberty is finally restored. As for Emma, she's on a speaking tour of Canada, but I will endeavour to send word as well.*

The joy these words cause! The relief that floods through Sasha's spirit! If nothing else, he now has a place to stay following his release, and won't have to live on the streets of Manhattan, sleeping under sheets of cardboard and begging for change. He writes Nold again, and tells him that he'll send the details of his release as soon as they are made known to him.

* * *

At first, imagining freedom veers upon the blissful. Sasha pictures himself getting up from an easy chair and deciding to have a walk; it is this agency, this ability to decide what he will do with himself from one moment to the next, that rings with the sublime. Or, he imagines himself in a room with a large window, through which light cascades. There are no other details; he can't describe the room, or any of the objects *in* that room. It is merely the size of the window that entrances him: in his imagination, it is huge, its very existence meaning that Sasha can walk up to it, *should he choose to do so*, and then look through it, or perhaps even open it, letting the resulting breeze cool his skin. Or: he pictures himself in a store, standing in front of two loaves of bread, one pumpernickel, one caraway rye, and, glory of glories, he's able to decide which loaf will take its place at his table. Sasha's imagination stops there, for he can't picture the person who sells him the loaf of bread, he can't guess where the store is located, and he has no idea whether the store is busy with people or whether he happens to be there during off hours, as picturing such details requires an energy that he cannot, as yet, muster.

As the days progress, he finds that his ability to dream begins to grow, his fantasies now coming to him fully rendered. That room with the window? It now has wallpaper, a large knitted rug, a vase filled with flowers. Or that walk he dreams of taking? Now, there's a path along the East River, the smell of fish in the air, the caw of seagulls, the gleeful shouts of playing children, Italian cart men selling cashews, Sasha's lungs inflating with salty port air. Or that trip to the bakery? It's on Third Avenue, now, between a shoe repairman and a Polish restaurant, and the older woman who works there has been replaced by a much younger woman, perhaps twenty-five years of age, and she has beautiful skin and wavy blond hair and a kindness about her. Days later, the fantasy takes on a self-aggrandizing tone, for as he places his order, her eyes narrow slightly, as though trying to place him, *oh my goodness! Aren't you Alexander Berkman, the anarchist? Yes, you are, I know you are, it's an honour serving a comrade, go ahead, take any bread you want, it's a gift from the people.*

Ludicrous, he realizes. Yet the contents of his fantasies are not important; it is the fact that he's able to generate them. He is teaching himself to want, to desire, to crave, to wish for things; over the past fifteen years, he'd smothered these inclinations, for he knew they wouldn't be fulfilled, and would only lead to a sort of lacerating frustration. Now, as freedom looms, he is relearning that most elemental of abilities, that being the ability to yearn. Even a baby has it: it wants food, sleep, love, warmth, and so now does Sasha. A week goes by. He is in the mess hall, eating with some of the other range men, and he takes a bite of the meat loaf they serve most days—it is grey and flavourless and has the texture of slurry. Sasha has just had a spoonful when he starts to imagine the food he'll eat when he gets out—a hot bagel, deli sauerkraut, a fresh tomato. But then, his elation abandons him. His spirits plummet. How will he purchase such delicacies? How will he make a living? How will he find employment in New York City, given that he has a criminal record? His thoughts cascade. Where will he live? What landlord would have him? Will he be homeless?

To ward off despair, he puts himself back in that Third Avenue bakery, talking to the comely young woman who works there, when it occurs to him that, in almost a decade and a half, he has made love to exactly one person, a gentle young convict named Johnny Davis. Will he still know how to relate to the female body? Will he be able to generate sufficient ardour? He doesn't know, his joyful anticipation abandons him; there's an elderly range man at Western named Jerome, and he always says to Sasha, *I doubt I'll be getting out, not in this lifetime, oh no, they'll be holding me forever*, and the thing that always strikes Sasha is the way he grins when he says it, as though relieved. Now, Sasha understands: the promise of freedom, while wonderful, can also activate a man's nerves, and fill his head with imagined catastrophe.

Another week goes by. Another week goes by. It has been a month and a half since the warden informed Sasha of his commutation. One afternoon, a terrible thought strikes him. What if his upcoming release doesn't exist? What if its promise is just another form of torture, psychological in nature, that the prison authorities have invented to torment political prisoners? What if he still has to serve the full twenty-two years of his original sentence? And yet, he can't stop himself, he awakes each morning thinking that this will be the day in which he walks free, only to find that it's just like any other day, the only difference being that each hour and minute and second has been slowed by the torture of hope. But no, it can't be, it'd be too diabolical, no one could be that cruel, not even them. Another week passes. Prisoners start coming up to him and saying *Hey Berkman I thought you was gettin' out?* This sparks a decline. His health begins to ebb and his head fills with suicidal fantasy—anything, he thinks, would be better than this agonizing wait. He begins contemplating a method. He could sharpen a spoon against the cold stone floor, and then fall on it in such a way that it slides between his third and fourth ribs. Or maybe, he thinks, I could obtain a length of canvas from a fellow prisoner in the sewing shop, which I could fashion into a lynching rope. He begins to make some inquiries. It would cost him a pack of cigarettes—real ones, not the burnt-rubber smokes issued by the prison. No problem. He still has comrades in Pittsburgh who could bring him some. With time, he becomes resolved: he won't allow them to toy with him in this manner. He will not be batted around like a helpless mouse. Then one day it is morning time, just after breakfast, and he is pushing his broom while contemplating his own oblivion. One of the guards—everyone calls him Smitty—comes up to him and says, "Hey Berkman, guess what? You better pack your things since tomorrow's the day."

*　*　*

That night, his hearing is enlivened by the prospect of liberty—snoring, the scurry of mice, wind against his leaky window, his own breathing, all are amplified, such that they meld into a roaring, featureless noise. He never falls asleep. Finally, there's the screech of cell bars opening and closing: it's 5 a.m., and the night captain is turning out the kitchen men to prepare breakfast. Sasha rises as well, and, as he has done on so many days during his incarceration, begins to pace, an action that helps to calm him. The gong rings at 6 a.m. He stands at the cell door, waiting. A guard travels down the range, unlocking every door, ordering every prisoner to fall in for breakfast.

He joins the lineup for chow, which winds down the stairs, past a lynx-eyed deputy in the middle of the hallway; slowly, they all enter the mess. Here, each man receives a chunk of bread, a bowl of soupy porridge and a mug of chicory coffee. He then returns to his cell—only lunch and dinner are taken communally—and eats, even though he's unnerved by the fact that none of the guards, or the range deputy himself, has acknowledged that he is leaving that day. Once again, he is beset with fear that his release is nothing more than a sadistic taunt.

When the cell doors open at seven-thirty, such that the prisoners might attend to their work details, a guard comes to his cell and says, "You ain't workin' today, Berkman." Instead, he's directed over to a line of a dozen men who are leaving as well. They all march toward the clothes room, where they remove their prison attire and subject themselves to the usual indignities: tongue out, lower your pants, lift your ball sack, bend over, spread your cheeks, stand up. They are all then given a cheap, ill-fitting suit of clothes, a small amount of money, and a thirty-cent train ticket to nearby Pittsburgh.

They're conducted to the prison gates. The gates open and Sasha steps into bright sunshine. The other eleven men have the luxury of either slipping away, or stepping into the outstretched arms of loved ones. As for Sasha, there are reporters, a half dozen of them, toting cameras, press cards in their hatbands, someone must have tipped them off. As their cameras pop, they shout questions: *Are you still an anarchist? What will you do now? Where are you going, Mr. Berkman?* He is not prepared for this; their aggressiveness frightens him, and the high, insistent pitch of their voices hurts his ears. So he waves them away and rushes off, which doesn't work, they just follow him, their voices growing louder and their feet moving quickly over the pavement behind him. As Sasha attempts to evade them, he rushes headlong into four tall men who, it seems, were waiting for him as well. Sasha pulls up and the reporters all but collide with him: now, he finds himself trapped in a claustrophobic scrum, reporters to his rear and those intimidating strangers to his front. One of the unknown men opens the lapel of his overcoat, revealing a policeman's star.

"Berkman," he spits. "You're gonna leave Allegheny by nightfall, on order of the chief of police. You got that?"

Sasha nods, and hustles off to the train station, which is just a few hundred yards from the prison gates, the reporters and the four police officers directly behind him, the journalists still shouting questions at his back, *Are you glad to be out, Mr. Berkman? Are you going to live with other anarchists, Mr. Berkman? What do you think about the revolution in Russia, Mr. Berkman? Are you still Emma Goldman's companion?* and so on and so forth, all he can do is hunch his shoulders and walk a little quicker and not engage with them in any way. He reaches the station just as a train pulls in; he jumps on as it pulls out and then he's away from the prison and the reporters and the police and everyone else who seemed so interested in his release.

He takes a seat, conscious that the other passengers are all looking at him. He breathes, slowly and deeply, and tries to make himself small. The train pulls into Pittsburgh, and he has no choice but to step down, his heart pounding so heavily he fears he might be suffering some sort of cardiac distress. (It wouldn't surprise him, given the calibre of tobacco he smoked in prison.) He pushes through the crowds at the station and stands on the street, entirely bewildered, assaulted by the noise and clamour. And the cars! Where did they all come from? They are everywhere, careening at unimaginable speeds, threatening to kill anyone who dares step in their path. Sasha is afraid to cross the street—to do so would be to take his life in his hands. But then there's a break in the traffic and a wave of people begins crossing, so he takes the opportunity himself, his eyes darting from side to side, fearful that some inattentive driver might ignore the traffic signal.

He's jostled by crowds. It's as though he is performing a dance he doesn't know, some foreign *pas de deux* that only results in him running into others. He turns one way and collides with a passerby, only to bounce into the path of another frenzied pedestrian. He panics, and seeks solace by glancing at a small baby in a stroller, the baby looking up at him and grinning. This helps, though only for a moment, as he notices that the four detectives who met him outside the prison have followed him to Pittsburgh—no doubt they're under strict instructions to re-arrest him should he commit the slightest offence. He is truly afraid, now, as it's obvious that the state wants him back behind bars, his commutation be damned. So he has to be careful: the slightest mistake will cost him his liberty. If he so much as looks at someone in a way that could be misinterpreted as aggressive, he'll be arrested. If he accidentally jostles against someone and, heaven forbid, knocks them down, he'll face the gallows. And who *are* all of these people! What *can* they all be doing?

He ducks down a side street and walks smartly. A trolley passes; he gives chase, yelling *Please conductor please!* When the conductor does show mercy and slows, Sasha jumps on and stays on, for block after block, a plan forming in his mind: he'll walk around Pittsburgh for several hours, during which time the detectives will tire and decide to retreat to Allegheny. Will it work? He doesn't know. It all depends on how determined the detectives are—if they've been instructed to pursue him to the ends of the earth, there's precious little he can do about it. This thought frightens him as well; there is so much noise, so much commotion, so many people, he can't think. After a few dinging stops, he leaps from the trolley, all but stepping into the path of another damnable automobile, its driver sounding the klaxon and hollering, "Watch where you're going, Mac!"

He is standing before a hat shop. Impulsively, he enters the store and, with some of the money bequeathed to him by the state, buys a large, dark Homburg; as luck would have it, the shop is on a corner and has a second entrance, leading to the cross street. Sasha sneaks out, the disguising hat on his head; then, he hurries through side streets. He travels a block in one direction, turns left for two more blocks, and then doubles back another couple of blocks. Finally, he stops, his back against a wall, looking up and down the crowded street for the detectives. He doesn't see them, which means one of two things. The first, and most likely, is that they are choosing to let him *think* that he's eluded them. The second is that they were never really following him in the first place, their task only to ensure that their target had made it to Pittsburgh, at which point they turned back.

Sasha keeps walking. When he comes across a telegraph office, he steps inside and sends a wire to Nold, telling him that he's out and in Pittsburgh and will take the morning train to Detroit. He then leaves the telegraph office, looking right and left for the detectives.

He walks around a bit more, and has a hot dog with relish at a diner. As he eats, it occurs to him that he should be delighted—his first meal as a free man! Instead, his nerves feel shattered and his vision blurry and he decides that what he really needs is rest and quiet.

He has coffee (real coffee!) and smokes a couple of cigarettes (fresh tobacco!) and this helps his morale. Again, on the street, he checks for the detectives: there is no sight of them, and he begins to think that they really did turn back. He finds a park and sits and collects himself. Again, he tries to savour his freedom and cannot, his mind still racing with concerns. He finds a cheap hotel, where he asks for a room on as high a floor as possible, thinking this will remove him, at least somewhat, from the noise on the street. The clerk nods and hands him a key and Sasha walks up six flights of stairs. By the time he reaches the top he is practically bent over, coughing, unable to catch his breath. He steps into his room; it has its own bathroom and, miracle of miracles, a large mirror. (They weren't allowed mirrors in prison, as it was feared the prisoners could shatter them and effect weapons from the shards of glass.) For the first time in fourteen years, ten months, two weeks and three days, he is able to really study his own reflection: he is an old man, now, his face hollowed and lined, his body grown spindly on the inadequate prison diet. As well, he is all but bald; the prison barber, acting under orders, had shaved off the few lengthy strands that had clung to the top of his head, leaving sickly patches behind. ("Looks good," he'd said in a French-Canadian accent. "It look real good.") And his glasses! About five years earlier, the spectacles he'd worn into prison had fallen and broken. The pair that the prison issued to him, which he'd received after enduring weeks of near-blindness, are round and heavy and look like something a pipe welder would use to protect his eyes from sparks.

Sasha lies down in the darkened room and savours the quiet. What, he asks himself, will he do when he returns to New York City, which is ten times as loud as Pittsburgh? He doesn't know, he can't say, it isn't as if prison was quiet—all day long, the place rang with the shouts of men and the clang of steel doors, opening and closing. Yet he became accustomed to those noises, as he heard them every day for almost fifteen years. It's the resonance of a modern city that so alarms him—the car horns, the trolley bells, the smack of feet against pavement, the call of vendors, the laughing of children, all of it a reminder that he's stepped back into a world he does not, in any way, understand. Yet up here, in his decrepit hotel room, the window closed against the world, he has quiet, which is arguably worse, for now that his ears have nothing to occupy them, they seem to conjure noises of their own. Shortly after dinnertime—or what would have been dinnertime, should he have chosen to eat—he ventures onto the street and finds a pharmacy. Here, he tells a kindly man in a white lab coat that he hasn't been able to sleep, of late.

"Now don't you worry," the druggist responds. "I believe I have something that will do the trick."

After watching the man fill a packet with powder, Sasha goes to the hotel and mixes the substance with the prescribed amount of water. He drinks, lies down, and is overtaken by darkness. He comes back to life shortly before dawn, having been missing from the world for close to a half day. He feels groggy and half dead. The coffee shops aren't even open, so he wanders the streets until he finds a brightly lit restaurant that services the early-morning traffic down by the train station. He enters, imagining he'll find the pursuing detectives eating bacon sandwiches in the corner. But no: he chooses a place at the counter, where he is served eggs and coffee by a dark woman with calloused hands. When he finishes, he stumbles to the train station and purchases a ticket. Mostly, he sleeps on the way to Detroit, still exhausted by whatever soporific is still in his system.

When he finally arrives, it is well past dusk. The platform is illuminated by pockets of lamplight; he has never felt so poor, so

afraid, so useless and dim-witted and drained. He looks along the
track and, after a time, spots Nold. He also notices that Nold is with
someone, a small woman with an awkward gait, he moves toward
them and sees that it's true, he can't believe it, she was supposed to
be on tour in Canada, but that isn't the case, oh no it's her, it's her,
it's his sailor girl, Emma.

twenty

AS THE CROWD on the platform thins, Emma starts to fear that Sasha missed his train and has been delayed in Pittsburgh. She lifts a fingertip to her mouth and starts chewing her nail, a recently developed habit that has reduced her fingers to gnawed-upon stubs.

Soon, there are only three people left on the platform (save for a handful of train station employees). There's her, there's Nold, and there's an old, bespectacled man at the end of the station, who is thin and stooped and wearing an oversized hat pulled down over his eyes. She watches as the old man turns his head and looks her way. When he starts moving, she recognizes his carriage. Emma gasps, and then she's running, which is not easy, not with the weight she's gained over the past fifteen years, and as she chugs toward her lover she starts crying, as the sight of Sasha causes her to recall a time in which she could run happily, and freely, all day.

She presses her damp face against his torso and squeezes him, melting into him, his body so insubstantial she feels like she could wrap her short arms around him twice. "Sasha," she moans. "My love, I can't believe it's you." And it's true, she really can't believe it's him, he's always been so hefty and strong, and if there's any remnant of the Sasha Berkman she loved a thousand years ago, in a land called the Lower East Side, it's his tobacco scent and the speeding timbre of his heart.

He returns the hug. Emma pulls him even tighter, falling within the veil of his coat, such that she disappears from view, just a pair of feet protruding from a well-worn overcoat. She can't stop weeping; so much time has gone by. That is the most painful thing, this relentless march forward called life. There are a thousand moments she remembers—a thousand sights, a thousand sounds, a thousand instances of touch. And yes, she can still picture him, on that day they first met, in Café Sachs, this young-yet-old man lifting a forkful of steak to his mouth, his forearms as big as a small man's thigh, and the way his fork had stopped, in mid-air, when he'd spotted her, walking into the crowded room.

Finally, they part. She takes her first good look at his now-craggy face: he looks indistinct, like something glimpsed through rain. She wipes away her tears and sees clearly. His cheeks are hollow, his eyes hidden behind prison glasses. His lips, so ridiculous and yet so sensuous, are even larger against his shrunken face. She starts giggling, embarrassed by her emotions. As for Sasha, he looks incredulous, as if unable to comprehend that this moment is occurring. "Emma," he says in a weak voice. "You're here."

"Of course I'm here."

"But they told me you were on tour."

"I was in Montreal. I quit as soon as I heard you'd be released."

"Carl…"

"Yes, yes, Carl wired me."

"Emma," he says. "I can't believe it's you."

She stands on her tiptoes and whispers in his ear. "Welcome home, fishlips."

Nold reaches them and gives his old comrade a manly hug, Emma feeling a mild concern when Nold slaps Sasha on the back. *Not so hard*, she wants to say. *Can't you see he's fragile?*

"Well well well," Nold says. "Alexander Berkman, resurrected."

"In the flesh," Sasha says.

"I've taken the liberty of planning a little dinner for you."

"Oh."

"But if you're exhausted, just tell me. I can easily cancel it."

"No, no, of course not."

"In that case, shall we?"

* * *

Nold has a sputtering jalopy that, for reasons that Emma doesn't quite understand, he refers to as "Ursula." As they walk toward it, Carl tells Sasha about his life: married, no children, a small house just outside of Detroit, working as a machinist in the city. "But don't worry, comrade," Nold concludes. "I haven't lost the fire, oh no, I'm still a believer, it just doesn't show as much, you wouldn't believe it, Sasha, there are more and more of us every day!

"If only that were true."

Emma stops. Sasha and Nold do as well. She has a puzzled look on her face. "Sasha," she says. "Why did you just say that?"

"We failed. I know this."

"And you know this... how?"

"They told me in prison."

"Who did?"

"The guards, the warden, the other prisoners, everybody."

"*Sasha*," she starts. "The government is running scared. Now that they've legalized the unions, it's us they fear. Everywhere I speak, I hear about police rounding up anarchists, beating them up, either throwing them in jail or deporting them. Suddenly, America is like Russia before the revolution, the only difference being that, in Russia, the tsarist police came in the middle of the night. At least *they* had the sense to be ashamed."

Sasha blinks, as if he barely understands.

"*Sasha*," she continues. "They arrested Johann."

250

"Most? Really?"

"He did a year in Blackwell's Island. You should see him now. I tell you, *Freiheit* is a shadow of its former self. He no longer believes in the 'propaganda of the deed.' Can you believe that? Sometimes, I think half the articles he publishes have been ghost-written by capitalists. If you ask me, I'd say he's afraid of going back to jail again."

"I never took him for a coward."

"Nor I. But you learn something new every day."

"And what about..." Sasha swallows; he can barely bring himself to ask. "What about Frick?"

"Frick is Frick, Sasha. Please, don't give him another thought."

They reach Nold's automobile. Emma and Sasha stand to one side while Nold starts it, a complicated process involving the turning of cranks and the shifting of levers and the pushing of buttons and a lot of looking up and away while listening intently. Finally, the engine grumbles to life. Sasha sits in the front passenger seat, while Emma crawls into a tiny pop-up seat in the back. Then, they are driving, the wind rushing in Emma's face, her hand placed atop her head to stop her hat from flying away.

"ISN'T THIS SOMETHING?" Nold yells over the wind.

From the back, Emma notices that Sasha is gripping the door frame with his hand. That's when she realizes something: it's his first time in a motorized vehicle. The speed is likely too much for him. Nold, however, is oblivious: "They're wonderful, these motor cars. I can get from my house to downtown in twenty minutes. Twenty minutes! Plus the engine doesn't shit all over my front yard."

He throws his head back and laughs. When Sasha doesn't respond, Emma leans forward and touches him—again, she feels like crying, it's his once-powerful arms, reduced to twigs. She wipes her eyes, and feels terrible. She is just about to suggest that they forget the supper, that they take Sasha home and get him the rest he deserves, when Nold pulls in front of a small tavern with stucco walls and thick, dark roof beams. They climb out of the car. Nold is whistling, while Emma holds Sasha's hand. Inside the restaurant, they're met with darkness and clamour. Their table is for twelve. The other guests, all of them Polish-born anarchists with names like Henryk and Stanislaw and Borkowski, all stand to greet Sasha and shake his hand and tell him what an honour it is to meet a man like him, a man who has sacrificed so much for the principles of the movement. Though he smiles bravely, Emma is convinced he doesn't want to be there. Nold's wife, a tall, light-haired woman named Kate, is there too. She kisses Sasha's cheek and says, "It's a privilege to meet you, Mr. Berkman."

Again: that shaky, unconvincing smile. He takes her hand. Though they are the same age, her skin is smooth and free from blemishes, while his is a patchwork of nicks and abrasions. They all sit. The others resume their loud, spirited conversations. Emma makes sure to seat herself across from Sasha; she wants to keep an eye on him, so that she can escort him from the restaurant if the occasion really does prove too much for him.

Upon taking his seat, Sasha removes his hat. Emma gasps—it isn't that Sasha is bald, as he never had that much hair to begin with. It is his pattern of baldness that upsets her, his scalp an ugly patchwork of denuded spots, caused not by genetics but malnutrition and disease. The few patches of tightly shorn hair are grey. Again, tears; she rushes from the table and hides in the bathroom, weeping. A few moments later, she hears knocking.

"Emma?"

"Who is it?"

"It's Kate. Can I come in?"

Emma opens the door and Kate steps inside. "You poor thing," she keeps saying. "You poor, poor thing."

"What they *did* to him in there."

"Shhhhhhhhh." She pulls a handkerchief from her purse and wipes Emma's face.

"Better?"

"Yes."

"Good. Best to be strong. Let's go back."

When they return to the table, Nold looks up and says, "Ahhhh, here they are! Looking as lovely as ever."

Emma sits. Sasha reaches across the table and touches her forearm, as if to say, *I know, darling, I know.* The food comes. To Emma, it seems almost an insult, given what prisoners across the nation are receiving, but there it is, the table covered with perogies, cabbage, pork chops, boiled potatoes, green beans, bread. Sasha looks stunned. Kate, sensing his hesitation, makes him up a plate, the steam rising into his blinking eyes. When he starts eating, he takes small, exploratory bites, as if fearful that food this tasty might, after all of his years in prison, have some injurious effect upon him.

"To Alexander Berkman!" Nold says, lifting his glass.

"To Alexander Berkman!" the others echo.

"And let's not forget Emma Goldman, who interrupted a speaking tour to be here. To Emma!"

"To Emma!"

Everyone drinks. Sasha too—when he pulls his glass away, his lips look stained red. Emma thinks that there's nothing as loud as a table full of anarchists with something to celebrate, all drinking and gobbling and laughing and talking and feeling glad to be alive. Someone drops a knife onto a plate; the clang cuts through the clamour. Sasha flinches. Nold leans over and says, "Sasha. There's something we have to talk about. A lot of people want to hear what you have to say. Emma and I have booked a hall in town for tomorrow night, and guess who's the main event? Again, if you're too tired, I could easily cancel the talk. But it'd be a shame."

"*Carl,*" Emma says. "It's a terrible idea. Of course he's too tired. Sasha, I'm sorry, we weren't thinking."

"Is that right, Sasha? You'd like us to cancel? It wouldn't be a problem. Everyone would understand."

Sasha puts down his fork. He wipes his mouth; the red on his napkin looks like blood. For a moment, Emma worries that his gums are bleeding. Could he have scurvy? When was the last time he had an orange? Her heart starts beating quickly. But no, she realizes, it's only the cheap wine. Just then, Sasha looks up and she peers into his sad, soulful eyes—the same eyes that had so attracted her, all those years ago. There is nothing as painful, she thinks, as the passage of years.

"It's all right," Sasha says in a soft voice. "Really, it's all right."

"Are you sure?" Emma says. "It's fine if you can't. We can cancel the thing like that." She inexpertly snaps her fingers in the air, the sound like two sheets of foolscap rubbing together.

For the first time since his release, Sasha grins, revealing teeth turned brown and small.

* * *

As the meal progresses, the guests make periodic toasts to Sasha's return, to Sasha's good health, to Sasha's talk the following night, which they are all anticipating, *oh yeah Sasha you're really going to knock 'em dead*, and when the wine turns to vodka they become louder, and more cheerful, and more rambunctious, the only exception being the guest of honour, who has started to look grey. He lights a cigarette, his hands shaking slightly.

Emma reaches across the table and holds his elbow; it isn't much bigger than a golf ball. She turns to Nold and says, "Sasha's exhausted. We've got to get him home."

"Yes, yes," he says. "It has been a long day. I tell you what. I'll give you both a lift back and then I'll return for the rest of the evening."

"Good," says Emma. "Good."

The three go outside, Nold repeating the histrionics required to make his car come alive. "Ursula," he comments as he cranks away, "can be a bit of a fuss-budget sometimes. Oh, wait, here we go!" and they drive off, winding through woods and past fields lit by moonlight. After twenty minutes or so, Nold slows and turns onto a long, wood-chip driveway that leads to a handsome cabin. Emma and Sasha climb out. "You'll get him settled?" Nold calls to Emma.

"Yes."

"Good! Kate put fresh towels on your bed. I tell you, I'm excited as hell. This is all going to be terrific! I'll see you both in the morning."

He reverses to the end of the driveway, waves, and then barrels back toward the city. Emma takes Sasha by the crook of his arm. There's the sound of crickets and not much else. They walk into the house; it's tidy and nice and Emma realizes that she's exhausted as well, for she's suffering the same thought that she always has when feeling depleted: maybe *this* is what I've needed, all these years, a nice warm home away from things. Not anarchism, not propaganda of the deed, not *attentats* and revolutionism and the demands of this beast called "the movement," but something quiet, something just like this. She chases the thought away, thinking *I'll feel better in the morning*. She kisses Sasha. His lips feel warm and she considers this a start. "Let's go to bed," she says.

Sasha nods and they walk into the bedroom with towels left on the bedspread. It's warm in the room, and they disrobe slowly. Emma laughs, though it's the sort of laughter that accompanies great sadness. "We've grown in different directions, the two of us. You thin, me fat." Emma continues looking at Sasha. It is different than before; not so much attraction as an admiration, so deep and fundamental it borders on the mystical. These are the bodies they wore, during all those difficult years, *and look, my love, we're still standing, the two of us, both alive, if barely*. Emma takes a step toward Sasha and hugs him, the rush of time making her rueful. His new frame—so withered and pale grey and bruised—is the body of their new, noncorporeal relationship, the one that will last them for the rest of their days and into their afterlives as well.

"In prison," he says, "you used to come to me." His voice sounds croaky and thin; the skin on his lips is dry. "When I was in solitary, you'd come to me, and sit with me. We'd talk, and you'd entertain me with stories. You always were such a talker. No one quite tells a story like Emma Goldman. Others came, too, like Modska and my father, but mostly it was you. If you hadn't, I would've gone out of my mind. So you saved me, Emma."

"But I didn't! If I hadn't helped with that stupid tunnel then they wouldn't have... oh Sasha I'm so sorry."

"Shhhhhh," he says. "Shhhhhhhhhhh."

"Let's make a promise."

"Okay."

"We'll get better together, all right? We'll eat better and we'll take walks and everything will be better."

They climb into bed and lie like spoons, Emma's arm draped over him, the two becoming twin halves of the same entity, Emma and Sasha, sailor girl and fishlips, the anarchist and her companion, together in essence if not carnality. It is a comfort; Emma's eyes are dry, now. She drifts off, only to awaken with a start: Sasha's side of the bed is empty. She sits up and hears a body, moving about the little house. Then, she hears the front door open.

Emma leaps from the bed and runs to the window, which happens to look out over the cabin's forested front yard. There he is, walking down the driveway. He reaches the roadway that runs in front of the house and stops. He looks to his left, and to his right. He reaches out, and rests a hand on the mailbox. From inside the house, she watches him take a deep breath, turn, and head back up the driveway. She rushes to the bed and climbs under the thin white sheet. The door to the room opens; he undresses and climbs in beside her. It is two-thirty in the morning. She rolls over and pretends to come awake.

"Sasha? Are you all right?"

"Yes."

"Are you sure?"

"I think so, yes."

The two remain silent, Emma holding him. Eventually, they sleep; it is almost lunchtime when they finally emerge from their room. Kate Nold is there. "Well look who it is! You two must have slept well."

"Where's Carl?" Emma asks.

"Why, he's at work. Come, come, you must be starved."

They sit at the kitchen table, Kate serving them kippers and eggs and toast and potatoes. Sasha picks at his food; Emma can't eat at all. The coffee, though, is hot and delicious. Later, Emma helps Kate with the dishes. Together, they stand over soapy water in a little galley that extends off the kitchen. In a low voice, Kate asks, "Is he all right?"

"He was away for a long time. They treated him terribly."

"Yes, but he's okay, isn't he?"

"No," says Emma, "I don't think that he is."

* * *

The dishes done, Emma approaches Sasha. "I've got an idea." She gestures toward the window. "Why don't you and I go for a stroll?"

"Mmmmmm, I'm feeling a little drained."

"It'll help. You're as pale as a tuna's belly. You need sunshine."

They stroll along a tree-lined country lane. They can hear cicadas and sparrows and a breeze in the trees. Above them, crows circle in slow, wafting arcs.

"Emma," Sasha says. "I don't feel well."

"What is it?"

"I don't want to speak tonight."

"I know."

"I *can't* speak tonight."

"You're still feeling fragile."

"No! That's not it. That's not it at all. Don't you understand, Emma? I'm nothing, a nonentity. Please don't make me speak to an empty hall tonight."

Emma allows herself a smile.

"It's not funny."

"Yes it is. You really don't know, do you Sasha?"

"Know what?"

"Tell me something. In all the years you were away, how many letters did you receive from me?"

"Four."

Her jaw drops. "Four! Those bastards. I wrote you *hundreds*. What about Modska? How many letters did you receive from him?"

"I got one on my birthday, shortly after I started my sentence."

"Dozens, fishie. Dozens. When you didn't respond, he thought you were mad at him for leaving the movement."

"No... I... dozens? Really?"

"*Really*. I tell you, Sasha. If I have my way about it, when the revolution comes prison reform will be our first priority. Imagine, cutting an inmate off from his loved ones. It's savagery, plain and simple."

They walk a little farther; from a distance, they must look like old people, out for a stroll. "Sasha," she finally says. "I need to talk to you about something."

"All right."

"I'm starting an anarchist journal of my own. But believe me, it'll be nothing like Most's rag. In the first issue, I plan to run an editorial, in which I vow to run articles reflecting all schools of anarchist thought, not just those that mirror my own. Do you understand what I'm saying? I want a free and co-operative publication, just like anarchism itself. I also want to expand the anarchist discussion, so that it includes things like women's issues, and the rights of marginalized cultures, like homosexuals and Native Americans. I've already raised quite a bit of money. I've even got my eye on some offices."

"When will you start publishing?"

"By the end of the year. But I've got a problem. I've had a look at my speaking schedule, and I'm going to be busy. There's no possible way that I'll have time to be the editor. I'll need someone."

"Who are you going to get? Solotaroff, maybe?"

Emma chortled. "You know, you really can be quite thick at times."

"I don't understand."

"*You*, fishie. Who else would it be? Don't say anything. You're perfect for the job. Now let's get you home. And no more coffee and cigarettes today. You're trembling like a leaf."

By the time they return to the cabin, Nold has come home from work. "I told them I was feeling sick and had to leave early. Would you believe it? The suckers bought it." He lends Sasha a suit, shirt and tie; though the suit is too big for him, he looks more than presentable. "Well then," Nold says. "We should go."

It is four o'clock in the afternoon; the talk is at five. Before they leave, Kate hands Sasha a small plate with a little whitefish, some bread and a cube or two of crumbly cheese. He waves it away.

"I'm sorry, I'm scared to death."

"Of course you are," Kate says. "I hate public speaking too."

"It's not that," says Emma. "He's afraid no one will be there. I've told him he's wrong, but..." She shrugs, and they all pack into Carl's jalopy. Sasha takes the tiny seat at the rear so that the two women can share the passenger seat up front. It's a tight fit, and Kate has to pull in her left leg every time her husband changes gears. They rumble along country roads, past fields and farms and cows and worn cedar fence lines. No one speaks. Every few minutes, Emma turns and looks at Sasha, as though afraid he might pitch himself from the car. Each time, he smiles weakly. They keep going; the fields turn into small homes, built far apart on gravel lots, some with lawns and some without, though each one seems to have an automobile parked in the front. As they approach the city proper, the houses close in on one another, as if bundling against the wind blowing off Lake St. Clair. Soon, there are tall buildings and people and cars honking at one another, one klaxon sounding after another. At a stop sign, Nold turns to Sasha and says, "We're just around the corner."

They keep going, a little slower, passing a park and a school and a row of houses before Nold turns a corner and parks behind a small building. He turns and winks at Sasha. "Odd Fellows Hall," he says. "Perfect for the likes of you, eh Sasha?"

No one laughs. Emma takes Sasha's arm. They enter through a door at the rear of the building, which leads into a basement. Everything smells like must and old coats. It is hot, down there, an old boiler clanking away. After a bit, they come to a set of stairs leading upward. As they climb them, the sound of the boiler gives way to another sound. Emma squeezes Sasha's arm. "You hear that, fishie?"

"Are those..."

"I don't know, Sasha, why don't *you* tell *me*?"

They climb the last few steps. Now, they're at the side of a wooden stage, standing behind a brocaded curtain. From beyond the curtain, they can hear the chatter of voices. Emma grins, light beaming from her eyes, as life is acting in a way that it rarely does. Sasha, however, looks confused, as if nothing about the moment makes any sense. He looks down at Emma; perhaps it's a form of magic, existing between them.

"Peek through the curtain, Sasha."

"No, I can't."

"Yes you can."

"It's a trick."

"Why would it be a trick?"

"I don't know."

"Who would want to trick you?"

"Everyone. No one. Emma I don't know."

"Sasha. Would you please take a god damn *look*."

She seems annoyed, now. There was a time when Sasha wasn't fearful of her moods. But now he fears everything; prison has done that to him, he's more a child than a man, but like all children he's curious, he can't help it, there must be some explanation for all of the noise he's hearing, all the coughs and hubbub and chatter, all the laughs and chair squeaks and sneezes, and just then he feels a touch of Emma's energy, emboldening him. So he reaches for the edge of the curtain, right where it touches the side wall, knowing that his final assessment awaits on the other side, the curtain scratchy and thick in his fingertips, more burlap than wool, it all feels so reminiscent, he's flooded with memories of his school days, all of his life rushing before him, such a maudlin sensation this is, thank goodness Emma is beside him, touching him, saying, "Go ahead, fishie, go right ahead," and he pulls the drape open, no more than an inch or two, just enough for the two of them to peek through and see people, so many people, close to a hundred, maybe even more, in their seats, looking forward, faces alive, waiting.

author's note

FOLLOWING HIS RELEASE from prison in 1906, Alexander Berkman served as editor of Emma Goldman's *Mother Earth* until its folding in 1915, at which point he founded a short-lived anarchist periodical called *The Blast*. In 1917, Berkman and Goldman were jointly arrested at the *Blast* offices, and charged with "conspiracy to induce persons not to register" for duty in the First World War. Both were sentenced to two years in prison: Berkman served his sentence at the Atlanta Federal Penitentiary, while Goldman was housed at the Missouri State Penitentiary. Upon their release in 1919, both were deported from the United States, the pair accepting residency in Russia. There, they were both shocked at abuses perpetrated by the Bolshevik government. After two years, the pair left Russia. Following a period of itineracy, they both landed in France, Berkman settling in the outskirts of Nice, while Goldman lived in a cottage in Saint-Tropez. There, the two wrote their memoirs, worked as editors, and penned books concerning various anarchist issues, most commonly the failure of the Russian Revolution. (Both survived thanks to patrons: Goldman's cottage was paid for by the socialite Peggy Guggenheim, while Berkman received an allowance from his cousin, Modska Aronstam, who had become a successful illustrator in New York City.)

Goldman, wishing to be close to her family in Rochester, settled in Toronto in 1934. Berkman, ill with prostate cancer and clinical depression, committed suicide in 1936, and was buried in a small cemetery in Nice. He was sixty-five years of age. Goldman died in 1940, following a stroke at age seventy. Only then was she allowed re-entry into the United States, her body laid to rest in the same Chicago cemetery containing the anarchists executed for their role in the Haymarket riot.

about the author

ROBERT HOUGH has been published to rave reviews around the world. He is the author of *The Final Confession of Mabel Stark* (Vintage Canada, 2002), shortlisted for both the Commonwealth Writers' Prize for best first book and the Trillium Book Award; *The Stowaway* (Vintage Canada, 2004), one of the *Boston Globe*'s top ten fiction titles of 2004; *The Culprits* (Vintage Canada, 2008); *Dr. Brinkley's Tower* (House of Anansi, 2012), short-listed for the Governor General's Awards for fiction and long-listed for the Giller Prize; *The Man Who Saved Henry Morgan* (House of Anansi, 2015), a finalist for the Trillium Book Award; and *Diego's Crossing* (Annick Press, 2015), shortlisted for the Arthur Ellis Awards. His last book for Douglas & McIntyre was *The Marriage of Rose Camilleri* (2021). Hough lives in Toronto, ON.